11.16

A Lifetime
Last Night

David Homick

A Lifetime Last Night
© 2014 All rights reserved
Published by Blue Knight Media
ISBN 978-0-9906126-2-9
Library of Congress Control Number: 2014948972

Cover design by David Homick and
Sulyn Bennett-Hennessey
Book design by Sulyn Bennett-Hennessey
Edited by Tahlia Newland

"It's never too late to be what you might have been."

~ *George Eliot*

Chapter 1

A young nurse hurried to the phone in the Intensive Care Unit. "Doctor Howard, your coma patient is awake."

She returned to the patient's bedside, checked the heart monitor, then adjusted the amounts of fluids and drugs that flowed through the two IVs. She smiled as she wrote on his chart while keeping an eye on his vitals.

Richard Dunham looked at the ceiling, unable to move. Blinding light forced his eyes closed. His brain spun up like an old hard drive as his physical systems slowly came online. He tested his arms. The sheets barely rustled. His legs did not respond at all. *Where the hell am I?*

A dull pain nagged from somewhere deep inside his head. He opened his eyes for a moment, but the light was too intense. Unable to focus quickly enough to identify his surroundings, he struggled to get his bearings. His arms and legs felt heavy, impossible to move.

Aware of someone else in the room, Richard opened his mouth to speak. Only a scratching sound emerged, accompanied by a burning pain in his throat. He blinked again.

Doctor Howard pulled back the privacy curtain and stepped inside. Though nearly six feet tall, his boyish features gave the impression that he was too young to be a doctor. He glanced at the patient, then looked at the nurse.

"I understand we have some good news?"

The nurse's excited smile greeted him. "Yes, Doctor. He's been stirring for the past ten minutes." She handed him the chart. "His vitals are improving, and brain activity has increased significantly."

The doctor sat on a stool and rolled over to the side of the bed. He looked at the chart in his hand and then to his patient.

"Welcome back. I was beginning to think you had left us for good." He held Richard's right eye open and waved a small penlight.

The pain that gnawed at the base of Richard's skull spiked, and he recoiled.

"Your eyes are going to be sensitive for a while," the doctor said.

Richard blinked several times, able to keep them open a little longer each time. He moved his lips, but again was unable to speak. The nurse offered him a few ice chips from a plastic cup, and he held them in his mouth until they melted, savoring the cold sensation on his throat.

The doctor waited for him to swallow. "I'm going to ask you a few simple questions, and I'd like you to blink once for yes and twice for no. Can you do that?"

Richard blinked once.

"Good. Now, do you know where you are?"

Richard blinked. A hospital. He could see a doctor and a nurse. The sound of the heart monitor added further validation.

"Okay. Do you know why you're here?"

He frowned and searched for an answer, but saw only flashes of images, like pieces to a puzzle he couldn't fit together. He blinked twice.

"I see." Dr. Howard wrote something before looking back to his patient. "You were brought to Springfield Memorial Hospital after a serious auto accident. You've been in a coma for three weeks. We'll unhook some of these tubes and wires after we're certain you're stable."

Richard closed his eyes.

"I should warn you that in cases such as yours," the doctor continued, "it's not uncommon to experience a temporary loss of memory and/or motor skills. We'll monitor you here in the hospital for a while. We want to make sure you're back to your old self before you leave."

Richard opened his eyes, which were growing more accustomed to the light, and stared in disbelief at the doctor. Memory? Motor skills? At the moment, he felt numb. *Am I paralyzed? Tell me the truth, Doc. Will I walk again?*

Doctor Howard studied the chart. "Okay. One more question." He looked up. "Do you know who you are?"

Richard blinked once. *Of course, I know WHO I am. What I need to know is HOW I am!*

"All right, Mr. Riordan, that will be all for now," the doctor said as he stood. "You're doing fine. Just relax and take it slow." He smiled. "I'll come by and check on you again in a few hours."

Richard watched him walk away and stop for a moment to speak with the nurse before he left. *Mr. Riordan? Who the hell is Mr. Riordan? He's asking me if I know who I am, and he doesn't know himself. Is he even old enough to be a doctor?* He'd heard of hospitals switching babies, but never full-grown men.

Richard swallowed hard. Somehow, he had to let them know, but he could barely move and had difficulty speaking.

I must be hearing things, he thought. Maybe the nurse's name was Riordan. He took a deep breath, but it wasn't enough to stop the weight that pushed against his chest. He needed to clear up this misunderstanding as quickly as possible.

He summoned his strength and attempted to raise his left arm, watching in frustration as it moved only an inch or two before falling back onto the sheet. His fingers responded more readily, so he walked his hand across the sheet like a crab, dragging his lifeless arm behind it. He walked it up his side, crossed his stomach, and stopped in the middle of his chest.

Richard lowered his chin as far as he could. He needed to see his name printed on the plastic bracelet encircling his wrist. You couldn't go to the bathroom without the hospital staff checking that bracelet to verify your identity. Someone would be looking at it soon enough.

He turned his arm and read:

RIORDAN, MICHAEL J.

Richard squeezed his eyes. His head began to throb as he opened them for another look. *What the—*

The pain spiked and commanded his full attention. He closed his eyes until he could think again. Nothing made sense. He half expected Rod Serling to appear from behind the curtain and welcome him to *The Twilight Zone*.

Richard surveyed the room, looking for a mirror or anything shiny. A chrome band covered the edge of the tray table next to his bed, reflecting a portion of the ceiling on the shiny surface. He needed a better angle.

His eyes followed the thick gray wire that looped around the bed rail and ended at a control switch. He walked his hand into position and pressed the large button in the center of the device. Nothing happened. He moved his finger to the top edge of the button and pressed again. An electric motor whirred and the top of the bed rose. He held the button and waited for the rest of the room to come into view.

Richard lifted his head until he could see directly into the reflective surface. A stranger's face looked back at him! The alarm on the bedside monitor squealed, and his head fell back to the pillow.

Moments later, someone entered the room. Richard no longer had the strength to open his eyes. The alarm stopped. He sighed, grateful for the silence.

A hand touched his shoulder, and a voice whispered, "We need to talk."

Chapter 2

Ten Months Earlier

"So … what are you going to do with all that money?" she asked, turning her glass in her hand.

Richard's laughter flowed as easily as the champagne had flowed from the empty bottle on the table between them. After all, it was a celebration of sorts.

He leaned over the table and whispered, "I can think of a few things, but if I told you, I'd have to kill you."

She studied him for a moment as a faint smile played on her lips. "Well then, I guess you'll just have to surprise me."

Attractive and witty, Carolyn Giordano had become more of a friend than a client. She knew the right thing to say at the right moment. Not only was she easy to talk to, but her frequent compliments boosted Richard's confidence, which had been sagging lately. Carolyn could be very convincing.

Their waiter appeared and cleared the table. He returned a few minutes later with two cups of coffee. "Will you be having dessert?" he asked.

Richard glanced at Carolyn, and she gave a quick nod. He ordered crème brûlée for both of them, and the waiter disappeared into the adjoining room.

He leaned back in his chair and watched the candlelight dance in Carolyn's ebony eyes. He felt better than he had for some time. Until the familiar feeling that it was too good to be true crept into his consciousness. He couldn't shake the sense that something sinister lurked in the shadows, waiting to drag him back to the mediocrity of his life.

His cell phone rang. He pulled it from his pocket and dismissed the call. "Whoever it is can wait."

Carolyn smiled, apparently pleased with his decision.

Before he slipped the phone back into his pocket, he noticed the time: almost ten. He'd have to invent some excuse for being out so late. Deceiving Emily was his least favorite part of this whole arrangement, but necessary for the time being. He leaned forward and sipped his coffee.

Carolyn soon pulled him back into conversation. They enjoyed their dessert, and laughed and chatted over a second cup of coffee, unaware that they were being watched.

∞∞∞∞

Samantha Riley observed Richard and Carolyn's little soirée from behind a large ficus plant. She'd happened on them unexpectedly and had been about to walk over to say hello when she realized that the woman with Richard was not her sister Emily. Samantha had ducked into a booth in a dimly lit corner of the room and set up surveillance.

She ordered a drink and recalled the first time that Emily brought Richard home to meet the family. While she wouldn't admit it to Emily, or anyone else, she'd been jealous the minute he'd walked through the door. Richard looked better than most of the guys Sam dated, even if he didn't have the kind of edge that usually caught her attention. His wavy brown hair had been longer back then, but his eyes were still as blue as the day she'd met him.

She crunched ice between her teeth and watched him sip his coffee. The woman laughed at something he'd said. Richard's great sense of humor had annoyed her after her divorce. Pretty much everything about him annoyed her after the divorce. At one time, she would have gladly traded places with her younger sister. Now she wasn't so sure.

She closed her eyes for a moment. When she opened them, she no longer saw Richard; she saw Matt and ... and that whore!

Samantha finished her drink and wiped a tear from the corner of her eye. Her relationship with Matt had died five years ago. Ancient history. She glanced at the clock on the wall and decided she'd seen enough. She slipped a ten dollar bill under her empty glass and left the restaurant, unsure of what to do with this new information.

∞∞∞∞

Richard drove home thinking about how and when he would break the news to Emily. He had to do it properly, and timing was everything. He looked at the split in the vinyl dashboard and smiled, realizing that the freedom to follow some of the dreams he'd all but given up on was now within reach. The restoration of this classic car sat near the top of that list.

Six years ago, Richard had thrown caution to the wind and bought the car he'd dreamed of owning since he was a child—a 1968 Ford Mustang Fastback. His friends and family called it a piece of junk, but the only way he could afford a car like that in tip-top shape was if he did the work himself. He didn't mind. It was a labor of love.

Richard knew a thing or two about tuning up an automobile engine, especially the older ones that didn't rely on computers. A good set of socket wrenches and a timing light were all he really needed. With a little elbow grease, he had the 302 small-block V8 purring like a kitten. Sure, the leather seats had torn in a couple of places, and the chrome had lost some of its luster, but Richard had vision. The car had a soul—a little worn and faded, maybe—but he would bring it back to life.

Two of his clients had already offered to buy "The Blue Knight," as he affectionately called it, for double what he paid. Richard vowed that he wouldn't sell his baby at any price.

He glanced at the keychain hanging from the steering column—a gift from Emily—and felt a twinge in his chest. It must be the champagne, he thought. He tightened his grip on the steering wheel, took a deep breath, and exhaled slowly.

He turned into his driveway and saw the downstairs lights through the windows. Apparently, Emily hadn't gone to bed yet. He turned off the car and sat alone in the darkness. Discretion was required. The last thing he wanted was to come clean too early and jinx the deal. As difficult as that might be, it was the most prudent course of action.

To avoid the impression that he was sneaking in, Richard closed the back door a little harder than usual and deliberately made some noise in the kitchen. Bogart, their four-year-old Labrador Retriever, padded up to him and nuzzled his hand. Richard knelt on one knee and held the dog's head between his hands, scratching him behind the ears as Bogey licked at his face.

"Hey, Boy. Have you been keeping an eye on things here?"

Bogey cocked his head and wagged his tail.

"I knew I could trust you." Richard grinned and scratched him again. "C'mon, you deserve a treat."

Richard took a biscuit from a bag on the counter and placed it in his palm. Bogey snatched it up. He gave him another pat on the head, turned off the light, and set off to find Emily.

He checked the living room and found her asleep on the sofa. With a sigh, he relaxed into the upholstered chair across from her and watched the rise and fall of her breathing. She lay barefoot with her head propped up on two large pillows. Her hair had fallen across her face.

A gentle wave of nostalgia washed over him and transported him back to the fateful day in 1985 when he'd first laid eyes on the woman he would marry.

Unseasonably warm weather had marked the spring semester of his junior year, and on the day they'd met, Richard had decided to take some work outside to his favorite bench in the quad. The fresh air and sunshine offered a respite from the long winter indoors and an opportunity for some inspiration.

He'd been working on an assignment for Professor White's Creative Writing class, an elective he'd added just before the drop/add deadline. His father had scoffed at his interest in music and literature, particularly within the context of school. "Those are hobbies, not something you do for a living," he would say. Many young men rebelled against authority by smoking marijuana or getting a tattoo. Not Richard Dunham—he wasn't quite that brave. He'd enrolled in a creative writing class.

Richard had sat and stared at the blank piece of paper in his lap. A warm breeze carrying a hint of intoxicating perfume had caught his attention and made it impossible to concentrate on his work. He'd raised his head and turned.

A female student strolled across the quad nearby. He'd been too preoccupied to notice her, and if it hadn't been for his nose, he might have missed her altogether. Richard had seen beautiful women before, but this one intrigued him.

Too shy to approach and ask her name, he'd continued to watch from a distance.

She'd walked barefoot in the grass, books in one hand and shoes dangling from the other. Her dark hair danced on her shoulders. When she turned her head, it swung as if in slow motion across her face before bouncing back into place, revealing the most beautiful, unguarded smile he had ever seen. He'd found his inspiration.

Richard's eyes had followed her until she'd walked out of sight. He'd picked up his pen, closed his eyes, and watched her once more in his mind's eye, remembering every detail.

Now, almost three decades later, he found it hard to believe he was still watching her, only this time she was asleep in their living room. She looked peaceful, even content. He wondered if she might be dreaming, and if he still inhabited those dreams.

Their relationship was on a downward slide and gaining momentum. He wanted to stop it, but he wasn't sure how. They weren't actually fighting, at least not in the traditional sense. They'd somehow disconnected emotionally, and the space between them grew. Even when there were no obvious signs of trouble, an underlying current of discontent ran just below the surface.

The Dunham men had never been comfortable discussing emotions, and this inability to communicate effectively added to their troubles.

He couldn't remember how or when it had started, but it hadn't happened overnight. It was more subtle than that—like a crack in a plaster wall that becomes more pronounced over time. As the years slipped away, so did the passion. Now, it seemed they talked less, touched less, and even had their own agendas.

They say familiarity breeds contempt, but in this case, the problem was more like indifference. No, it wasn't even that. Richard still loved her. But other demands, other priorities, seemed more time sensitive. He always thought: As soon as he'd taken care of this, or when that was finished, there would be time for Emily. And then somehow, there wasn't time for Emily at all.

It didn't make him feel any less guilty about what he was doing, but when the dust finally settled, they would both be better off. He thought it easier to beg for forgiveness than ask for permission.

Richard stood and brushed the hair from her face, then grabbed the afghan from the back of the sofa and covered her. Before leaving the room, he noticed the toes of her right foot peeking out from under the edge of the blanket and pulled it down just enough to hide them.

"Goodnight, Em," he whispered before turning off the lights and heading to his room alone. He'd dodged another bullet and avoided a confrontation. A bittersweet smile crossed his face.

Richard stared at the ceiling of the guest room. Lights from the street crept across the top of the wall as traffic passed. The new sleeping arrangements offered personal space in a relationship that had become a little too confining. He'd never expected to feel this way and couldn't explain how, or even when, it'd started. At least for now, sleeping alone in this room was more of a preference than a punishment.

Why were these memories bubbling up tonight? He'd heard that people's lives pass before their eyes just before they die. He wondered if the same might be true of a dying relationship. *Dying relationship? Is that what this is?*

A surge of emotion followed by mild nausea turned the contents of his stomach. He couldn't blame this one on the champagne. A disturbing mix of guilt, fear, and nostalgia replaced the exuberance he'd felt earlier that evening.

The compressor in the air conditioner started with a rumble. He tossed and turned for another half-hour, worried that the confrontation he'd avoided tonight would be waiting for him when he awoke.

Chapter 3

Richard slept late the next morning, which rarely happened when he shared a bed with Emily. An early riser, she usually had him out of bed by the time she got out of the shower. But these days, she let him do what he wanted.

Eventually, he made his way downstairs and discovered that she'd made breakfast for both of them. She stood over the sink, humming a tune, apparently unaware of his late arrival the night before.

Richard walked around the oak table that was set for two. He paused near the counter where the stainless steel coffee maker sputtered out its last few drops. He drew in a long, delicious breath.

Sunlight spilled into the kitchen through the large window above the sink, creating a shimmer along the edges of Emily's silky brown hair. The two stained glass sun catchers that hung in the window painted a kaleidoscope of colors on the counter around her.

Emily turned and smiled. "Good morning."

"I guess it is."

"I hope you're hungry. I made blueberry pancakes."

He secretly pinched himself. *Nope, this is real.*

They ate breakfast together, smiling and talking as if they had stepped into a time machine. He half expected their daughter Lexi to run in, jump on his lap, and help finish his breakfast as she had when she was little.

They were still sitting at the table when he began to

wish it were a dream.

"I think it's time to start planning the kitchen project," Emily announced.

Richard choked on his coffee.

"Are you okay?"

"Yes." He cleared his throat. "Just went down the wrong pipe."

"So, I was thinking," she continued, "we must have enough money in the account by now to get started. I'll have to check it first so we know what our budget is."

Richard cleared his throat again. "Em ... please, let me take care of the financial stuff. You need to pull together the design elements—paint chips, tile and counter top samples. Have you found a contractor yet?"

"No, but I was thinking of getting a quote from the guy who did my parents' kitchen last year."

"Sure. He did a great job." Richard needed to redirect the conversation away from anything financial. "So, what have you got planned for today?"

"I don't know. It's beautiful outside. I think I might take the day off."

Richard considered this for a moment. "Let's go to the park."

Now *she* choked on her coffee. "Really? Together? Since when do you blow off work to spend time with your wife?"

"What do you mean?"

"You're not exactly Mr. Spontaneous."

"I'm spontaneous. I do things ..." he swallowed hard, "... spontaneously."

"Yeah, right."

"When do you want to go?"

She just stared at him.

He made a sweeping gesture, indicating the breakfast dishes.

"As soon as we get this mess cleaned up, we're outta here."

"Sounds like a plan." She stood and slid her chair under the table.

oooooo

Franklin Park, situated within the city limits, encompassed approximately sixty acres of woodlands and recreation areas. Richard and Emily walked together along the trail that encircled a large pond near the center of the park. The stone fountain in the middle of the pond sprayed water into the air in every direction, providing a picturesque backdrop.

Richard glanced up at the Overlook, an observation platform built into a large rock formation at the north end of the pond. Countless relationships had started or ended there. Lovers visited day or night, stealing a kiss or a tender moment in each other's arms, or just watching the lighted fountain churn up the water some twenty feet below.

Richard and Emily were no exception. He remembered their first kiss, and the day Emily had brought him there to announced her first pregnancy. Over the years, it had become a landmark in their lives together.

It occurred to Richard that it had been a while since they'd been there together. He couldn't remember exactly when, and that bothered him. *Mr. Spontaneous.*

A comfortable breeze blew just enough to provide the perfect complement to the summer sun's heat. He told himself to just relax and enjoy. About halfway into their first circuit, Emily reached over and took his hand. He welcomed the gesture and they reminisced about the past.

"Do you remember the first time you brought me here?" she asked.

"Hmmm …" He rubbed his chin, barely concealing a

smile. "Can't say that I do."

She lifted an eyebrow. "Oh, really?"

"Well ... I've brought so many women here over the years, you can't seriously expect me to remember—"

"Yeah, right." She punched his shoulder. "You were such a Ladies Man."

"Hey—"

She ran ahead. "Come on!"

Richard scratched the back of his head. *What's gotten into her today?* He looked around for signs of hidden cameras. When he didn't see any, he jogged after her.

He reached the Overlook and stopped to catch his breath. Emily, in their spot on the left side of the platform, leaned against the railing and looked over the pond.

She turned to face him. "Glad you could make it."

He exhaled sharply. "What's going on, Em?"

"Do you still love me, Richard?"

The question caught him off-guard. "Yes ... of course, I love you," he said between slightly labored breaths.

"I want to hear you say it like you mean it."

Richard hesitated. His phone rang, and he reached for it instinctively. Emily rolled her eyes. After the second ring, he sent the call to voicemail and looked up. "I'm sorry."

"I know." She sighed. "Let's go."

She took a step, and he grabbed her arm. Without thinking, he placed his other hand behind her head, pulled her toward him, and pressed his lips against hers. She didn't resist.

Twenty-five years disappeared in an instant. For a moment, the past and the present were one, and Richard had some trouble distinguishing between them. His attention returned slowly, almost reluctantly, to the here and now. Her smell, her taste, her touch brought back a flood of memories that were much stronger than he expected and reminded him of how powerful their connection had once been. He pulled back just far enough to take a breath and look into the big green eyes that had once rendered him powerless. He wondered if she'd felt it, too.

Emily remained silent. Those eyes studied his.

Why? He wondered. Why today? Why here? What was she doing? The moment vanished as quickly as it had arrived. His brain took over and tried to make sense of the sudden shift in her disposition. What was she up to? He thought she must have staged this little outing to end up here until he realized it'd been his idea to come to the park in the first place. Perhaps his guilt fueled his paranoia.

"Richard?"

A few seconds passed. "Hmmm?"

"Where were you?"

"Uh ... I'm here, I was just ... remembering."

"It was a long time ago. Longer than I'd like to admit." She sighed.

"Yeah, me, too."

Richard's phone rang again. He looked at the screen—Carolyn—and then back at Emily. It rang a second time and he almost dropped it.

"Go ahead, answer it."

"No, it's work." He sent the call to voicemail. "And I'm not working right now."

Emily studied him for a moment. "Richard, what's going on?"

"What do you mean?"

"With us."

His chest muscles tightened and his heart thumped. It was a valid question, but he didn't have an answer. They walked on in silence. Richard stole a glance at her from the corner of his eye.

After a few minutes, Emily spoke. "Richard?"

He hesitated, anticipating a continuation of her previous line of questioning.

"Are you afraid to die?"

He slowed down and looked at her. *Oh my God, is that what this is about? Is she dying?* "Why ... why would you ask that?"

"No reason. It's just that we're not getting any younger."

"True, but we've still got a good thirty or forty years, don't you think?"

"Perhaps."

He stopped walking and grabbed her arm just above the elbow. "Emily, are you okay?"

She smiled. "I'm not sick, if that's what you mean."

He let go and blew out his breath as they began to walk again. More silence.

"I started a bucket list," she said.

"You did?" He'd seen the movie. A bucket list refers to the things you want to do before you 'kick the bucket', but they'd never discussed the idea. His heart still pounded. He wanted to lighten things up a bit. Get back to where they were when they started this walk.

He smiled. "So tell me ... what's number one on your list?"

"Guess."

He hated guessing. "I hope you don't want to go skydiving or running with the bulls."

"No. I want to go to Ireland."

"Really?" He scolded himself for not knowing, but he hadn't been paying attention for a while ... a lot longer than he wanted to admit.

"Grandma McKenna and I were very close. She used

to tell me stories about growing up near Dublin. I want to walk the streets she walked, maybe somehow connect with her spirit."

"Her spirit?"

"Would you come with me?"

He hesitated before a smile crossed his lips. "I couldn't have you wandering around the Emerald Isle chasing ghosts all by yourself, now could I?"

"Richard, I don't want to wait."

"What … what do you mean?"

"I want to go soon."

A lump formed in Richard's throat and he swallowed hard. "Define *soon*."

"We could go in the fall," she said.

"This fall? What about the kitchen? We can't do both. You just said—"

"I want to go *before* we do the kitchen," she said. "I have to do this."

Richard raked his hair back and started to calculate the costs of the kitchen remodeling *and* the trip. The only way they could do both was if his recent investment with Carolyn paid off quickly.

Stay calm, Richard. Stay calm.

"It's your kitchen … your call," he said, trying to act casual. They reached the parking lot, and he looked at her across the top of the car. She looked happy for the moment. He wondered how long that would last.

∞∞∞∞

At home, Emily changed her clothes and went outside to work in the garden. Richard stood near the kitchen window watching her weeding the flowerbed by the driveway as he tapped Carolyn's number on his phone. "Hey, Carolyn, it's Richard."

"I've been trying to reach you," she said.

"I know. I've been busy."

"I just found out SkyTec received FCC approval for their towers. They're going to announce it tomorrow. It should cause a nice jump in the stock."

"How exactly did you find out something like that?"

"I have my sources."

"It sounds like something you're not supposed to know, let alone tell anyone."

"You're not *anyone*, you're my partner. Now, don't be such a boy scout; this is good news."

"You're right. I really wish I'd bought more." He silently berated himself for being so conservative. But he'd been reluctant to empty their entire savings account, so he'd taken only half of what they'd accumulated over the years. He hadn't mentioned it to Emily, hoping for a big score before she missed the money. It was the forgiveness versus permission thing again.

"The press conference is at eleven. I'm sure there'll be activity ahead of the announcement, but you should still have time to get in if you buy as soon as the market opens."

"I can do that." The lure of a big payday trumped his usual trepidation. It might be the closest he'd ever get to a sure thing. He'd been around long enough to see that life rarely hands out second chances. The stock had been performing very well since they bought it— the reason for their celebration the night before. The trip Emily planned meant he would have to raise the stakes.

His financial pressures had been mounting for some time. Richard's Internet consulting business did reasonably well, but it wasn't growing as fast as he'd hoped. They'd been saving for nearly five years to remodel the kitchen, and now Emily wanted to go to Ireland in the fall. He'd like to visit places and do other things as well, but when would any of that happen? He'd wanted to finish restoring the Mustang for too long. Impatience nagged at him.

Richard slipped the phone into his pocket; time to put up or shut up. Tomorrow morning couldn't come fast enough.

Chapter 4

By the time the market opened on Friday, Richard had already transferred the rest of the money from their savings account into his brokerage account. By nine-thirty, he owned just over 36,000 shares of SkyTec stock. He'd never done anything like it before. He picked up his phone from the desk, sank back into his office chair, and called Carolyn to share the good news.

Richard found it increasingly difficult to work as the day unfolded. The stock ticker on his computer drew him like a moth to a flame. By noon, the stock had risen fifteen percent on the news of the FCC approval. By two o'clock, it was up twenty. He felt practically giddy, but if he didn't find some sort of distraction, he'd spend the rest of the day watching his computer screen. He shut it down and went outside to cut the grass.

The sun burned the back of his neck as he drove around the yard on his big John Deere. Unlike most of the other maintenance work around the house, Richard didn't mind this particular job. It normally took about an hour and allowed him some alone time to think. He'd left his phone inside, severing his Wall Street connection for the time being. He wondered how the day-traders did it all day every day, particularly when the chips were falling in the other direction.

Sweat beaded on his forehead and trickled down the sides of his face, but a strong breeze from the west brought some welcome relief. He watched Emily whenever the mower travelled in that direction. She knelt beside the flowerbed with her hands in the soil, then sat back on her heels for a moment to wipe her brow on her sleeve. As Richard approached, she turned and offered a tentative smile. Unable to be heard above the rumble of the mower, he touched the brim of his ball cap and nodded. His gaze lingered as he wondered how all this cash might affect their relationship. Perhaps she would appreciate him a little more.

By the time he finished the lawn and a few other chores, the stock market had closed. Emily had gone out, hopefully to pick up something for dinner. He walked into the house and grabbed his phone from the kitchen counter. SkyTec had given back some of the earlier gains, but finished the day up sixteen percent. He did some quick math and came up with a profit of $2,400. Not a bad day's pay for nothing more than a few mouse clicks.

After a quick shower, Richard reclined on the sofa in the living room. Bogey wandered over and set his chin down on the edge of the cushion next to him. He gently stroked the back of the dog's head.

"I made a boat-load of money today, Bogey," Richard said, appreciating the opportunity to tell someone.

Bogey's head remained still, but his eyes looked up at Richard.

"Anything you need? Just tell me and I'll buy it for you." Bogey lifted his head and barked once.

"Really? I like your style." Richard chuckled and scratched his dog behind the ears.

Eventually, Bogey curled on the floor next to the sofa. Richard clasped his hands behind his head and lay back on one of the big pillows. His gaze wandered around the room as he thought about his unexpected good fortune. He stopped at the framed photo of him and Emily that sat on the piano, and once again, he found himself lost in memories. Lately, a small voice in his head, or perhaps his heart, asked, "What kind of memories are you creating today?" and he would have difficulty breathing.

It happened again. Richard swung his legs over the edge of the sofa and sat up, nearly stepping on Bogey. He inhaled sharply as the dog scampered to his feet. It took a few minutes before he could breathe normally again.

Emily stood in the doorway. "You don't look so good," she said. "Are you all right?"

"I'm fine." He lied. "What's for dinner?"

∞∞∞∞∞∞

The sun blazed in a vivid blue sky on the day of Frank McKenna's annual 4th of July bash. A few majestic white clouds floated by every now and then, and the temperature was expected to top out around eighty degrees. By all accounts, the heat wave that was burning up the Midwest wouldn't make it to Springfield until later in the week.

Dozens of people milled about in Frank's sprawling backyard. The event that had started as a picnic for a few family and friends had, over the years, morphed into something resembling a block party. Many of the adults clustered in the shade of two large Japanese Maple trees, while others hovered around the drinks table on the veranda. Children waited in line near the ten-foot slide, situated at one end of the kidney-shaped pool. Those already in the water laughed and squealed.

Richard picked up a beer and wandered over to where Emily's brother, Frank, stood at an over-sized gas grill. "How's the project going?"

Frank was presently knee-deep in the restoration of a 1969 Dodge Charger, the muscle car popularized in the *Dukes of Hazard* television series.

"I was about to call and ask for your help again," Frank replied flipping steaks with a pair of tongs. "I need an extra set of hands to get the dashboard back together."

Frank was Springfield's top cop. His appointment to Chief of Police two years ago did not sit well with his older brother, Tommy, who was convinced the job should have been his. Fortunately, the powers-that-be had made the right decision. Everyone, with the exception of Tommy and a few of his close friends, knew he had an edge that was better suited for working the mean streets. Tommy didn't like to follow rules or regulations. Frank, on the other hand, wasn't wound as tightly, and possessed a more conventional sense of justice and diplomacy.

"Sure, I can help with that." Richard took a swig of his beer.

"Great." Frank moved on to turning sausages, and Richard stole a glance at Emily, who laughed and talked with two other members of the McKenna clan by the pool. Thankfully, when Emily wasn't around her family, she didn't act at all like one of them. He glanced at Frank— present company excluded.

"How about next weekend?" Frank moved a couple steaks away from a burst of flame.

"Sure. Consider it done," Richard replied, still watching Emily. Sometimes, you'd think she'd been switched at birth in the hospital, but you could see the similarities between them whenever they got together like this.

Frank loaded the meat onto two huge platters. "Let's go feed the masses," he said.

Richard carried one of the platters to the table and

added it to the extensive array of salads, fruits, fresh bread and pickles. He picked up a plate and moved to the end of the line.

When he'd finished eating, Richard sat in the shade of one of the big market umbrellas and scanned the festivities. Emily's sister, Samantha, sat next to the pool talking with Tommy. Both had been divorced at least once and, unlike the rest of Emily's siblings, were not presently married.

Tommy obviously had a couple of screws loose. Samantha, on the other hand, was a bit more interesting. A twenty-year veteran of the Springfield police force, she was attractive in a tomboy sort of way—no comparison to Emily in terms of beauty and fashion sense, but far from unattractive. Today, she wore cut-off shorts and an Aerosmith t-shirt. She'd tied her Auburn hair in a ponytail and pulled it through the back of a baseball cap.

When he and Emily started dating, he often caught her watching them together with an envious eye. He never admitted it to anyone, but he rather enjoyed the attention at the time.

She looked in Richard's direction and he waved. Samantha did not reciprocate. He watched her talking with Tommy for a few minutes before she turned and headed toward the house.

"Hey, Sam," he said as she walked past.

She glared and continued on her way.

Every time he'd get close to figuring her out, there would be another setback. Today's reaction was cold, even for Sam. Sure, she often called him *Dick* just to push his buttons, but that's what she was—a button pusher.

It started after her divorce. Matt had cheated on her five years ago and, when she found out, it wasn't pretty. Matt was lucky she wasn't carrying her gun the night he got caught, or she might have put a bullet in the middle of his forehead. Perhaps *lucky* isn't the right word. The poor bastard probably still sleeps with one eye open.

Richard stood up, grabbed another beer, and followed her into the house. He found her alone in the kitchen.

"Hey, Sam, you're awful quiet today."

She looked at him with an unexpected intensity. "I know what you're up to, Dick."

"What are you talking about?"

"You better stop sneaking around and tell her."

Richard swallowed, wishing he was still outside. "Tell her what?"

"I don't like people lying to my sister. I'm funny that way. You—"

Frank's sixteen-year-old daughter, Meghan, entered the room and walked over to the refrigerator.

Samantha stopped talking and glared at him for a moment. She took a step closer and pointed a finger in his face. "If you don't tell her, I will," she whispered.

Richard watched her turn and walk away, before glancing at Meghan, who retrieved a large dessert tray and left quietly. He inhaled, then slowly exhaled. He didn't know what to do next. Did she expect him to tell Emily here at the party? Was *she* planning to tell her today? How long did he have? He needed to buy some time, another week. *Why can't you just mind your own damn business, Sam?*

The beautiful day just turned sour.

ooooo

Richard sat in Carolyn's office at the restaurant admiring the decor. The white-walled room with its polished black desk and leather chairs looked more like the office of a

Park Avenue executive than that of a restaurant owner. Carolyn had worked in New York City before returning to Springfield to run the family business when her father died three years ago, and he wondered if she'd brought the furniture with her when she moved back. A little over the top for Springfield. He imagined there weren't too many things that Carolyn wanted and didn't get.

He'd come to discuss his current predicament and see if she could offer any advice. He'd shared the details of yesterday's conversation with Samantha and his fear that Emily would find out about the missing money. A phone call had interrupted them, and Carolyn had excused herself to settle a dispute in the kitchen.

"Don't ever own a restaurant," she said when she returned.

"I wasn't planning on it."

"Good. Now, where were we?" She sat in the big leather chair on the other side of the desk.

"You were talking me down off the ledge."

"Oh, yeah." She smiled. "I have some good news. My source keeps raising his expectations. He hinted at more positive news to be released next week."

Richard shifted in his chair. "That doesn't really help my immediate situation, does it?"

"This is not the time to be getting cold feet," she said. "This company is on the verge of taking off. You'd never forgive yourself if you got out now. I don't want to see you regretting this for the rest of your life."

"I don't either, but there could be serious consequences at home."

"You could always stay with me," she said with a coy smile.

Richard didn't know how to respond, so he looked

away and said nothing.

"How upset is Emily going to be if you come home a month from now and hand her a check for fifty or sixty thousand dollars? Do you really think she's going to be mad at you? That she won't immediately forgive you for investing the money?"

He hesitated. It was a simple question, and he was pretty sure he knew the answer, but he remained silent.

"It's a lot of money, Richard. You may never get another chance like this."

He nodded. She was right.

"I have an idea." Carolyn walked around the side of her desk and swung her long, dark chocolate brown hair over her shoulder as she sat in the chair next to his. The coolness and self-assurance in her eyes drew him in.

"You're up sixty percent right now," she said. "You could sell off your initial investment of twenty thousand and still have roughly twelve thousand in play. Obviously, you're reducing your earnings potential, but your savings account would be back to where it was when you started. No harm, no foul."

He raised an eyebrow and looked at her for a moment before a smile slowly crossed his lips. "That could work," he said, thinking out loud, "as long as Samantha keeps her mouth shut until then."

"Trades take three days to close. If you sell today, you could have the money back in your account by Monday."

"Hmmm ... that does make me feel a little better. Thank you."

"Anytime," she said with a smile as they both stood. She gave him a hug.

Richard was so pleased to be leaving with a plan that he didn't notice how tightly she squeezed, or how long she held on. Before she let go, she kissed his cheek and whispered, "Don't worry, dear, everything is going to work out for us. You'll see."

∞∞∞∞

Richard awoke early Saturday morning and took the Mustang for a drive. Four days had passed since the party, and Emily had not confronted him about the money. Apparently, Samantha intended to give him more time to tell Emily than he'd expected. But how much time did he have?

He pushed it into fourth gear and pressed the pedal towards the floor. Houses and small farms on this lonely stretch of Route 7 began to bleed into one another as they rushed past his window. The speedometer passed eighty and he squeezed the steering wheel.

Richard hadn't taken Carolyn's advice about selling. He'd had every intention of doing so when he'd left her office on Wednesday, but the stock was on fire, up another ten percent, and he couldn't bring himself to pull the trigger.

Eighty-five.

He wanted to double his money. Was that too much to ask?

Ninety.

Richard frowned. He felt a slight shimmy in the wheel. He tightened his grip.

Ninety-five.

Yesterday, his stock had been up almost ninety percent. Just a little bit more.

One hundred.

The shimmy returned, and Richard struggled to steady the wheel. The speed amplified every movement. His tires bit into the gravel on the shoulder and he pumped the brakes. The speedometer needle fell, but the back end of the car fishtailed. Gravel flew. He wrenched the wheel and pumped the brakes again, struggling to regain control.

The needle passed fifty on its way down, and he jumped on the brake pedal. The Blue Knight skidded to a stop, sideways across the northbound lane. His heart beat in his throat as he backed the car onto the shoulder.

Richard climbed out of the car, walked around to the passenger side, and leaned back against the fender. He watched the morning mist crawl across an open field, chased by the rising sun. A surreal stillness surrounded him momentarily before a crow's throaty call admonished him from a nearby tree.

∞∞∞

When he returned home two hours later, he found Emily in the kitchen.

"You were up early," she said. It felt like an accusation.

"I went for a drive."

"Oh."

After last weekend's unexpected thaw, their relationship was beginning to freeze over again. He sat at the table without a word.

"You missed breakfast," she said in a flat tone.

I almost missed a lot more than that. "I'm good. I stopped and had something to eat in Riverside."

She shot him a curious glance. "Riverside? What were you doing up there?"

"I stopped at a little diner up there and had breakfast on the patio overlooking the valley. It's a great spot."

"How nice." She made no attempt to disguise her

sarcasm. "Were you alone?"

His eyes narrowed. "Was I alone?"

"It's a simple question."

"Of course, I was alone." He walked over to the refrigerator, a little surprised at the sudden inquisition. "Why? Who did you think I'd be with?" he asked as he poured a glass of water.

Apparently, Emily didn't feel the need to elaborate, and an awkward silence descended on the room. Richard set his empty glass in the sink.

"I guess I'd better get moving if you still want me to clean out the garage today."

She didn't respond.

He grabbed a banana from the bowl on the table, left the room, and headed upstairs to change his clothes. He hated this situation. He could feel the sweat on his forehead and wondered if Emily had noticed. It won't be long now, he thought. *Once the money is back in the account, I can stop feeling like a criminal. No harm, no foul.*

Chapter 5

After a mostly warm, dry week, which included a picture-perfect day for the holiday, no one complained about a little rain on Monday. The clouds hung low like a heavy gray ceiling, giving the day an ominous feel—the kind of morning that made it easy to stay in bed. Richard took his time getting up.

He finished his breakfast just before noon and walked into his office with Bogey at his heels. The first order of business was to check his brokerage account to make sure everything was proceeding as planned.

Richard had placed the sell order just before the market closed on Friday. Samantha's ultimatum left him little choice. He didn't want to wait until Monday, first because he didn't trust himself, and second so he could relax over the weekend knowing he'd taken care of it.

As his computer booted up, he looked through the mail that had arrived on Saturday—the usual junk with a couple of checks mixed in. Being self-employed meant that, rather than receiving a steady paycheck, he had to rely on the U.S. mail and the schedules of his clients' accounts-payable departments to get paid.

He frowned and shook his head at the numbers on the screen after logging in to his account. *This has to be a mistake!* Richard hit the refresh button a couple of times, but nothing changed. He checked the daily chart. The stock had opened as expected at eighty-nine cents. Then, except for the occasional bounce, the line headed south until it flatlined at around eleven o'clock. The stock price had remained at seventeen cents for nearly an hour.

Then he noticed over 36,000 shares still in his account. *No. This isn't happening.* Sweat prickled beneath his forehead. The temperature in the room had just risen fifteen degrees. *What the hell is going on here?* He searched through the day's news for an explanation. It didn't take long to find one. The headline read:

SEC Suspends Trading of SkyTec Communications.

He shook his head; he wasn't knowledgeable enough to sort this out on his own. He needed help.

Bogey, sensing a problem, wandered over from his usual spot in the corner and stood next to Richard's chair.

"Not now, boy," he said, nudging him as he reached for his phone. He dialed Carolyn's number, then got up and closed the office door. "Have you seen the news?"

"Yes, I've seen it. I'm trying to get some answers, but I haven't been able to reach my contact at the company."

"So, what do you know?" He paced around the office and nearly tripped over Bogey who watched him with a helpless expression.

"Apparently, the SEC announced this morning that they're investigating SkyTec for illegal practices … including insider trading. When investors found out, they began dumping the stock. So many shares were being traded and the price was falling so fast that the SEC stepped in and froze everything. They do that to try to protect the investors. Right now no one can buy or sell any shares."

"Well, that's just brilliant." He didn't hide the sarcasm in his voice. "What happens now?"

"We wait."

"Don't you get it? I don't have time to wait."

"No, Richard, I don't get it. I thought you cashed out

the twenty thousand. That would mean, technically, you haven't lost anything."

His jaw tightened. "Well … technically … I didn't sell."

"Oh, no," she moaned. "What happened?"

"Do you want to know what happened? I'll tell you what happened." He realized he was nearly shouting and lowered his voice. "Richard got a little too goddamn greedy, that's what happened."

"Richard—"

"I was going to take care of it as soon as I left your office, but the price was climbing again and I held out for more. What I don't understand is why the order I placed on Friday was canceled."

"What type of order was it?"

"I don't know. It was an order … the usual kind, I guess." He sat down. "Why?"

"There are different types of orders. What time on Friday?

"Late … about quarter to four."

"Penny stocks don't typically trade as quickly as other listed stocks. If you placed a market order and it wasn't executed before the bell, it would have automatically been canceled. Market orders are only good for the day."

Richard stood and resumed pacing. The temperature rose again. "How would I have known if it was a market order?"

"Market orders are the default. You would have had to specifically request a different type of order."

Richard groaned. He hadn't specifically requested anything. In his inexperience, he'd just placed the order. Another brilliant move, he thought as he slumped in his chair.

He wanted to blame Carolyn—first for getting him

involved in this debacle, and again, for not explaining something as important as how to place an order—but the only person he could blame was himself. Foolishly, he'd made an effort to sound like he knew what he was doing to impress Carolyn. But the bottom line was that he had gotten greedy. Plain and simple.

∞∞∞

Richard stood in his usual spot for a Saturday evening, on his deck looking down at two savory New York strip steaks on the grill. If grilling was an art form, then Richard was Picasso. Each week he would produce another masterpiece, properly seasoned and cooked to perfection. Tonight, however, his heart wasn't in it. It'd been a long, stressful week. He'd watched helplessly as their hard-earned money was flushed down the toilet.

Richard and Emily were approaching their twenty-fourth wedding anniversary, and over the past ten years, Saturday night steak dinners had become something of a tradition. For a short time after Joshua, their youngest, had moved out of the house, the evenings had taken on a relaxed and sometimes even intimate atmosphere. Lately, however, it was beginning to feel like one more casualty of their deteriorating relationship. Richard wasn't sure if they continued to do it out of habit, or if a deeper, more symbolic, reason existed. Perhaps neither of them was ready to let go.

Emily walked in and out of the back door, setting the table and preparing the remainder of the meal. Every now and then, Richard turned to steal a glance at her. She was still as beautiful as the day he'd met her, and he wondered why she'd chosen him to share her life with—why she'd put all her faith in him. He didn't quite understand it, but he didn't want to lose her.

He looked across the backyard, feeling guilty for his recent transgressions, and wondered how he could explain himself. A cool breeze blew across the deck. He shivered. It had barely reached sixty degrees during the day. The fickle northeastern weather could be hot one day and cold the next with little regard for the season. Tonight, his shiver didn't come from the unseasonably cool air but from the chill that had descended upon their relationship.

Somehow, he had to tell Emily that he'd gambled with their life savings and lost. He hoped it wouldn't be the end of them. He kept wondering how he could've been so stupid.

"Richard!" Emily shouted.

Startled, he turned. She stood pointing at the grill.

"Shit!" He grabbed the fork, rescued the steaks from the raging inferno, and deposited them on the front edge of the grill. He examined them, hoping he hadn't turned tonight's masterpiece into a mess.

"What happened?" Emily asked.

"I don't know. I … I guess I wasn't paying attention."

She studied him with a slight frown.

Richard held her gaze for a moment before turning back to the meat. "No worries," he said with a forced smile. "I think we caught them in time."

Emily walked over to the table and gathered up the plates and glasses. "It's a little cool out here. Why don't we eat inside?"

"Sure."

"Don't forget to turn off the gas," she called over her shoulder as she disappeared through the kitchen door.

Inside, the air didn't feel much warmer. The meat was a little overcooked, but neither of them complained. They spoke little and when they did, their words seemed stilted, mostly meaningless small talk. The distance between them seemed to have increased, as if a chasm had opened up and the ground crumbled beneath their feet. Too often, they had to step back to avoid falling in.

Richard helped Emily clear the table. He couldn't tell if she had something on her mind or was simply reacting to his distant behavior. He'd never been one to talk openly about his problems and didn't have the courage to start tonight.

After dinner, Emily stood in front of the sink, rinsing the dishes and loading them into the dishwasher. Richard walked up behind her and slipped his arms around her waist. A peace offering. She flinched at first, but then flashed a guarded smile. He read it as permission to press in a little closer. He still liked the way their bodies fit together.

"I'm sorry, Emily," he whispered in her ear.

"What's going on, Richard? Even when you're here, it's like your mind is somewhere else."

"It's nothing." He lied, and his heart rate increased.

"I think it is something."

"I just have a lot on my mind." *Here's your chance, Richard. Do it. Tell her now.* He loosened his hold and took a half step back so she wouldn't feel the hammering in his chest.

Emily stopped. "What is it?"

Richard hesitated. "It's … complicated," he said. "I'm tired. I could really use a break." *Coward!*

Her body stiffened. "A break from *me*?" She turned around to face him.

"No," he reassured her, "we're good."

She studied him carefully.

"We're good," he said again.

Something in her eyes troubled him. Did she not believe

him, or was there something *she* was not telling *him*? He needed to dial it back. *Say something nice.*

"You seem tense," he said. "Maybe when you're done here, we could open a bottle of wine and relax."

"Are you serious?"

"Yes. Maybe we both just need to chill out a little."

The fear and uncertainty that only a moment ago shrouded her face gave way to a tentative smile. She kissed him on the cheek. "That would be nice."

Emily turned and continued to clean the sink, and Richard rubbed her shoulders for a few moments before heading outside.

He sat down in one of the more comfortable deck chairs and leaned back. A few stars winked at him as the sky faded to black. How much longer could he do this? He'd been telling so many lies lately that he was losing his grasp on the truth. He'd wanted to put his foot down before things got too far out of control, but sadly, it seemed a little late for that now.

The door opened, and Emily appeared wearing a sweater and carrying a bottle of wine in one hand and two glasses in the other. He hoped this wasn't a mistake. Now more than anything, he needed to act normal and convince Emily there was nothing to worry about. He would worry enough for both of them.

He watched her pour wine into the two glasses and thought that perhaps alcohol might be just what they both needed. Richard started a fire in the metal pit between them.

They sat for a while in silence, sipping the wine and watching the flames dance. He moved the wood around periodically with a metal poker, releasing flurries of tiny glowing embers into the air. He remembered happier times when he would allow Lexi and Josh to stay out after dark and make s'mores around the fire.

Life seemed so much simpler back then. Not to say it hadn't been hectic sometimes and exhausting most of the time, but as young parents, Richard and Emily knew their purpose in life, at least for the foreseeable future. That changed when Lexi and Josh grew up and moved out, leaving him and Emily alone to redefine their roles.

"Richard?"

"Hmmm?" he said absently.

"You left me again."

He poked at the fire and watched more embers escape into the night. "No, I'm here, I just—"

"What's wrong, Richard?"

"Nothing."

"Then why have you been so distracted? Are you sick? Are you having an affair? Are you in some kind of trouble?"

He looked her in the eye. "No, no, and no."

She absently twirled a few strands of her hair and studied him for a moment before accepting his answer. They sat in silence, neither one knowing what to say next.

After twenty minutes, Emily stood and announced she was going to bed. She disappeared through the back door, and left him alone with the stars. *That went well.* He finished the wine.

His dilemma raced back to fill the mental void that had been temporarily occupied by Emily's presence. After two weeks, there was no indication that Samantha had said anything. Had she changed her mind? *Not likely.* What was she waiting for?

Richard pushed the glowing embers around the dying fire. He watched tiny flames flare for a moment and then burn out while he explored the possible outcomes of his present situation. He was playing with fire in every sense of the word.

Chapter 6

Sunday morning, Richard allowed himself to stay in bed a little longer than usual. This laziness, the result of his waning motivation, had become a disturbing trend. Adding to his discomfort, the heat wave, which had mercifully passed them by last weekend, had apparently reconsidered and returned with a vengeance. Any outside work would have to wait. His time would be spent in close proximity to an air conditioner.

After showering and donning shorts and a T-shirt, he strolled barefoot downstairs to get some breakfast. A note from Emily lay on the kitchen table.

Went out for coffee with Sam and then some shopping.

Suddenly, he wasn't hungry. He raked a hand through his hair and read the note again. The chair felt heavier than usual as he dragged it from the table. He sat and slowly blew out his breath, unaware that he had been holding it. He suspected that Samantha had arranged this little get-together to rat him out to Emily.

Nervous energy built inside him like a pressure cooker. He wanted to pace around the room, but fear paralyzed him where he sat. He couldn't have got up to save himself if the house was on fire. How did he get into such an impossible situation? More importantly, how was he going to get himself out?

ooooo

Earlier, at the Starbucks on Mission Street, Emily waited for her sister. She sat alone at a table next to a large window that overlooked the street and watched an elderly couple stroll by holding hands. They appeared to be at least eighty years old, and she wondered where she and Richard might be when they reached that age. Tomorrow would mark their twenty-fourth wedding anniversary. It seemed like a long time—and by today's standards, it was—but in comparison to the couple who'd just passed in front of her window, she was practically a newlywed.

In the past, Richard had been enthusiastic about every anniversary, even when they were dating. On their one-month anniversary, he'd brought her a single red rose. Every month after that for the first year, he'd added another rose. After they were married, he'd kicked it up a notch, with each year's gift an attempt to outdo the last. Eventually, his enthusiasm had waned, as had the originality of his ideas.

She tried to convince herself that anniversary surprises were not a true measure of a man's love, but she couldn't shake the feeling that it was somehow a barometer for the overall health of a relationship.

Emily picked up her phone and checked the time. Samantha was almost fifteen minutes late, which wasn't unusual. Sam's ex-husband Matt had always been the timekeeper.

Emily scanned the room and noticed several patrons sitting alone. She wondered if they too were waiting for a punctually challenged friend or relative. She glanced out the window again to see the elderly couple disappear around the corner. When she turned back, Samantha walked through the door.

"Hi, Em."

"Hey, Sam. Glad you could make it." The sarcasm was

lost on Samantha, who never acknowledged when she was late. Emily wondered if she was even aware of it.

"God, Em, you don't look so good. Are you okay?"

"Thanks for noticing," Emily said with a contrived smile. "I haven't been sleeping well. What's your excuse?"

They fell silent for a moment before laughing together at Emily's remark as they walked up to the counter to place their order.

"So, what's been keeping you up at night?" Samantha asked when they'd returned to their seats.

"I'm not sure … I mean, something isn't right, but I don't know exactly what it is."

"You and Richard having trouble again?"

Emily hesitated. "This time it's different. He's distracted all the time—distant—like his body's there, but his mind is somewhere else."

"Maybe that's not such a bad thing. If the sex is good, men don't really need to talk all that much. Most of what they say is a load of crap anyway."

Emily looked at Samantha as if she were a misbehaving child. Samantha raised her eyebrows, grinned, and shrugged.

"Last Saturday, he gets up earlier than me and takes a drive to Riverside," Emily said. "What's in Riverside? I ask. Nothing, he says. He stopped and had breakfast. Then last night, he's grilling steaks—and you know how particular he is about that. So I can hardly believe it when I walk outside and he's staring off into space while the steaks are on fire. If he was standing any closer, he would have gone up in flames with them."

Samantha remained silent for a moment. "Do you think he might be seeing someone else on the side?"

"The thought crossed my mind," Emily admitted, "but—"

"Didn't he have an affair a couple years ago with that Cruz woman?"

"No, Sam. We've been over this before. Nothing happened."

Samantha slowly sipped her coffee.

Emily stared into her cup and lowered her voice. "He promised me, and I believed him."

"Oh, I see. So that means it didn't happen."

Emily ignored her remark. "I asked him last night, and he assured me that he wasn't."

"God, Emily, do you know how many times I asked Matt before I caught him with his pants down?"

Emily glanced around and motioned to Samantha to lower her voice.

"Men are cowards," Sam continued in a slightly more subdued manner. "They don't like to admit things like that, and never the first time you ask."

Emily stared out the window until Samantha spoke again.

"I hate to break it to you, Sis, but Richard is just like all the rest of them. In my courtroom, men are guilty until proven innocent. Don't be fooled by—"

"Stop it, Sam. I never should have said anything."

"You didn't have to. It was all over your face." Samantha leaned forward. "I'm sorry, Em, but I just don't want to see you get hurt like I did."

"Really? Why would I get hurt like you?"

Samantha glanced away and shifted in her chair.

"Sam … is there something you're not telling me?"

Samantha bit her lower lip.

Emily raised her voice. "Sam?" Fear rose in her chest and formed a lump in her throat. Sam's obvious discomfort added to the mounting anxiety. Emily swallowed hard. "If you know something, please tell me," she said in a softer voice.

"All right," Samantha said. "I didn't know whether I should say anything."

"Whatever it is, just tell me."

"About three weeks ago, we had a retirement party at Adrianna's Restaurant. As I passed by one of the dining rooms on the way out, I saw Richard. I was going to say hello to my favorite sister when I realized that the really attractive, forty-something woman with him wasn't you. So I ordered a drink and found a spot in the corner where I could see them, but they couldn't see me."

"Richard has a lot of female clients. I'm sure it was just a business meeting. He's had quite a few lately."

"Business? I'm no expert, Em, but this didn't look like a business meeting."

"What do you mean?"

"I saw a bottle of champagne on the table, and they were laughing and carrying on like a couple of high school kids."

"How many drinks had *you* had at that point?"

"I know what I saw."

"I think you were seeing you and Matt all over again."

After Matt had cheated on Sam and she'd promptly divorced him, Emily had detected a hint of jealousy from her sister. Sam had become much more sarcastic in her comments, projecting her disdain for her ex onto men in general, and Richard in particular. Richard was nothing like Matt, a fact which must have become painfully obvious to Sam after the divorce.

"Look, Em, I'm telling you what I saw. You can do what you want with the information."

"I'm sure it wasn't as bad as it looked. I know Richard wouldn't do that to me."

"Yeah, I knew Matt wouldn't either," she scoffed. "Sometimes, you're so naive."

"Naive?"

"Look at the facts, Em." She set her cup down and clasped her hands together. "He's out a lot, he's distracted, he's been spotted carrying on with a beautiful woman at a fancy restaurant …" She paused to look her sister in the eye.

"So?"

"Any changes in the bedroom?"

Emily hesitated; the conversation had begun to feel like an interrogation. She sighed and avoided eye contact. "He's been sleeping in the guest room for a couple weeks."

Samantha let the words hang in the air between them.

Emily set down her cup and studied her sister. Samantha built a pretty good case, but it was all circumstantial.

"I'm sorry, Em, but a girl's got to protect herself, you know?"

Emily didn't respond.

They talked for another fifteen minutes, but Emily's mind was no longer on their conversation. She'd fixed her attention on a single dirty little word, an accusation. *Naive*— not a word she'd use to describe herself. Did Samantha mean naive only in matters of the heart, or was it evident in other areas of her life, as well? Perhaps one's naiveté was a selective mechanism, allowing a person to believe only the things they wanted to believe and reject those that were too painful to consider.

Emily wasn't prepared to admit defeat or throw twenty-four years of marriage away on circumstantial evidence. But she wasn't ready to confront Richard yet, either. She'd be a little less *naive* and wait to see how the anniversary thing played out. She wasn't ready to put him on trial, but if she did, it would be in her courtroom rather than Samantha's.

∞∞∞∞

Richard didn't hear Emily enter the house. He sat in his office talking on the phone with Carolyn. His computer screen displayed updates on the SkyTec situation.

"I'm home," Emily said.

Richard jumped in his chair and turned toward the door, making no attempt to cover the contents of his screen. "Hang on a minute, Steve," he said into the phone before pulling it away from his ear.

"I didn't hear you come in." He wondered how long she'd been standing there and if his attempt at subterfuge was too little, too late. "You're home early."

"I didn't feel like shopping. I'm going to go lie down."

He watched her turn and leave, praying it was the heat that had gotten to her and not something Samantha had said.

"Look, Steve, I gotta go," he said into the phone and then hung up.

∞∞∞∞

Upstairs, Emily adjusted the settings on the air conditioner before lying down on her bed. Her conversation with Samantha had emotionally drained her and she just wanted to sleep, perhaps for the rest of the day. She closed her eyes and soon realized that it wasn't going to happen, at least not right away. She considered taking a couple of sleeping pills, but normal people didn't take sleeping pills in the middle of the day, and normalcy was something she needed to maintain at this point in her life.

Damn it, she thought. *It used to be called trust, now I guess it's considered being naive.* She thought marriage was about trust, so why would she enter into it always looking over her shoulder or second-guessing her partner? If that's what Sam meant, then she was guilty as charged.

Emily closed her eyes again and saw her sister rattling off a list of symptoms that could have come straight out of the *Cheater's Handbook*. She quickly opened her eyes and stared at the ceiling for a half-hour before drifting off to sleep.

She awoke just before five o'clock. After freshening up, she wandered downstairs, not sure where she would find Richard or if he was even home. She followed the smell of garlic to the kitchen where she found him preparing dinner.

How sweet ... perhaps I was overreacting. Don't be so naive, Emily. She chastised herself for the latter thought but couldn't dismiss it altogether. Then she noticed the large bouquet of pink and purple hydrangea that stood in the middle of the table. Flowers for no reason—another symptom from the handbook. She wondered if a neatly wrapped package from Macy's or Neiman Marcus wasn't lurking nearby.

"What's this?" she asked, startling him.

"Hi ... it was getting late, and I figured you might be hungry when you woke up." He smiled, and she studied his face for any obvious signs of guilt before returning her gaze to the flowers.

"Thank you. They're lovely," she said, as she gently touched one of the large blooms. *Could this be a precursor to the big surprise he has planned for tomorrow? Don't be so naive.* She really needed to get off this emotional roller coaster.

∞∞∞∞∞

The next morning, Emily found Richard talking on the

phone at the kitchen table. She stopped to smell the flowers.

"I'll do that ... okay ... goodbye." He ended the call and set the phone down.

Who was that?"

"Nobody."

"Nobody? You were having a conversation with nobody?"

"It was the cable company, all right?"

"What did they want?"

Richard took a deep breath. "They want their money."

"Didn't you pay them?"

"Don't worry. I'll take care of it."

Emily watched him stand and push his chair under the table, wondering how many other things might be falling through the cracks. She made a mental note to look into their finances. "Richard, you really need to—"

"I said I'll take care of it."

Richard spent the rest of the morning in his office and the afternoon out with a couple of clients ... *allegedly*. He texted Emily at five to say he wouldn't be home in time for dinner. She swallowed her disappointment once again and ate alone from a box of leftover Chinese as Bogey watched.

"Fancy dinner we're having, huh?" She looked at the dog and sighed. "Happy Anniversary, dear." She tossed the last piece of pepper steak on the floor and watched Bogey snatch it up.

She looked around the room and felt a sudden twinge of guilt. At first, it seemed irrational. She wasn't the one who didn't care any more, who was out God-knows-where on their anniversary. She'd tried to make it work. But a more compassionate voice within her asked if she were ready to throw in the towel? Was there nothing else she could do?

What do you want, Emily?

She stood and took two wine glasses from the cupboard, then opened the liquor cabinet and removed a bottle of Merlot, Richard's favorite. He'd be home soon, and she wasn't going to go down without a fight.

ooooo

Emily's chin touched her chest and her eyes opened. She raised her head slowly, moving it from side to side as the muscles in her neck protested. An empty wine glass sat on the end table, an open photo album spread across her lap. Another glass and a half-empty bottle of Merlot sat on top of the piano.

She'd planned a romantic evening of wine and happy memories, hoping the images from the past would rekindle the passion they'd once shared. But as she sat alone and the evening had worn on, the faces in the photos turned to ghosts of some long-forgotten time. Bittersweet memories at best.

Emily didn't know what time it was or if Richard had returned, but at this point, she no longer cared. She turned off the lights and climbed the stairs to her room.

She changed and slid into bed, and a few minutes later, Richard's slow, deliberate footsteps climbed the stairs. She didn't bother to get up. Likewise, Richard did not show his face, and she assumed he went straight to bed.

The son-of-a-bitch never even acknowledged our anniversary! A chill traveled up her spine, and she pulled the covers over her head. He seemed perfectly content to go on living like roommates, but she was not at all happy with the arrangement. *This isn't what I signed up for.*

Emily wondered if his so-called client meetings included time between the sheets. That possibility hurt the most.

Sleep was out of the question. She threw back the sheet, jumped out of bed, and marched downstairs.

She grabbed the bottle of Merlot from the piano in the living room, walked into the kitchen, and turned on the small light above the stove. It bathed the immediate area in a soft glow, and she stood beneath it, barefoot on the tile floor. She poured a glass and drank it. The fire that had been smoldering inside her flickered into life. It wasn't wise to mix alcohol with fire, but she poured a second glass, anyway.

Emily took a drink, and then another, while she contemplated the worst day of their entire relationship. Richard had really blown it, but she feared that, whatever this was, it ran much deeper than a forgotten anniversary. She emptied her glass again, and that dirty little word crept back into her thoughts. *Naive.*

She reached for the bottle again, but stopped, startled by a buzzing sound in the room—not loud, just unexpected. A soft blue light shone on the wall above the table by the door. Emily set down her glass and walked over. A text message lit up Richard's cell phone.

She picked up the phone and read the message. A vise tightened around her chest as the screen went dark. She pushed a button on the edge of the phone. It lit up and she read the words again.

I have a solution to your problem. Keep smiling, dear.
We'll get through this together.

Emily sucked in a breath. She wasn't going to put up with his shit any longer.

Chapter 7

T he door slammed against the bedroom wall, and Richard bolted upright in bed. The light from the hallway pierced the darkness. Emily stood silhouetted in the doorway, her hands on her hips.

"Get out!" she shouted.

"What?" He shielded his eyes against the light.

"Get out! You have to leave!"

"Seriously? Can we talk about this in the morning?"

"You won't be here in the morning!" She threw his phone at him.

He turned away and it bounced off his shoulder. "Dammit, Emily! What the hell are you doing?"

She grabbed the comforter and yanked it off the bed. He reached for it too late. She flung it onto the floor. "Get up."

"Where am I supposed to go at this hour?"

"You can go to hell for all I care. I'm sure your girlfriend would be happy to put you up for the night."

Richard rubbed his eyes. "My what?"

"You heard me. Now, get the hell out of here."

"You're the one with the problem, Emily. Maybe *you* should leave," he shot back. He was not in the mood for this, whatever *this* was.

She glared at him.

"Go back to bed, Emily." He closed his eyes and squeezed the bridge of his nose.

"What part of *get out* don't you understand?" She grabbed his clothes from the chair and hurled them at him.

Richard knew from experience that only Emily's passion surpassed her stubbornness, and together they made a formidable opponent. If he were to get any sleep tonight, he would have to do it elsewhere.

"Fine!" He snatched his clothes and swung his legs over the opposite side of the bed. He pulled his shirt over his head in slow, deliberate movements, stealing an occasional glance in her direction. She watched him like a security guard escorting a fired employee from the building, and he despised her for the way it made him feel.

"Move it!" she shouted.

Richard looked up in time to see her grab a framed picture of the two of them from the dresser and fling it in his direction. It narrowly missed his head and the glass shattered against the wall behind him.

"Stop it!" He stood and faced her.

"Or what?" She put her hands back on her hips. "What are you going to do, Richard? You going to hit me? Make me stop? Is that how much I mean to you?"

Richard stared at her. He closed his eyes and shook his head, hoping this was all a bad dream—that he was still asleep. Unlikely. He opened his eyes and sat back on the bed, but this time, he kept a steady eye on her.

He wasn't about to run away with his tail between his legs like a frightened animal, but the thought of leaving in an ambulance wasn't very appealing either. He'd only seen her this upset once before. At this point, saying anything else would just be spitting into the wind.

He finished dressing, careful to avoid the broken glass. When he reached the end of the bed, his foot kicked something on the floor. He bent down and picked it up.

"Jeezus, Emily. My phone?" He slipped it in his back pocket, as he brushed past her on his way toward the door.

"See you in the morning," he said with a *this-isn't-over* sneer.

She let him pass without a response until he reached the top of the stairs. "Happy Anniversary," she called.

Those two words stopped him in his tracks. He turned. She stood in the bedroom doorway. The biting sarcasm in her voice and the look of contempt in her eyes didn't quite mask a deeper pain. It sucked the air from his lungs like a cold December wind.

Richard's throat tightened. He whispered, "Emily, I'm—"

"Just go."

She followed him downstairs, keeping a safe distance between them. There'd be no more conversation tonight. He stepped outside and the door locked behind him with a click.

Richard's head spun. He turned around, walking backward toward his car, and looked at the house. He took a deep breath, remembering how he'd felt suffocated and wanted some breathing room. He had plenty of that now.

Be careful what you wish for, he thought as he reached his car and opened the door.

∞∞∞∞

Emily watched through the blinds as her husband backed out of the driveway. The day had felt more like a funeral than a wedding anniversary. She pounded the door with her fist and stared at the empty driveway. Their life together flashed before her eyes.

It had started with love-at-first-sight, Hollywood style. They met in college, dated for two years, and married shortly after Emily graduated. The first five years brought them two beautiful children, Alexis and Joshua. The next fifteen flew by in a blur of baby toys, books, bicycles, and backpacks.

Apparently, keeping up with the kids, the house, and their careers had taken a toll. At some point, her husband had put his life on autopilot, and their relationship had begun to show signs of neglect.

Neglect was one thing, but sleeping around was quite another. It was a betrayal of the worst kind. Richard had suggested separate beds, not her. She couldn't deny that they were having some problems, but it seemed a little strange that he would advocate such a thing. Apparently, she'd been too naive to suspect anything more than a temporary bump in the road. The reason was painfully obvious to her now—he'd found someone else.

Her anger gave way to fear. She couldn't believe what had just happened. It didn't seem possible—not for them, anyway. When she stepped away from the door, the room began to spin as if a black hole had opened beneath her feet and slowly sucked in everything she'd ever cared about. She leaned her back against the door for a moment to steady herself before sliding slowly toward the floor. She sat alone on the cool tile as the drama of the past few minutes replayed in her head.

"Oh, my God. What have I done?" she whispered to an empty house. She didn't try to stop the flood of tears. *How did we let it get to this?*

Emily cried until she could cry no more. She was alone. She didn't like to be alone.

Bogey poked his head around the corner and stared at her. He approached slowly, nails clicking on the ceramic tile. His big, sad eyes searched hers as if he sensed her pain and wanted to comfort her. Moved by what she saw in the animal's eyes, she couldn't help thinking that none of this would be happening if Richard had half as much compassion as his dog.

Emily had never spent much time with Bogey, but she was glad to see him tonight. He moved closer and she reluctantly allowed him to lick her face a couple of times before he curled up beside her on the floor. At least I won't be alone, she thought as the two sat in silence.

After what seemed like hours, she pulled herself up off the floor, rubbed her swollen eyes, and stumbled toward the stairs. Bogey followed without a sound. On her way through the dining room, she opened the door to the liquor cabinet and reached for the tequila. She stared at the bottle in her trembling hand. Bogey watched silently, as if waiting for her decision. "This is definitely not how I planned to spend my anniversary," she said.

The dog continued to watch as she walked away. She stopped and turned. "Are you coming?"

Bogey hung his head and moved slowly in her direction. Emily waited silently before they continued on to her bedroom. She had a feeling sleep would not come easy.

Chapter 8

Richard arrived at the Holiday Inn on Montgomery Street and parked in the lot behind the building. He turned off the car and sat for a moment gathering his thoughts. *Did I really just forget our anniversary?* That mistake would leave a mark.

Forgetting your anniversary was second only to infidelity in terms of relationship killers. He wondered where secretly gambling with your life savings appeared on that list. Evidently, he'd worked his way up to number two. Could number one be far away? He didn't want to think about it.

"Who the hell am I?" he asked the rear view mirror.

Richard entered the hotel through the back door and walked down the long, lonely hallway, past the empty pool. Something, perhaps the smell of chlorine, caused a tremor to rock his stomach. Just before he reached the lobby, a wave of panic washed over him. Unsure what to expect, he pushed open the men's room door, raced to the nearest sink and splashed cold water on his face.

The waves of fear subsided as the water cooled his hot skin. *How could I have forgotten our anniversary?* He turned off the faucet and watched the water drip from his chin. A face, paler and older than he remembered, stared at him from the mirror. He squeezed his eyes shut, but when they reopened, the image hadn't changed. He grabbed a couple of paper towels and dried his face.

"Lighten up," he said, leaning in toward the glass. His

voice was a bit shaky at first, but gained strength as he continued. "It's only one night. It's a nice hotel. It'll be like a mini-vacation." The man in the mirror relaxed a bit.

"There. You see?" He grinned, feeling better, until he realized he'd been talking aloud to himself in a public place. *Come on, get a grip.* He listened for signs of anyone else in the room and did a quick scan under the stall doors before he stepped into the hallway.

At the front desk, a girl younger than his daughter Lexi greeted him with a smile. He suddenly felt old. He asked for a room for the night, and a wave of relief washed over him when she told him that one was available. While the clerk began the registration process, Richard reached into his back pocket for his wallet. Another tremor. This time, the ripples were much larger. His pocket was empty.

He checked another pocket, and then another. Heat built up around the inside of his collar. *This can't be happening. Think, Richard. Where did you leave your damn wallet? God, please don't let it be back at the house. Maybe it fell out in the car.*

A voice brought him back. "Excuse me, sir?"

"I'm sorry, what?" Richard replied, realizing where he was.

"How will you be paying for this tonight?" she asked, eyes wide.

That's a good question. He patted his pockets. "I ... uh ... I think I left my wallet in the car. I'll be right back." He turned and hurried back down the long, lonely hall in the opposite direction.

He stepped out of the building into an oven and, grimacing at the sudden temperature change, raced to his car. He opened the door and inspected the area around the driver's seat. *Nothing.* He knelt on the seat to check the passenger side and caught his reflection in the mirror.

"Don't look at me like that," he said. "This is all your fault."

He shoved his hand between the seats, but thirty-five cents was all he found. Nothing on the ground outside the car, either. He kicked the rear tire. "Dammit!"

Richard sat in his car with the door open, head in his hands and feet on the pavement. His sense of security had fallen away, leaving him adrift on a stormy sea. This wallet debacle had single-handedly eliminated all but a couple of his options. He looked into the backseat and considered spending the rest of the night there. He surveyed the inside of the vehicle for anything he could roll up and use as a pillow, but found nothing. The backseat of a '68 Mustang had barely enough room for a child to sleep. The heat was another problem.

The homeless shelter might be the only remaining port in the storm now raging around him; not a very comforting thought, though more appealing than going home and facing another confrontation with Emily. An aftershock rolled through his stomach at the thought. He took a deep breath, slipped the key into the ignition, and drove off.

∞∞∞∞∞

The Blue Knight rolled up to the curb and came to a stop in front of a large, three-story brick house just outside the city's business district. Richard sat behind the wheel for a moment, and then bent down to look out the passenger window at the Lighthouse Homeless Shelter. He'd volunteered there for almost two years. Tonight, however, he faced the unwelcome prospect of becoming a resident.

The dashboard clock showed a little past midnight. At least the day was finally over. His twenty-fourth wedding anniversary had been a disaster.

Richard leaned his head against the headrest, closed his eyes, and took a deep breath. He exhaled slowly before opening them. Traffic rolled along State Street up ahead. He wondered where they were all going at this hour and imagined that, like himself, each one had a story to tell. His story had taken a turn for the worse tonight, one he hadn't seen coming. Or had he?

Richard stared at his reflection in the rear view mirror. *Is this what your life has become, Richard?* He looked at the building again and saw his friend John in the window. From the corner of his eye, he noticed the sign in the bank parking lot alternately displaying the current time and a temperature of seventy-nine degrees. He offered a little prayer of gratitude for the cool air that blew from the vents in the dashboard.

He turned the mirror so he could see his reflection again and stared into the eyes that gazed back at him. "This is a fine mess you've gotten us into this time," he said with a half-hearted smile. His attempt at humor, one of his trademarks, fell short this time, and his face took on a more serious expression. "So, what are we going to do now?" He looked deep into those eyes and found that he barely recognized them.

After a few moments, he sighed, as if the lack of response to the rhetorical question disappointed him. He pushed the mirror back to its normal position and sat up. *It's showtime.* He opened the door, stepped into the heat, and scanned the empty block before walking toward the shelter. At the front steps, he paused, unable to lift his suddenly heavy feet up to the first step. *I can't do this.* He turned and walked back to his car.

Richard stood beside the driver's door and watched John

through the office window. His peripheral vision picked up movement farther down the street. An old man walked—if you could call it that—down the sidewalk towards him. He listed to one side like a ship taking on water and dragged a large bag or suitcase. *Where the hell did he come from?* The street had been empty a minute ago.

The man approached his car and put his hand on the rear fender. "Excuse me," Richard called.

The man, probably in his mid-sixties, looked up. Something was wrong.

"Are you okay?"

"It's a little warm out." He ran his hand through his thick gray hair. Richard walked around the back of the car. "You've got that right. Can I help you?"

The man eyed Richard for a moment. His baggy pants and faded shirt looked old, but neat. "I hope so." He leaned his back against the side of the car, his breathing labored.

"Where are you headed?" Richard asked.

The man inhaled slowly. "I haven't a clue. I seem to have lost my bearings and forgotten where I was going. Now I'm just wandering around hoping I might remember."

I know the feeling, Richard thought. "It's too hot to be out here. Where do you live?"

The man pulled a folded handkerchief from his pocket and wiped his shiny forehead and the back of his neck. "I'm not from around here."

A strange answer. Richard wasn't sure, but he thought one corner of the man's mouth turned up ever so slightly.

"Do you need a place to stay tonight?"

"I guess I do. Do you know someplace?"

Richard grinned. "You're not going to believe this, but we're standing in front of a homeless shelter, and I happen to know the guy on duty tonight."

The man looked at the building and then back at Richard. "That would be perfect," he said as he returned the handkerchief to his pocket. He smiled. This time Richard was sure of it.

"Come on, then, let's get you inside before you keel over from this heat." He bent down to pick up the suitcase.

"Thank you, Richard."

Richard stopped and straightened up. "What did you just say?"

"I said thank you."

"No, after that. How do you know my name?"

The little man's eyes widened. "What did I say?"

"You called me Richard."

"Did I?" He hesitated for a moment. "Yes, well, you remind me of a friend of mine. Perhaps for a moment, I thought you were him."

"For the record, my name is Richard Dunham."

"Arthur," the man wheezed and tugged at his collar. "My name is Arthur Mulligan."

"C'mon, Arthur," Richard said, picking up the suitcase. "Let's go inside."

Together they headed up the stairs and through the door into the welcome relief of cooler air. Richard set the suitcase down and watched Arthur shed his tattered backpack and place it near the door.

John ushered them into the office and offered to get them something to drink. A large man of African-American descent, his beefy arms strained the fabric of his shirt sleeves. He could have been a bouncer or played linebacker for any NFL team, but his broad smile, punctuated by a wide gap between his two front teeth, offset his otherwise imposing presence.

John was a Lighthouse success story. When Richard

volunteered two years ago, John had been a resident. After a brief stay, he became a volunteer himself as a way to give something back to the organization that helped him get on his feet. After six months, management offered him an overnight staff job.

When John returned, he handed them each a glass of ice water, and Richard explained how he happened to meet Arthur out front. When he told John that they both needed a place to stay for the night, the big man looked confused.

He ran a hand over the top of his smooth head. "Both of you?"

Richard shrugged.

John turned to Arthur and smiled. "Let's take care of some paperwork, so we can get you boys settled for the night." Then he led him to the chair beside his desk.

Richard sat in the corner of the room and studied Arthur as John explained the shelter's rules and procedures. The man's coarse gray hair stuck out in all directions as if it had a mind of its own, reminding him a little of Albert Einstein. His clean, thrift-store clothing contrasted with his otherwise disheveled appearance, and a little twinkle in his soft blue eyes gave Richard the distinct impression there was more to this stranger than his appearance suggested.

Richard closed his eyes and replayed the events of the evening. He'd been thrown out into the street and was, at the moment, homeless. He squeezed the bridge of his nose and fought back his growing irritation.

John finished with Arthur and ushered him into the living room to wait until he could get a bed ready. "Next," he said when he returned.

Richard opened his eyes.

"So, my friend," John said, "what are we supposed to do with you?"

"I just need a place to crash for the night," he replied, "and I was hoping we could skip the paperwork."

John grinned and nodded. "I hate paperwork."

"Good. Maybe I could sleep in the purple room."

The small overflow room on the third floor that Richard referred to didn't figure in the shelter's official capacity. It held two single beds and not much else. A local contractor had donated the purple paint when they'd renovated.

"Okay, but here's the bad news. We were full before you guys showed up tonight, so I'm going to have to put Arthur in there with you."

"You're kidding …"

"That's how it's gonna have to go down, at least for tonight."

"Fine. He's a little strange, but I guess since I'm the one who brought him in, I shouldn't be complaining, right?"

John smiled. "The guy looks beat. He'll probably go right to sleep."

Richard stared at a photo of the director and his wife on the desk. "I hope you're right. It's been a rough day."

"So, what happened, Richard?" Richard looked up. John's expression had turned serious. "Why are you here?"

He sighed. "It's a long story, and even if I understood it, right now I don't have the strength to tell it."

John raised an eyebrow. "Are you okay?"

"I'll be fine. I just need to get some sleep."

"Okay then, let's get you two settled."

Neither of them noticed Arthur watching from just outside the doorway.

Chapter 9

Richard lay on the twin bed with his hands clasped behind his head and stared into the darkness.

"Do you mind if we talk for a few minutes?" Arthur whispered.

"I guess not," Richard replied, curious about the man on the other side of the room. "What do you want to talk about?"

"You," he said.

"Me?"

"Yes. You seem a little out of place here. If you don't mind my asking, how is it you ended up here tonight?"

"I'm still trying to figure that one out myself." He thought of leaving it at that, but something in Arthur's voice made him want to continue.

"My wife Emily and I have been having some issues lately, but the problem tonight is that I forgot our anniversary. Twenty-four years, and it just slipped my mind. Well, it didn't slip hers. She got her panties in a bunch and threw me out. Woke me up an hour ago and told me to leave. Just like that. Frankly, I don't think the punishment fits the crime."

"Do you still love her?"

The question surprised Richard. He hesitated before replying. "Yes."

"Then, what's the problem?"

"What's the problem? Are you kidding?" Richard pushed himself up on his elbows and looked in Arthur's direction. "For starters, we're having this conversation in a homeless shelter. Yesterday was my wedding anniversary, and all I got was the boot."

"No, Richard, that is the *effect*. I was asking about the *cause*. They are two very different things that you must be able to separate if you are to have any chance of fixing this. You can't fix a problem if you don't know what's causing it."

Richard opened his mouth, but found he had nothing to say.

"The truth will set you free, my friend."

"The truth, huh?" Richard thought about it for a moment. "I'm not sure, Arthur," he began, "it's like we've been growing apart. Other things have somehow become more important—things to do, deadlines to meet. With Emily, I guess I just figured there's always tomorrow."

Arthur sighed. "There was a time when I thought the very same thing, but I was mistaken. It wasn't until my wife died that I realized how foolish I'd been. It's pretty arrogant to believe we always have tomorrow."

"I'm sorry for your loss."

"I've made peace with it." An awkward silence followed.

"We used to be close," Richard continued. "We used to want the same things. She used to tell me she loved me, but I don't think that's true any more."

"So you're not really sure how she feels because she doesn't tell you?"

"Yeah, I guess you could say that."

"Do *you* ever tell *her*?"

"Tell her what?"

"How you feel."

Richard paused for a moment and then admitted a little sheepishly, "No, I guess I don't."

"I see. So, neither of you really knows for sure how the

other one feels. You're letting your minds create a picture based on what you *think* the other is feeling."

Richard remained silent.

"It sounds to me like a communication problem."

"I don't recall asking for your opinion," Richard said, suddenly frustrated with the old man's meddling.

"All I'm saying is that everything we do is a choice. We are constantly choosing what to think, what to say, how to act. We are free to choose as we wish, but each one of those choices has consequences. We must pay attention."

"Let me ask you something, Arthur. If you're so smart, how did you end up here in a homeless shelter? You *chose* this? I certainly didn't."

"Sometimes, all it takes is a couple of bad decisions."

Both men waited. Arthur's last words hung in the dark room.

"Wouldn't it be something if we could see the consequences of our decisions while there was still time to change our mind?" Richard asked.

"Do you think it would make a difference?"

"Well, sure. Don't you?"

Arthur said nothing.

"There's something else ..." Richard hesitated. "I guess you could say I made a bad decision."

"How so?"

"Without discussing it with Emily, I emptied our savings account—a considerable amount of money—and made a bad investment. The money is all but gone, and I haven't been able to tell her. I've been a wreck, and I think she's starting to suspect something. Then I throw gasoline on the fire by forgetting our anniversary. I've never done that before, but I was just so damn distracted."

"Hmmm, I see."

"You see? What do you see? Help me out here, Arthur, because my life is suddenly in the shitter." Richard waited in the silence that followed, hoping for something, anything, that he could use.

"Honesty isn't just the best policy; it's the *only* policy," Arthur finally said. Not exactly what Richard wanted to hear. "You have to tell her the truth if you want this relationship to continue."

"You're probably right," he sighed, not looking forward to *that* conversation. *There has to be another way.*

"As always, my friend, it's a choice—your choice. You have been given the power. You are in control."

"Control? I wish."

Arthur remained silent.

"If I'm so in control, why am I here having this conversation?"

"I'm afraid I can't answer that."

"I didn't think so." Richard snorted. "Look, at this point, I just want my old life back. It doesn't look so bad from where I'm sitting now."

"Is that what you've always wanted for yourself, a *not-so-bad* life?"

"Well, it was certainly a hell of a lot better than this."

"I know, but my point is you should be asking for more."

"But it was enough for me. I guess you could say I was content most of the time."

"Apparently, it wasn't enough for Emily. It seems to me perhaps *she* wanted more."

Richard thought about this for a moment. "That's the problem," he explained, "she always wants more. It's like nothing I ever do is good enough."

"What do you do?"

Arthur's probing pushed Richard's buttons. He felt the

need to defend himself, as if he were talking to Emily again. His difficulty in answering only added to his frustration.

"Well, Richard?"

"You're starting to sound like Emily," he replied.

"And I imagine you are sounding like Richard."

"What is that supposed to mean?" Richard shot back.

"It means the two of you are never going to get anywhere if you're constantly defending yourself like this."

"Hey, you don't know Emily, and you've only just met me, so maybe you shouldn't be talking about things that don't concern you." Richard had had enough of this conversation.

"True. I don't know you all that well, but I—"

"Look, Arthur, I'm really tired. I'm going to sleep now," he said firmly and rolled over to face the wall.

Arthur fired one more shot. "Is this another one of your tactics?"

"Goodnight, *Emily*," Richard called over his shoulder, hoping it would end the conversation.

"I'm just trying to help you," Arthur said softly.

Richard spun around to face the old man's silhouette. *"You?* Trying to help *me*? You'd probably still be wandering the streets if it wasn't for me."

"Perhaps," he said with a sigh. "You were very willing to help me earlier tonight, and I appreciate that. Now, let me return the favor."

Richard hesitated. "Unless your backpack is full of hundred-dollar bills and you're willing to part with them, I don't see how you can help me."

"You really don't get it, do you?"

"Get what?"

"The problem isn't the money. The problem is the choices you've been making."

"Thank you, Dr. Phil, but here in the real world, it doesn't work like that."

"The real world, huh?"

"Yeah, the real world, where shit happens and you have to play the hand you've been dealt. It's just the way it is."

"I see," Arthur said. "Have you ever played Draw Poker?"

"Yes, but—"

"Good. Then you know that you start out with five cards. How you got the cards is not important. The important thing is that you have a chance to draw, to change your hand. You get to choose which cards to keep and which ones to throw away. No one chooses for you. It's called free will, and the best part—"

"Okay, enough. I don't need you to explain the game of Poker. That's not life. This is life. Right here and right now. The good, the bad, and the ugly."

"So, you look around yourself and you think this is all there is? The immovable, unchangeable, like-it-or-leave-it *real* world?"

"I'm afraid so, old man."

"And there's nothing you can do about it?"

"From where I'm sitting, I just don't see it."

Arthur fell silent.

In the darkness, Richard was unable to see the sly smile that crept slowly across the old man's face.

Chapter 10

J ohn opened the bedroom door and found Richard lying on one of the beds in the small room, face down in the pillow.

"Hey, buddy, time to rise and shine."

Richard didn't move.

John walked to the bed and tugged on his arm. "Hey … Rip Van Winkle … it's time to get up."

Richard stirred. "Hmmm?"

"What do you think this is? Some kind of a resort?" John laughed as he watched Richard pull himself into a sitting position. "We've got work to do. No free rides, not even for you."

Richard looked around the small green room. His bed sat next to a wall with a dormer window like you'd find in an attic. His clothes lay across the foot of a neatly made twin bed on the other side.

Richard frowned, a little disoriented. "Where am I?" he asked, rubbing his eyes

John raised an eyebrow. "You're at the shelter."

"Yeah, that part I remember, but I fell asleep in the Purple Room."

"The Purple Room?" John shook his head slowly. "What are you talking about? Ain't no purple rooms here."

"Of course, there is. The extra room on the third floor."

"That's where we are now, but it's never been purple."

"Look, I might be a little groggy, but I'm not stupid."

"Richard, you and I painted this room in the spring with paint leftover from the living room. Surely you remember that."

Richard hesitated. The look on John's face changed from confusion to concern. He had no recollection of painting this room, or any other room, with John. He didn't want to send up any red flags, at least until he could figure out what was going on, so he used a little humor to diffuse the situation.

"Of course I do," he said. "And stop calling me Shirley."

John studied him for a moment, then laughed out loud. "There you go," he said and placed a beefy hand on Richard's shoulder. "Come on downstairs. I saved you some breakfast."

"Thanks, I'll be right down."

John disappeared into the hall, leaving Richard sitting on the bed searching for answers. Suddenly, he jumped up and ran to the top of the stairs. John was already halfway down.

"Where's Arthur?" Richard called after him.

"Arthur?"

"Yeah, Arthur. The guy who slept in the other bed last night."

"Nobody named Arthur has been through here lately."

"Sure he has. He came in with me last night. You set us both up in the … uh … *green* room." Richard's voice trailed off.

John folded his arms across his chest and frowned. "What's with you this morning? You came in here alone last night. You said Emily threw you out and asked if you could stay the night 'off the books.' I did you a favor, man, so don't make a lot of noise and get me in trouble. Okay?"

"Yeah, sure thing," he muttered and watched John continue down the stairs.

Richard dressed quickly and ate breakfast alone at the big dining room table. Midway through the meal, his struggle to understand the bizarre circumstances of the previous night stole his appetite. He remembered Arthur and their conversation in great detail, but couldn't ascertain the man's current whereabouts. What confused him the most, however, was that no one else remembered seeing him.

Richard had watched John do the intake paperwork. *Am I losing my mind along with everything else?* He picked up his plate and rinsed it in the kitchen sink.

The first thing he needed to do was search for his missing wallet. He drove home, forcing himself to entertain only positive thoughts about finding it, hoping it would somehow influence the final outcome. He couldn't bring himself to consider the challenges he would face if it were not there. But the single most important event of the morning, and possibly the rest of his natural life, would be his encounter with Emily.

She threw me out of the house in the middle of the night, he thought. For God's sake, I messed up, but I certainly didn't deserve that kind of treatment. I forgot our anniversary. What happened to good old-fashioned forgiveness?

Emily's car wasn't in the driveway when Richard arrived at the house, and the garage door was closed. From where he sat, he couldn't see whether her car was parked inside. He hadn't considered the possibility that she wouldn't be home. He might be able to slip in, get cleaned up, and prepare for his afternoon meeting. He'd show up that evening with some flowers and a bottle of wine and, by then, everything would be just a bad memory.

Richard got out of the car feeling much better and walked toward the house. He stopped in front of the garage and looked in the window. Emily's car sat quietly on the other side of the door as if taunting him. He swallowed hard, opened the door, and stepped into the empty kitchen.

The echoes of last night's drama hung heavy in the air like the smell of gunpowder after a battle.

Emily walked into the room. Her lips tightened when she saw him.

"Hello, Emily," he said, testing the water.

She planted her hands on her hips, her eyes red and swollen. "What are you doing here?"

"I live here."

"Not any more you don't."

He'd seen that look before and knew enough to tread lightly. "Em ... I ... I came to talk."

"I've already heard everything I need to hear. So you can just turn around and leave."

"You've got to be kidding. This can't be how you want to play this."

"Play? I'm not playing, Richard. This is serious."

"Look at us, Emily. What the hell is going on?" he said, not sure how much she knew.

"I think you know what's going on."

She must have found out about the money. Damn you, Samantha. That wasn't a conversation he wanted to have right now. "Look, I'm very sorry about our anniversary. I've been distracted lately with—"

"You're distracted, all right," she said as if she knew exactly what he had been up to.

He squirmed a little. "I'm not even sure how this whole thing started."

She folded her arms in front of her chest. "That is SO like you, Richard."

"Emily, I'm sorry. C'mon, whatever this is, we can get past it. You know I love you."

"Maybe *you* can, Richard, but I'm not so sure I can get past this one. And what about you? You checked out of this relationship a year ago." She hesitated for a moment and her voice softened. "Why, Richard? How long has this been going on?"

"Emily, please." He held out his arms and moved toward her.

"Don't touch me." She recoiled from his advance. "I can't do this."

"Emily," he pleaded.

"I said no!" Her hands were back on her hips. "Now, why are you here again?"

"Look at me," he said as he raised his arms. "I need to take a shower. Then I need to do some work. My office is here in the house, remember? I need to prepare for an important meeting this afternoon."

"Of course, another important meeting," she said. "Our marriage is falling apart, but don't miss any meetings, Richard."

"We need the money. For crissakes, Em, this is important."

"That's exactly my point. There's always something—or someone—more important than me." She glared at him.

"That's not fair."

"Oh, so I'm the one who's not being fair?"

"Look, I can't do this right now, I have to get cleaned up."

"Fine." She stared at him. "But you have to leave after that. I can't have you here during the day, either. You're going to have to find someplace else to work."

"No." He attempted to put his foot down. "I can't just work someplace else. My—"

"I thought you told me you could do your job from anywhere. So take your little laptop and your cell phone and go find another place to sit and do whatever it is you do."

"It's not that easy."

"Why not?"

"Because all my stuff is *here*," he argued. "I have files and other things I can't take with me."

"You'll think of something." She turned and walked away.

Spitting into the wind.

Chapter 11

"That went well," he said to himself on the way upstairs. *What the hell is wrong with everyone today?*

He found his wallet on the floor of the guest room where it had apparently landed when Emily threw his clothes at him. After a quick shower and a change of clothes, he spent the next hour preparing for his meeting, grateful that Emily had left him alone to work.

He packed his briefcase and walked through the dining room into the kitchen, wondering where she'd gone. When he looked in the living room, he noticed she hadn't cut him out of any of the photographs. That was a good sign.

"Em?" he called on his way back to the kitchen. No answer. She'd been in the habit of telling him when she was leaving and where she was going, but apparently, everything had changed overnight.

Well, maybe not everything. Bogey ran toward him from the den as if his tail was on fire. Richard squatted to greet him.

"Hey, Bogey! It's good to see you, boy," he said with a big grin. He held the dog's head with both hands, scratching him behind the ears as Bogey licked at his face. "Did you miss me, boy? Yeah, I missed you, too."

Richard leaned back and looked the dog in the eye. "Has she been taking good care of you? Huh? You'll tell me if she doesn't, right?"

Bogey barked and Richard laughed. "That's a good boy!"

Richard played with Bogey on the hallway floor for a few more minutes before heading for the back door. He stopped in the kitchen and looked at the photo fixed to the refrigerator by a magnet. Their granddaughter Kayla's smile lit up his heart, as it always had.

"Hello, Little Miss Sunshine," he said, using the pet name he'd given her when she first smiled at him as an infant.

Bogey watched from a few feet away. "It's OK, boy. I'll be back soon," Richard said as he lingered for a moment. He wondered what tonight would bring. He didn't expect a reception like the one he'd just got from his four-legged friend, but he hoped Emily would have calmed down enough by then so they could talk.

The wind had picked up, and the back door slammed harder than usual behind him as he left. He hoped it wasn't an omen.

∞∞∞∞

The meeting couldn't have gone worse. Not only did he fail to walk out with a fat check in his hand as he'd hoped, he didn't get the job at all. It was a devastating blow, but the way his problems were piling up, it probably wouldn't even make the top three.

Richard stopped at Winslow's Bar & Grille, his favorite watering hole, on the way home. He sat at the bar and ordered a sandwich and a beer, reluctant to face Emily again on an empty stomach.

The bartender said little—unusual for him. Richard rubbed his chin as he scanned the room. The whole place looked different.

"Hey, Charlie. When did Winslow put in all the

TVs?" he asked.

Charlie stared at him.

"It's like a sports bar, all of a sudden."

"When's the last time you were in here?"

"Last Friday. I had lunch." He glanced around the room then back at Charlie. "You were here. We talked. Don't you remember?"

Charlie folded his arms across his chest and frowned. "They were installed in January, just before the Super Bowl." A phone rang at the other end of the bar, and he walked away.

Richard decided to let it go.

∞∞∞

When Richard arrived home, he found Emily crying on the sofa. He approached cautiously.

"What's the matter, Em?"

She looked up at him dumbfounded and wiped the tears from her cheeks. "What's the matter? Seriously, Richard? I'm mourning the death of our marriage, and you just go on about your business like nothing happened."

"I'm sorry, Em, but—"

"Well, don't be. Just leave me alone." She got up and left the room.

She clearly wasn't in the mood to have a rational discussion, and Richard wasn't looking for another fight. He climbed the stairs and walked into the bedroom. She'd made it clear he wouldn't be staying there tonight, so he grabbed a duffel bag from the closet floor and filled it with enough clothes and personal items to get him through the next couple of days. When finished, he sat down on the bed next to his bag and, not looking forward to staying another night at the shelter, considered other options.

His parents lived only a ten minute drive away, but their house was small, and he hesitated to get them involved in this situation, at least not until he knew what was going on himself. Richard's mother would be sympathetic in her own way, but his father would not approve of any of this. The thought of crawling back home and feeling like a failure in his father's judgmental eyes did not appeal to him. He would rather sleep in his car.

Richard had a fair number of business associates, but no close friends. At least not close enough to show up on their doorstep with an overnight bag. He shook his head.

The broken picture stared up at him from the floor beside the bed. He squatted down and picked up the damaged frame. Two smiling faces looked back at him through a spider web of shattered glass. He carefully removed the photo from the remains of the frame.

Emily's younger face—a face that had changed his life forever—reminded him how it felt to be in love. The memory unsettled him. Though angry at her, a part of him just wanted to go back to a time before the mess began. He swallowed as he stood and slipped the photograph into the side pocket of his bag. He left the house without a word.

ooooo

Richard considered returning to Winslow's for another drink before heading back to the shelter, but he had a ten o'clock curfew. If he didn't get back before they locked the doors, or was clearly under the influence, he might be forced to spend the night in his car. While the shelter would struggle to garner more than a single star on any rating system, it beat the hell out of sleeping in the backseat of a

'68 Mustang. And he couldn't afford to waste money that he didn't have at the Holiday Inn.

He made it back with a few minutes to spare and slipped upstairs to his room. Richard paced from one corner of the small room to the other, thoroughly frustrated by Emily's reluctance to talk to him about their predicament. His attempts to reach her by phone had failed. The first two had gone unanswered. The third time he'd called, she'd answered and promptly hung up.

Though Emily's sister was the last person he wanted to talk to, in desperation, he sat on the bed and dialed Samantha's number. He needed some answers.

"Hello, Samantha, it's Richard."

"Richard *who*?"

"Come on, Sam. You know who it is."

"You mean the *Dick* who left my sister?"

"Very funny. You might want to check your facts."

"What do you want?"

"I want to know what's going on with Emily."

"Why don't you ask her?"

"She's not exactly speaking to me at the moment."

"Do you blame her?"

"Yes, I do. I think she's being unreasonable. We had an argument. Married couples have them all the time."

"Is that what you're calling it, an argument?"

"Yes, an argument. What are you calling it?"

"Oh, I don't know … abandonment?"

"I didn't abandon her. For your information, *she* threw *me* out."

"I would have thrown you out, too."

"That doesn't surprise me."

"Are you having an affair?"

"What?"

"You heard me."

"No, of course not. Why would you ask that?"

"You're sure?"

"Yes, I'm sure."

"I don't believe you."

"You don't have to believe me." His hand tightened around the phone. "Did you say something to Emily? Is that what's going on? Does she think I'm having an affair?"

"How could you do what you did and not expect some type of volatile reaction? You know she has issues."

"First of all, I didn't do anything." That wasn't entirely true. He did lose their money, but he certainly wasn't having an affair. "And second," he continued, "how long is everyone going to keep babying her because of something that happened forty years ago? She's a big girl. Don't you think she's over that by now? Don't you think you should *let* her get over it instead of—"

"No, Richard," she cut him off, "she may never be over it. And now I can pretty much guarantee it. You hurt her where she was the most vulnerable."

Richard said nothing.

"Well?" she prodded.

"Well, what?"

"Are you happy now?"

"Of course I'm not *happy* now. I wasn't trying to hurt her. I don't want that. I love Emily."

"You sure have a funny way of showing it."

"You don't know what the hell you're talking about." The phone call was clearly a mistake.

"I used to think you were different, Richard." Her tone softened a bit. "But now I can see you're just like all the rest—a jackass. A clueless, inconsiderate jackass."

"Matt was a jackass, but you can't keep—"

"This isn't about Matt!"

"I think it is."

"I'm sorry, Richard. I have to go."

"Wait." His voice softened. "Can you please just tell Emily that—"

"I'm afraid you're going to have to tell her yourself."

"But, Sam—"

"Goodbye."

Richard sat with the phone next to his ear, listening to the silence. He brought his arm down and stared at the dark screen. He shouldn't have expected anything more from Samantha. He'd married into a family full of narrow-minded, judgmental, over-protective cops. They were circling the wagons, and he didn't stand a chance against them.

The day had been one bizarre episode after another from the moment he woke up, and he couldn't wait for it to end. Before he turned off the light, he looked at the four green walls, still unable to reconcile some of the day's events. He flopped down on the bed and closed his eyes.

Chapter 12

At breakfast the next morning, Richard's phone rang. He picked it up from the table—Carolyn.

"Please don't tell me you have more bad news," he said.

"Hello to you, too."

"I'm sorry, I just don't think I can handle any more problems right now. I've reached my quota ... for the year."

"That's why I'm calling. Didn't you get my text?"

"No. When did you send it?"

"Night before last. I'd expected to hear from you by now."

"Yeah, well, it's been a rough couple of days." He sighed. "What did you want?"

"I have a plan to get us out of this mess."

"You do?" *Could there really be a light at the end of this tunnel?*

"Let's meet and I'll share it with you."

"Where?"

"My place."

Richard knew where she lived, though he'd never been inside. "I can be there in half an hour."

"Good, I'll be waiting."

Richard had barely been able to eat anything for the past two days and had been pushing his food around on his plate when Carolyn called. Suddenly, everything looked more appealing, and he surprised himself by finishing it all. After a quick change of clothes, he jumped into his car and drove to Carolyn's house.

Carolyn Giordano had never overtly made a pass at Richard, but he had sensed on more than one occasion that she was about to. Each time he had politely redirected the conversation to avoid an uncomfortable scene. Clearly, she had wanted to take him some place that he was not prepared to go, but it frightened him to think how easily something might happen given the right circumstances.

His optimism turned to apprehension when he turned off his car in her driveway. Carolyn stood on her front porch wearing a short yellow sun dress which provided a stunning contrast to her well-tanned legs. She'd pulled her long brown hair into a ponytail.

"Come on in. I made some tea." She watched him climb the stairs and held the door as he stepped inside.

An almost undetectable chill embraced him when he followed her into the living room. Her sophisticated, expensive décor felt more like a fancy hotel, rather than a comfortable living room. *Don't touch*, rather than *make yourself at home.*

Her smile did little to put him at ease. He took a deep breath, remembering why he had come.

Richard sat on the sofa and berated himself for not choosing the chair when Carolyn sat down beside him. He slid over a couple of inches on the stiff cushion as he watched her pour two tall glasses of iced tea from the pitcher on the coffee table. "So, you said something about a plan?"

"Has Emily discovered that the money is missing?" she asked without looking up.

"I don't think so. Why?"

She relaxed into the sofa and met his gaze. "How would you like to put it back before she finds out?"

"I think you know the answer to that," he replied. "But how?"

"I could write you a check. In fact, I already have." She reached into the pocket of her dress, pulled out a folded piece of paper and held it up between them.

Richard's eyes moved to the check, then back to Carolyn. "Why would you do that?"

"I like you, Richard. I think you know that."

Richard did not respond.

"I think that's why you're nervous right now. Look at you." She rested a hand on his knee.

Was it that obvious? His skin tingled under her touch. He reached for his glass and took a long drink.

"You can relax." Her voice softened, and she retracted her hand. "We'll just call it a business deal. I buy your position in SkyTech for what you paid. You're whole again and everyone is happy."

"But the stock is worthless," he said as he set the glass down.

"It may appear that way at the moment, but I like to think there's always hope." She raised her eyebrows and a flicker of a smile crossed her lips.

"You're serious."

"Of course, I'm serious. You see, I don't gamble with money I can't afford to lose." She leaned closer. "We're friends, Richard. Friends help each other out."

"Yes, but ... but that's very generous. I don't know how I can ever repay you."

"I don't want your money."

She was close, now. Too close. "But—"

Carolyn put a finger against his lips as she slipped the check into his shirt pocket. The air suddenly left the room and it was impossible to breathe.

She removed her finger, leaned in and kissed him on the lips. She pressed herself against him, and he closed his eyes.

More time passed than he would like to admit before he disengaged. He leaned back in, only to stop abruptly.

Get a grip, Richard! He wanted to run, to get as far away from her as he could, but he didn't want to jeopardize an opportunity to fix the financial mess he had gotten himself into.

"I can't do this right now," he whispered.

"Why not?"

"I'm ... my head is a mess. I need to get the money back into the account before Emily finds out. Maybe then I can relax. You understand, don't you?"

"Sure, Richard." She studied him. "You're no good to me all nervous and jerky like this, anyway."

He forced a smile. He had just bought himself some time. When he stood, Carolyn offered him her hand, and he helped her to her feet. She smoothed her dress with both hands.

"Don't be a stranger," she called as he walked out the front door.

Walking down the steps with her money, he had the unsettling feeling that, once again, he had made a poor choice. He had no one else to blame. He had met the enemy, and it was Richard Dunham.

∞∞∞∞

Richard walked into the bank wearing a baseball cap and sunglasses and stood in line feeling like a criminal waiting to deposit his ill-gotten gains. He scanned the room, his eyes drawn to the little red lights on the security cameras mounted every twenty feet along the outside walls.

"Next," a teller called.

Richard shuffled forward in line. The large, gray room

was sterile and uninviting. A client of his walked in and entered the maze of chrome stanchions and velvet ropes. Richard ignored his wave.

He nearly turned and ran when he reached the teller window. His neighbor, Gail Jensen, stood on the other side of the counter ready to handle his otherwise covert transaction. If you looked up the word *busybody* in the dictionary, you would find her picture.

"Hi, Gail."

"How can I help you today?"

He removed his sunglasses, which apparently weren't fooling anyone, with the possible exception of Gail. "It's me, Richard." She would see his name on the check, anyway.

"Richard?" she asked with a blank look.

"Richard Dunham. Your next-door neighbor. On Kirkland."

She frowned. "You must have me confused with someone else. I've never lived on Kirkland."

Richard glanced around the lobby. Everything else appeared normal. His client waved again. Richard closed his eyes and squeezed the bridge of his nose before looking back at the teller. *Yup, still Gail.* Normally, you couldn't shut this woman up. She had a laugh that could rattle the teeth in your head. Not today. She acted as if she had never seen him before.

He endorsed the check and slid it across the counter.

She examined it then cleared her throat. "Can I see some ID?"

"Are you kidding?"

Gail flinched. "No, sir. I'll need to see your driver's license."

Richard exhaled sharply. He pulled his license from his wallet and placed it on the counter. She set it next to her keyboard and punched some numbers into her computer. Richard tapped his fingers on the counter.

The transaction took longer than he thought it should, and Gail's sideways glances fueled his growing concern. Richard leaned over the counter. "I'm in a bit of a hurry, Gail," he whispered.

"I'm sorry, Mr. Dunham. The system is running a little slow today."

Maybe the check was no good. Maybe Carolyn—

"Oh. There we go." She handed him the receipt. "Have a nice day, Mr. Dunham."

He forced a smile, replaced his sunglasses, and headed for the door. *That was weird.*

Richard decided to stop by his daughter's house on the way home. He hadn't seen Lexi for a couple of weeks and missed three-year-old Kayla's big inquisitive eyes and positive energy. He could use a dose of her sunshine to lift his sagging spirits.

He climbed into his car and slid the keys into the ignition. His phone rang and he pulled it from his pocket. Emily. He took a deep breath, tapped the speaker button, and set the phone on the passenger seat.

"Where are you?" she asked.

"That's it? No *hello*, just where are you?" His heart sank.

"Why didn't you answer my calls last night?"

"Why won't you talk to me, Emily?"

"Maybe I would if you'd answer your phone."

"Oh, that's all I have to do? You've been blowing me off for two days, then you call me once and it's my fault we don't talk?" He slammed on the brakes to avoid hitting the car in front of him.

"It was four times."

"What?"

"I called you four times last night."

"I never got your calls, probably because I'm staying in a goddamn homeless shelter." His voice rose. "Every night, they lock all the goddamn cell phones in the goddamn office. So, I'm pretty sure that's why I didn't hear your four goddamn phone calls." The light changed, and he stepped on the gas.

"You don't have to swear like that."

"That's the first thing you've heard me say this whole conversation. Evidently, I do."

"This is why I don't talk to you," she said.

"No, this is *because* you don't talk to me."

"What were you thinking calling Samantha?"

"I was thinking that I would prefer to talk to you, but I might have to settle for Sam. I was hoping to get some information, maybe even have her intercede on my behalf."

Silence.

"Emily, what is going on?"

"Please don't call my family again."

"Then talk to me, Em."

"I can't." There was sadness hidden in her almost-whispered words.

"So, you didn't want to talk, you just wanted to tell me to leave your family out of this." He glanced at the speedometer and let up on the gas a little. "I don't get it, Em. When are we going to talk?"

"Sure. Now you want to talk. You should have thought about that before you—"

"Emily, please don't shut me out."

"Don't shut *you* out? That's a good one." The attitude was back.

"Son of a—"

"Goodbye, Richard."

She ended the call as he pulled into Lexi's driveway. He turned the car off and pounded the steering wheel. *God, Emily! Why are you doing this to me?*

Richard walked up the steps and past the porch swing where he and Emily had sat the few times they'd watched Kayla. He knocked on the big wooden door, then let himself in.

"Hello," he called from the foyer.

Kayla appeared in the living room doorway. She beamed an enormous smile and ran toward him. "Grampa," she squealed.

Richard got down on one knee, scooped her up, and gave her a big hug. "Hello, Little Miss Sunshine." He squeezed her again before he set her down.

She held out her hand. "C'mon, Grampa, let's play."

He extended his index finger, and she wrapped her little hand around it. Lexi watched from the kitchen. He offered her a smile and a little wave with his free hand. Kayla led him past the muted TV set into her little corner of the planet, inhabited by a multitude of dolls, stuffed animals, and plastic kitchen appliances.

For fifteen minutes, Richard sat and listened to Kayla talk about all the wonderful things that were going on in her little world. Her vivid imagination amazed him, and he wondered if she saw things he couldn't. He'd read somewhere that young children often retain the ability to see beyond their physical reality for several years. They sometimes communicate with spirits that are just beyond the physical sight, if not the belief systems, of most adults. The common, psychological explanation is that the child had simply created imaginary friends with which to play. Looking back at his own childhood, Richard recalled a friend or two only he had been able to see. They'd certainly seemed real at the time.

Kayla's attention was suddenly drawn to a character on the television screen. He unmuted the sound for her and walked into the kitchen to talk to Lexi.

"Hi, honey."

"Done playing?" She removed a cookie sheet from the oven, set it on top of the stove and slid another one in its place.

"For now." He laughed. "Smells good in here."

"Chocolate chip. Kayla's favorite." She set the timer, then turned and gave her father a hug.

"How are you holding up?" he asked.

"I'm fine. How about you?" He sensed she wasn't being totally honest.

"I'm staying at the homeless shelter."

"The homeless shelter?" Her expression fell.

"It's not so bad." He shrugged. "I had nowhere else to go."

"I wish I could ask you to stay with us, but—"

"I know, Lexi. I couldn't put you in the middle like that."

"Are you hungry?"

"No, I'm fine." He forced a smile. "How's your mother?"

"Dad … don't," she warned.

"I was just wondering if you've seen her since …"

"Then you should ask her. I told you I don't want to get in the middle of this. Somebody says something to me and I don't know if I'm supposed to be telling the other one. I don't like it." She blinked and pressed her lips together, as if fighting back tears.

"I'm sorry, Lexi. I don't want to make you uncomfortable. It's just that I—"

"Thank you," she said, clearly not wanting to discuss it any further. "I told Mom the same thing."

"She asked about me?" He tried to sound nonchalant.

"Yes." She stared out the kitchen window, her facial muscles tense.

Richard knew she wanted her parents back together—as it used to be. He wanted the same thing. Maybe not the way it was, but the way it should have been. He walked over to the sink and gave her a hug. "Everything is going to be all right, Lex." Her arms remained at her side.

"You don't know that," she said as she stepped back.

He didn't respond.

Lexi looked away, chewing her bottom lip. A demanding little voice broke the silence.

"Mommy, I'm hungry." Kayla bounded into the kitchen where they both stood, oblivious to the adult drama she'd interrupted.

"The cookies will be done in a few minutes."

Kayla hopped around the kitchen on one foot and, with a look, Richard and Lexi silently agreed to finish their conversation another time.

He left the house and walked to his car with the strange feeling that they would never get the chance.

Chapter 13

Richard sat on his bed in the *green* room at the shelter and shook his head. Carolyn had solved his immediate financial problem, but it was a hollow victory and temporary at best, which only added to the sinking feeling in his gut.

Something else bothered him. This didn't feel like Kansas any more. The people, places, and things around him were somehow just a little bit off. Not enough, however, to suggest any reasonable explanation or confirm his growing suspicions.

The first text message arrived just before ten in the morning. It was innocent enough. Richard responded in-kind. By the afternoon, they were becoming more frequent with increasing degrees of ... familiarity.

Richard closed his laptop. He left his phone in his room and went for a walk. He needed to find a better place to work, but at the moment, his options were limited.

Another text message from Carolyn awaited him when he returned: *Don't forget to bring the wine.*

He typed a reply: *Sorry, can't do dinner*

Carolyn: *Don't u want to know what's on the menu?*

Richard: *No*

A few minutes passed before his phone signaled another incoming message.

Carolyn: *I lost Emily's number. Can u give it to me?*

Richard: *Stop it*

Carolyn: *I should probably tell her in person*

Richard: *Thought this was a business deal*

Carolyn: *It is. U work for me now ;-)*
Richard: *I quit*
Carolyn: *I love your sense of humor*

None of this was funny. Apparently, Carolyn was stepping up her timetable. His life was beginning to look like a bad movie.

Carolyn: *C U @ 8*
Richard: *Told u I can't make it*
Carolyn: *I wasn't asking*

He threw the phone on the bed just before it chimed again.

I have something special planned

I'll bet you do, he thought as he sat on the edge of the bed with his head in his hands. His mind fleshed out a probable storyline. He stopped just before the X-rated part and forced himself back to reality. *Seriously? What the hell are you doing, Richard?* He stood and paced the room, wringing his hands. How could he have gotten himself mixed up in blackmail?

Another message arrived.

Don't forget the wine

Richard turned off his phone.

He fell backward onto the bed and closed his eyes. After a few moments, he heard Arthur's voice. "Everything we do is a choice. We are free to choose as we wish, but each one of those choices has consequences. The problem isn't the money. The problem is the choices you've been making."

Richard opened his eyes and scanned the empty room.

When he closed his eyes again, he heard, "As always, my friend, it's your choice. You are in control." He sat up. *Damn it! It is my choice.*

He'd created one impossible situation after another. Hiding behind the lies was like trying to catch a falling knife. Each time, it cut a little deeper. It had to stop, and he was the only one who could stop it.

∞∞∞∞

Richard stood on Carolyn's porch a few minutes before eight and stabbed the doorbell. He took a deep breath, shifting his weight from one foot to the other and back again.

Carolyn opened the door and smiled. Her ebony eyes sparkled with anticipation. "Hello, Richard. I'm so glad you could make it."

Richard held up his hands. "Slow down, Carolyn. I can't stay long. I just came to talk."

"Oh … well, please come in. Perhaps I can change your mind." She touched his arm as he stepped into the house and closed the door behind him. She gestured toward the living room. He didn't move, and her smile disappeared.

He had no intention of getting comfortable, if that was even possible, but he didn't want to have the discussion on her front porch. "That's not going to happen."

She frowned. "What do you mean?"

"I made a mistake. I shouldn't have taken your money, and I'm going to pay it back … every cent."

"I thought you wanted it—needed it—to stay out of trouble. I was just trying to help you." She stepped towards him, palms out.

He stepped back. "You were trying to help yourself. There were strings attached, and you know it."

"Well … I guess I was hoping you would be … grateful." She stepped forward again, flashed a coy little smile and traced a line on his chest with her finger.

He brushed her arm away and took another step. His back pressed against the door.

She gave him an accusatory look. "You had no trouble accepting my offer in the first place."

"I wasn't thinking straight at the time. All I know is I can't go through with this."

Her back stiffened. "Of course, you can." Something in her eyes troubled him.

He held her gaze for just a moment before looking away.

"You know ... I've grown pretty accustomed to getting what I want." She relaxed again, and he eased his back off the door.

"Well, it's not going to happen this time."

"Why not, Richard? You didn't seem to mind when I kissed you yesterday."

He shook his head to clear it. That was yesterday. He wouldn't let her siren song lure him again.

"Well?" A harsh edge crept into her voice.

He said nothing.

"Let's sit down so we can talk about it." She motioned to the living room. Again, he didn't move. "Can I get you something to drink?"

"Don't waste your time, Carolyn. I've made up my mind."

"Oh, you have, have you?"

His jaw tensed at her condescending tone. "Yes. I love Emily. We have a history together and a family, and I can't just throw it away for ..."

"For what, Richard? For me?" She flicked a curtain of lush brown hair over her shoulder.

"For anything."

"You told me you weren't happy. You didn't hesitate to deceive your precious Emily when you had the chance. So why are you getting all holy now?"

"That was wrong. I shouldn't have done that."

"You *wanted* to do it."

Richard shifted his weight to his other foot. "I admit I got carried away, and perhaps I let things go a little too far, but—"

"I didn't twist your arm."

"You didn't have to. Beautiful women don't need to twist arms." He avoided her stare.

"So … you think I'm beautiful?" She cocked her head and raised an eyebrow above a playful smile.

"Stop it! I came over here to tell you I can't take your money, and that *this*," he pointed at Carolyn and then to himself, "isn't going to happen."

"I'm sorry, lover boy, but I think it's a little late for that." Her eyes narrowed and her tone hardened, all traces of the smile gone.

"So this is how you want to play it?"

"No, Richard. This is not how I *want* to play it, but you leave me no choice."

Richard's heart sped up. He took a deep breath and exhaled slowly, willing himself to stay calm. He'd applauded Carolyn's cunning and resourcefulness when they worked together, but she reeked of danger now. "What the hell are you talking about?"

"You're not going to have much of a chance with her after she reads this." She pulled a folded piece of paper from her pocket.

"What's that?"

She held it out in front of her and took several steps back towards the living room. "Why don't you come see for yourself?"

Richard walked over, snatched it from her hand, and took a few steps back before he unfolded it. A smile crossed Carolyn's lips as she watched him read.

His jaw dropped slowly as he read. When finished, he looked at her in disbelief.

"It's a great story, don't you think?" she asked, apparently proud of her work.

"It's a load of crap, and you know it."

Carolyn just smiled, too sure of herself. "But Emily won't know it, will she? She just might believe it. The expensive gifts you've been buying me with her money. And the plane tickets you bought for our getaway."

"Maybe you forgot—the money's not gone. It's back in the account, thanks to you."

"You know I don't leave anything to chance ... except maybe that foolish investment we made ... but I've learned my lesson."

Richard swallowed. His heart raced as he wiped his palms on his jeans. How could he deal with such a formidable opponent?

"Don't underestimate her as you've done with me," she said. "Emily might put two and two together. And just in case she can't add, I made a copy of the check." Her voice changed, taking on a contrived innocence. "Oh, Emily, I ... I just couldn't go through with it. As much as I care for Richard, I wouldn't be able to look at myself in the mirror knowing I'd broken up your marriage. Richard tried desperately to convince me to go with him, but I had to say no."

"You conniving little bitch!"

"I'm glad you like it."

"So what? This is supposed to make me *want* you?" Richard shook the piece of paper. "It isn't going to work. I'm going over there right now to tell her the truth before you can tell her your lies."

She walked over to the phone. "If that's the way you

want to play it. Perhaps I should call and read it to her. The mail can be so slow sometimes."

Blood rushed to Richard's head. He glared at her, fighting back the panic. "You're bluffing."

"Am I?" She picked up the phone.

"Stop it! Why on earth would you do that?"

"I thought this might happen, Richard. You'd come over here with your do-the-right-thing story." She shook her head slowly. "You're such an altar boy."

He shoved the paper into his pocket and turned to the door. The grandfather clock chimed, and his stomach twisted. Time for him was quickly running out. He yanked the door open and stepped across the threshold.

"Go ahead, Richard, tell her. Buy her flowers and tell her how sorry you are, but don't come crawling back here when she doesn't believe you. That's when you're going to be sorry," she called after him.

"I'm already sorry ... sorry I ever met you," he said and slammed the door.

He hurried to his car, slipped inside, started it up, and threw it into reverse. At the end of the driveway, a horn blared behind him. He slammed on the brakes. A car squealed past, barely missing his back bumper.

Pay attention, Richard!

His heart pounded in his chest as he backed into the street, slammed the stick into drive, and pushed the accelerator to the floor.

Chapter 14

Richard raced toward Emily's house—his house—hoping to make the fifteen minute drive in ten. The clock in the dash said twenty minutes to nine. He didn't want to have this conversation right now, but he no longer had a choice.

Richard pounded the steering wheel. Damn Carolyn for forcing his hand! He would've liked the opportunity to tell Emily on his own terms. He needed more time.

If he'd been honest in the first place, none of this would be happening. He could see that now. Sure, he would've had to take his lumps for not telling her about the money, but it wouldn't be half as bad as trying to convince her now that he'd not been unfaithful. The whole thing was blowing up in his face. He pounded the steering wheel again.

The wind picked up as he sped south on Route 7, and a wall of low dark clouds swirled before him in the half-light. Richard pressed the speaker button on his cell phone and speed-dialed Emily's number. No answer. Plan B was to bang on the door until she let him in. He had to talk to her, and it had to be tonight.

Rain burst from the sky and the wet pavement swallowed up his headlights. He rehearsed what he would say and wondered how Emily would receive it. Would she believe him or Carolyn? Carolyn was a master of persuasion.

Something flashed in Richard's headlights. He squinted into the light. A deer stood, frozen in his path. Richard veered into the other lane, hoping the animal wouldn't move until he passed.

Light from an approaching vehicle washed across his windshield. Richard swerved back into his lane, heart pounding from the near miss. Where had it gone? He studied his rear view mirror. In the corner of his eye, a stop sign flashed past his window.

Holy shit!

He hit the brakes hard. Light suddenly flooded the car from the passenger window. His stomach twisted. The impact sounded like a shotgun blast. Time unfolded in slow motion as tiny diamonds of glass sprayed inward, sparkling in the light. Some raced across his vision only inches in front of his eyes. Others seared into the skin on the side of his face and neck. Metal scraped against metal with a gut wrenching sound, and the car flipped sideways.

For a moment, up was down and down was up. The seatbelt bit into his chest and air escaped his lungs like a deflating balloon. The car turned over three more times before stopping against a large oak tree.

Richard blinked, barely conscious, but grateful for the stillness. Only the slow spinning of one of the wheels broke the silence.

Arthur's voice echoed in his mind. "It's pretty arrogant to believe we always have tomorrow."

Blackness engulfed his vision. It started at the edges and advanced inward until it filled his sight and swallowed him whole.

Chapter 15

"We need to talk."

Richard opened his eyes and blinked at the man in hospital scrubs who stood next to his bed, his hand resting on Richard's shoulder. Their eyes met and the stranger smiled.

"Hello, Richard … or should I say, Michael?"

Richard frowned and pointed to the cup of ice chips on the table. The man picked it up and held it to Richard's lips. With difficulty, he swallowed some of the cold liquid, but still couldn't manage more than a whisper.

"Do I know you?"

"My name is Arthur."

Richard studied the man's face. *Nothing.*

Arthur sat on the stool next to the bed. "You had an accident."

Richard nodded.

"It happened nine months ago. It was a fatal accident."

Richard hesitated, then lifted an eyebrow. "Who died?"

"You did, I'm afraid."

"What?" He paused to swallow again. "I'm still alive … aren't I?"

"Yes, but the Richard Dunham everyone else knew died in that accident."

"I'm not following you." He closed his eyes. His head hurt.

"Perhaps you should get some rest before we continue."

"Rest? How am I supposed to—"

"Do you remember anything after the accident?"

Richard thought for a moment. "No ... I thought I remembered my name, but I'm not even sure of that any more."

"Hmmm ..." Arthur rubbed his chin. "Then I'm afraid we'll have to do this another time." He stood.

"Wait."

Arthur patted Richard's forearm. "Get some rest. I'll be back soon." He turned and walked away.

"Wait," Richard said, straining his vocal chords, but Arthur had already gone.

∞∞∞

The doctor walked into the room followed by a petite blonde nurse. "I stopped by an hour ago, but you were asleep," he said.

Richard forced a smile.

"You're a lucky man," the doctor said as he studied the numbers on one of the monitors. "For someone who's been in a coma for three weeks, you're doing quite well."

Hadn't Arthur said the accident was nine months ago? "Three weeks?"

"Your accident was three weeks ago, Michael. You've been in a coma since then."

"Why do you keep calling me Michael?"

The doctor stared at him. His mouth opened slightly before closing again. He shot a glance at the nurse.

Richard looked from the doctor to the nurse, then back at the doctor. "Somebody tell me what's going on."

"It appears you have suffered some memory loss," the doctor replied. "In most cases, it's only temporary."

"I remember enough to know that my name isn't Michael."

"I see," the doctor replied. "Can you tell me your real name?"

"Of course, I can. It's Richard Dunham."

The doctor glanced at the nurse before he spoke. "What makes you think your name is Richard Dunham?"

I don't know. What makes you think your name is Doctor ... he squinted at the pin above the pocket of his lab coat ... *Howard?* His throat was on fire again. He stared at the doctor, but said nothing.

"Hmmm ..." Doctor Howard flipped through the pages of the chart and stopped to write on one of them. "That name sounds familiar, but I can't place it."

Now who's got the memory problem? Richard pointed to the cup. The nurse stepped forward and handed it to him with a tentative smile. He raised it to his lips slowly, studying the doctor's face. *How did you ever make it through medical school, Doogie?*

Richard took a few ice chips into his mouth and crushed them between his teeth. The cold water felt good going down. "There must be some mistake," he whispered.

After more chart writing, Doogie clicked the top of the pen with his thumb, slipped it into his pocket, and looked at his patient.

"All right, then." He pointed to Richard's head. "I'm going to schedule some tests to make sure everything is working properly up there. In the meantime, I'll see if I can clear up this confusion. We'll talk more later."

Richard nodded slowly.

"I apologize if I've upset you." He patted Richard's shoulder, then turned and said something to the nurse. After a brief conversation too low for Richard to hear, he hung the chart on the foot of the bed. "I'll schedule the tests for the morning and stop by in the afternoon with the results.

I'll have someone notify your family, but no visitors until I give the word. You'll be here in ICU for a couple more days. Hang in there, Michael."

What else could he do? *And stop calling me Michael.*

The doctor disappeared behind the curtain, leaving Richard—or Michael, or whoever he was—alone to think.

The next morning, well-meaning technicians poked, prodded, and scanned him in an exhausting array of tests. Doctor Howard came by in the afternoon with the results. They indicated that everything in his head appeared normal.

Before the doctor left, he introduced the therapist who would help him to walk again. A muscular woman, she looked like she could throw Richard over her shoulder and carry him if need be.

"We'll start tomorrow," she said with a slight German accent. She waved a beefy hand before leaving.

Michael looked at the doctor. "Should I be frightened?"

"She's very good at what she does." He smiled. "And remember, the catheter won't be coming out until you can walk to the bathroom on your own."

With nothing to do, time passed slowly. Lunch was all Richard had to look forward to, and it was dreadful—cream of something-or-other that didn't require teeth. He needed to take it slow, but his brain kept screaming *cheeseburger.* The fact that a nurse had to feed him the mush only added to his misery.

∞∞∞∞

The following day, Richard woke to find Arthur sitting on the stool beside his bed, his neatly pressed green shirt in stark contrast to the otherwise colorless surroundings. "Good morning, Michael. You don't mind if I call you

Michael, do you?"

"Go ahead. Everyone else does."

Arthur smiled. "From now on, my friend, your name is Michael. You need to get used to it."

Arthur, a little man with wild gray hair and soft blue eyes, felt vaguely familiar. "Are you going to tell me who you are … and what's going on?"

"Of course, but you'll have to keep an open mind." His voice was calm, yet authoritative, giving the impression of someone he could trust. No one else seemed to know what was going on.

"Right now there's nothing in it. Is that open enough for you?"

Arthur chuckled.

"That's somehow funny to you?"

"Well, no … I … uh … maybe a little." Arthur smiled and shrugged his shoulders.

Richard stared at him.

"Let's just say that you were in trouble, and I've offered to help."

"Do you work for the hospital?"

"Not that kind of help."

"Then, what—"

Arthur stood and pulled the covers back, exposing Michael's legs down to the knees.

"Hey, Einstein! What do you think you're doing?" Michael flinched, surprised by the amount of pain from the sudden movement.

"It looks to me like you're going to need a little help if you want to get out of here quickly," Arthur replied.

Michael frowned. "Wait a minute. What exactly are you trying to do?"

"Just relax," Arthur said in a soothing tone, "this isn't

going to hurt unless you make it."

"But—"

"Shhhh." Arthur closed his eyes and raised his hands in front of his chest, palms facing, about six inches apart.

After a few moments, he leaned over and placed his hands on Michael's legs, just above the knees. Michael gasped at the unexpected heat emanating from the man's hands. Arthur looked at him, but said nothing. Michael closed his eyes and let his head sink into the pillow.

When Arthur finally removed his hands, Michael opened his eyes. Arthur took a deep breath and exhaled through his mouth.

"What was that?" Michael asked softly.

"That, my friend, will cut your recovery time in half." Arthur pulled the covers back over Michael's legs and sat back on the stool.

"How?"

"It's called Reconnective Healing," he replied. "The body was designed to heal itself, but after centuries of negative energy on this planet, it's forgotten how. It has the ability to reconnect to a time when it was whole and perfect. All I did was remind it how to do that."

"We're not in Kansas any more, are we?"

Arthur smiled. "Not exactly."

"I'm confused. Apparently, I've had an accident. The doctor says I've been in a coma for three weeks. Then, you show up from God-knows-where with a different story and some sort of healing energy shooting out of your fingertips. Is this a dream?"

"Not exactly."

"Again with the *not exactly*? How about telling me *exactly*. I need to know what's going on here! Who are you? If this isn't a dream, what is it, some kind of time travel thing? Am I in the future?"

Arthur raised his eyebrows and looked at Michael. "Are you finished?"

Michael paused, then nodded slowly.

"Time is a funny thing," Arthur said. "It only exists here in the physical world. You left this world temporarily. Where you went, a minute, an hour, a year, 1000 years—it would have felt the same to you."

"What's that supposed to mean?" Michael shook his head. "What's going on, Arthur? I need some real answers."

"If you had all the answers, there would be nothing to learn, no way to grow." Arthur smiled and placed his hand on Michael's arm. "You're going to have to figure some things out for yourself."

"Okay, but how about at least getting me up to speed? I don't remember anything."

"Yes, well, that is not uncommon with *Walk-ins*."

"With *what?*"

Arthur proceeded to give him the *Reader's Digest* version. "Nine months ago, you had an automobile accident. You—"

"Wait a minute. Nine months ago? I thought the doctor said I was in a coma for three weeks."

"That's true." He paused. "Perhaps if you let me finish, you'll understand."

Michael nodded.

"Richard died that night in the hospital, nine months ago. The other driver, Michael Riordan, was pretty banged up, but he survived."

Michael couldn't help it. He interrupted again, "Can I ask a question?"

Arthur smiled. "If you must."

"How did I get to be this Riordan guy, and why am I still in the hospital after nine months?"

"That's two questions."

Michael waited.

"I'll answer the second question first." Arthur shifted his weight on the stool before he continued. "Michael had been having a difficult time. He never fully recovered from the death of his wife six years ago. Her death was an accident, but he blamed himself. He'd been doing better until his automobile accident with Richard last July. After that, he became depressed, started drinking again, and pretty much gave up on life. He was involved in another accident three weeks ago. In fact, this one wasn't an accident at all."

Arthur stopped and took a deep breath. Michael had more questions, but he decided to wait until the man finished.

"That brings me to your first question. After you died, the transition was, shall we say, unconventional. You refused to go. Unfinished business, you called it. So we conceived a plan for you to return as a Walk-in. It was important to bypass the usual time required to mature from infant to adult."

Michael opened his mouth, then closed it again.

"It's not done all that often," he continued. "But a procedure exists whereby one soul that is incarnated here on Earth and wishes to leave can swap with another who wishes to be here—usually for a specific reason—such as yourself. They both agree, and one *walks in* as the other *walks out*, so to speak. Only the physical body remains the same."

"How is that even possible?"

"You'd be surprised what's possible."

"And I went along with all this?"

"It was practically your idea."

"I still can't follow the timeline."

"Your accident was in July. It's the end of April now."

"So, where have I been for the past … nine months?"

"Waiting."

"For *what*?"

"For a suitable match."

"You make it sound like I was on a transplant list."

"In a sense, you were. That's a good way to think of it. Specific criteria had to be met. You couldn't come back as a twelve-year-old girl, now, could you?"

Michael grinned. "I was thinking more like a twenty-something with—"

Arthur cut him off. "It appears your sense of humor has returned. That's good. You're going to need it."

"Why?"

"You're going to have to lighten up, play along. Stop insisting that you're someone who died in a car accident months ago, or they'll be moving you to the psych ward. Do you think you can do that?"

"I'll work on it."

"Good. Staying locked up in here isn't going to help you get back to Emily."

Michael raised an eyebrow. "Emily?"

Arthur just stared at him.

"Well?" Michael pressed.

"The sooner you get your memory back, the better," Arthur said.

Michael titled his head in Arthur's direction. "You want to do that thing with your hands again?"

Arthur chuckled. "I'm afraid it doesn't work like that. I'm sure your memory will come back eventually. It's normal in these types of cases for there to be a period of … *adjustment.*"

"So tell me, Arthur. Who's Emily?"

Arthur clasped his hands in his lap and met Michael's gaze.

"Emily is Richard's wife. She is the reason you came back."

"Where is she now?"

"She lives here in Springfield."

"I have to go see her. I have to let her know I'm ..." His voice trailed off as he realized she wouldn't recognize him. She'd never believe it if he told her the truth. He wasn't sure he believed it.

"Is she okay? Was she heartbroken?"

"She's fine at the moment. Emily's heart broke, but it was more from events that took place prior to your death than from your actual death. I'm afraid the two of you were not doing well before you died."

"Why? What happened?"

Before Arthur could answer, the bulky therapist he'd met the day before arrived for his first road test.

"Time for your exercise, Mr. Riordan," she said as she eyed Arthur suspiciously. He nodded politely and got up to leave.

"Wait," Michael said. "When will you be back?"

"Soon," Arthur replied as he disappeared behind the curtain. The nurse watched him go before turning to Michael with a toothy smile.

Nurse *Schwarzenegger* helped him out of bed and steadied him as he took his first steps in almost a month. The intensity of the pain in his muscles and joints surprised him, and he managed only a few steps before returning to his bed. It felt as if he'd been on his back for three months not three weeks. He would have to accept the fact that it might be a while before he was back to his old self. *Whoever that was.*

Chapter 16

Getting out of bed the next day wasn't as much of an ordeal, and Michael wondered if Arthur's little hands-on healing had made the difference. Arthur hadn't returned as promised. I'll be back soon, he'd said, but what did that mean? What did any of this mean? Arthur seemed to be the only one who understood his situation.

With a little help, Michael walked to the window and looked outside. The therapist waited patiently while he stared through the glass at the parking lot. A woman walked to her car, and he wondered about Emily. He wanted to meet her, to learn more about her. Most of all, he wanted to remember.

"Let's try some more walking," the nurse suggested.

Michael turned around. "What day is it?"

"Today is Thursday," she replied.

He nodded, but realized that without an earlier point of reference, the name of the day was meaningless. He guessed it'd been two days since Arthur's last visit, and he had no way of telling when he would be back. The man didn't seem to operate under the same rules of time and space as everyone else.

Michael walked to his bed and sat down. "I think that's enough for now."

Nurse *Schwarzenegger* shook her head. "Are you sure?"

"I'm tired. Maybe later."

"Okay." She helped him into bed. "I'll be back."

Michael stared at the ceiling, frustrated by the accident,

his memory loss, and his inability to perform basic functions on his own like walking or using the toilet. If he didn't reach the bathroom tomorrow, he'd remove the tube himself.

At least he had his own room. They'd moved him to a private room earlier that morning, and he wondered who was paying the bills. He didn't know anything about Michael Riordan except that the man had been in the wrong place at the wrong time nine months ago, which resulted in his attempted vehicular suicide several months later. Arthur hadn't actually used the s-word, but he'd implied it. He knew very little about the past or the present occupant of his broken body.

The nurses did more than their required duty to assist in his recovery. Some brought him magazines and extra food; others offered warm smiles and practical advice. Even Nurse *Schwarzenegger* had grown on him with her patience and surprisingly gentle touch. He no longer referred to her as *The Terminator*.

After lunch, a conservatively-dressed couple in their seventies appeared in his doorway. They were strangers, yet vaguely familiar. A wave of relief washed over the gray-haired woman's face and she moved—faster than he thought possible for someone her age—to his bedside. Her hands trembled as she took his head in her hands and kissed him on the lips.

"It's a miracle," she said through tears. "We were so worried, Michael."

Mom?

The tall, well-built man had thick white hair and well-tanned skin, giving the impression of someone who spent a lot of time outdoors. He leaned over and kissed Michael's cheek. Unaccustomed to such displays of fatherly affection, Michael felt a wave of embarrassment.

The woman sat in the chair next to the bed. Her soft brown eyes watered and she wrung her hands. Michael muted the television mounted on the wall.

"At first we thought you might have—"

"Mary, stop it." His father glared at her, then turned to Michael. "We're just glad you're back, son. It's been a long time."

What weren't they saying? How much did they know about his condition?

His mother pursed her pale lips and wrinkled her brow. "We flew in this morning," she said, still fidgeting.

"Flew?" He glanced from one to the other. "From where?"

"From home, dear."

"Denver," his father added, looking across the bed at his wife.

"Angela was supposed to meet us at the airport when we arrived, but she never showed up. Has she been to see you?"

"Angela?"

"Your sister, Angie." She shot a worried look at his father. "Are you all right, Michael? Do you know who we are?" she asked, placing her hand on her son's forearm.

"Mary!" his father scolded.

She looked at him with narrowed eyes. "I have to know if my son recognizes his own mother." She began to cry.

Michael placed his free hand gently on hers. The tears rolled off her cheeks and onto the sheet. He couldn't let her suffer. "I … I can't remember much right now, but I could never forget you, Mom."

"Oh, Michael." She squeezed his hand and her sobs became tears of joy.

A nurse passing by stopped and stepped into the room.

"Is everything all right?"

Michael smiled and nodded, and the nurse continued on her way.

The three made guarded small talk for the next half-hour. The Riordans seemed grateful to have any conversation with their son again. His mother brought him a robe and slippers so he wouldn't have to walk around in those skimpy gowns showing everyone his backside. He thanked her for her thoughtfulness.

The nurse who'd entered the room earlier returned. "Mr. Riordan needs to rest now," she said, looking at him for a sign.

He nodded.

A few moments later, they said their goodbyes and walked to the door.

"We'll be back to see you tomorrow, son," his father said before they left.

The nurse walked them out, then returned to Michael's room. Michael studied her as she walked past the foot of the bed. She was petite, perhaps mid-twenties with a crooked little smile that must have caused a few heart palpitations both in and out of the hospital. He wondered what it was about Emily that had caught his eye.

"Thank you," he said.

She adjusted the window blinds. "You're welcome." She turned toward him and smiled. "You looked like you could use some help."

"It can get pretty awkward when your parents come to visit, and you don't know who they are."

"Oh, dear." She wrinkled her nose. "If you think it'll help, I can have the nurses take names of all your visitors and announce them before they let them in."

"That would be great. Could you?"

"Absolutely." She walked over to his bed.

"I wouldn't mind if you stopped by once in a while to say hello ..." He checked her name tag. "... Danielle."

"Sure," she replied, "but I wasn't kidding about the rest."

Michael shrugged. "Not much else I can do, is there?"

"I guess not." She gave him a little wave. "See you later."

Shortly after Danielle left, Doctor Howard returned. "Feeling any better today, Michael?" he asked.

Michael remembered what Arthur had said about having a sense of humor and playing along. *Showtime!* He smiled. "Much better, Doc. When do you think I might go home?"

"I'm glad you're feeling better." He grinned. "But your legs need to be much stronger before I can release you. And ... there seems to be a problem with your memory."

"My memory's fine. No problem there. Go on, ask me anything."

"Okay." He paused. "If your memory is working again, then surely you must know your name."

"Of course I do. It's Michael Riordan ... and stop calling me Shirley."

The doctor laughed. "Well, it seems Mr. Riordan has developed a sense of humor since I last saw him." He wrote something on the chart. "That's a good sign."

"Well?" Michael asked.

"First things first, Michael. You need to be able to walk to the bathroom on your own before I could even begin to consider discharging you."

"No problem, Doc. I'll do it today."

"That's great, but I have to warn you that you won't be going straight home."

"What do you mean?"

"You'll need to spend a couple weeks at the Ridgemont Rehabilitation Center before you can go home. You don't just wake up from a coma one day and walk out of the hospital the next."

"But Doc—"

"No buts, Michael. I'm impressed with the progress you've made so far. You seem to have a good attitude—do the work and you'll be home before you know it."

Michael's heart sank, but he decided to use his disappointment to strengthen his resolve.

That evening, with the help of Nurse *Schwarzenegger*, he made it as far as the bathroom.

∞∞∞

Michael was relieved when the catheter was removed the next day. A nurse brought him a cane and he ventured into the hall on his own. He walked down to the nurse's station and bowed to a round of applause. His month-long odyssey had made him something of a local celebrity.

An hour later, he left his room for a second trip. He walked to the end of the hall and stood in front of a vending machine, eyeing the rows of snacks standing single-file between the coils.

An attractive woman with espresso-colored hair bouncing on her shoulders walked up to a nearby coffee machine. Michael watched her slender hands feeding quarters into the slot, wishing he'd thought to bring some money. While she waited for the machine to dispense her beverage, she glanced his way and flashed a smile that could make you forget your name.

He returned his gaze to the snack machine and inhaled slowly before stealing another look at the woman. "Excuse me," he said after regaining his composure, "I seem to have a bit of a problem."

Her eyes moved from his head to his feet and back again. Apparently, she decided he looked harmless enough in his robe and slippers. "Perhaps I can help," she said.

"You see, Ma'am, I got me a real hankerin' for one a'them there Slim Jims." He tapped the glass on the front of the machine. "But at the moment, I find myself a little short on cash." He turned the pockets of his robe inside out.

The woman laughed. "Okay, cowboy, how much do you need?"

"It says seventy-five cents right there," he said, tapping the glass again, "so, I reckon I need ... seventy-five cents."

"I think I can handle that." She reached into her purse and handed him a dollar bill. "Here you go."

He fed in the money and extracted his prize from behind the trap door.

"I thought my husband was the only one who ate those things," she said.

"I reckon there's two of us now." He smiled and handed her the change. "Much obliged, Ma'am."

She laughed again. An awkward moment followed.

"What brings you to these parts?" Michael asked.

"I'm visiting my daughter. She had a baby. The machine upstairs was empty so I ..." She held up her cup.

"I see. Well, then I'd say congratulations are in order."

"Thank you." She turned and walked back down the corridor.

Michael tipped an imaginary hat. "You have a nice day," he said just before she disappeared into the elevator.

Michael walked back to his room feeling better than he had in ... more than nine months. He tore open the wrapper and took a bite of his Slim Jim.

He found his parents in his room with a younger woman, presumably his sister Angela. Cut flowers sat on the tray table. As soon as he stepped into the room, Angela rushed toward him with her arms extended. She wrapped him in a tight hug, kissed his cheek, and stepped back to look at him.

"God, Michael, I was afraid I'd never get to do that again." She swiped at the tears rolling down her cheeks, then punched his arm. "Twice in less than a year? You're done now, I hope. I can't take another one."

Angie was nearly a foot shorter than he and younger by a few years. Her sandy blonde hair had a slight wave and was layered to just below her ears. She appeared to be low-maintenance; the type that could get out of bed in the morning, run her fingers through her hair, and be good to go. It worked for her.

When Michael looked into her soft brown eyes, he felt the bond the two shared. He smiled. "It's good to see you again, too."

He walked to where his parents sat by his bed, patted his father's arm, and kissed his mother on the cheek. His muscles and joints complained as he straightened, and he climbed gingerly into bed.

Angie handed him a stack of mail. "I thought this might help."

"Thank you." You can tell a lot about a person by going through their mail.

For more than two hours, Michael's family answered his questions and helped him remember his life before the accident. He began to piece together a picture of what Michael Riordan's life had been like.

A knee injury in his senior year at college had derailed his dreams of making it to the big leagues. Baseball had been his life. He'd gone into a tailspin and become addicted to pain medication and alcohol. Then he met Jessica, and his life turned around. She helped him get clean and stay that way. At her suggestion, he took a job working with children at a state-run facility and found his purpose.

Michael had returned to school and earned a degree in social work. He'd eventually married Jessica, but after twenty-one years of marriage, she died in a boating accident. Devastated by the loss, he'd teetered on the brink again. In an effort to outrun his demons, he'd retired and moved far away. Angie, who'd just been through a rather difficult divorce and was battling her own alcohol addiction, followed him to Springfield where he'd bought a house. The two lived together for eighteen months, where they began to pick up their respective pieces.

When Angie moved out, Michael used the time alone to follow his dream of writing a novel. He wrote about a young man's struggle to make sense of life as he sought an answer to the question of where—and perhaps if—he belonged in its plan. Pulled from personal experience, as well as his twenty-plus years of working with children in similar circumstances, it took fourteen months to write.

The story moved Rhona Williams, a literary agent who took him on as a client and secured him a publishing deal with a sizable advance. The book had been selling reasonably well, and Rhona had been pressing him to begin writing the next one.

His family left when visiting hours were over, and Michael closed his eyes, exhausted. At the moment, he knew more about Michael Riordan than he did about Richard Dunham. While everything they'd said was news to him, he couldn't shake the feeling that somewhere deep inside—within every cell of his body—he already knew it. He wondered what would happen as he gained greater insight into Michael's life. Would Richard be lost forever?

Chapter 17

Nine Months Earlier

E mily stood with Lexi and Josh alongside the open casket in one of the Victorian-style sitting rooms at the White Chapel Funeral Home. Flowers spilled from dozens of vases crowded on the polished mahogany side tables.

The children had spent the previous night gathering photos of their father from scrapbooks and old shoeboxes and had assembled the visual remembrance that rested on a large easel near the entrance to the room. A gilded guest book sat on a pedestal just inside the door to record the names of those friends and family that came to offer their sympathy and say a final farewell to her husband.

Calling hours were about to begin, and Emily was not looking forward to standing for three hours listening to how sorry everyone was for her loss. She stole a glance at the casket from the corner of her eye. The mortuary had done a nice job of patching him up and making him presentable for the viewing. Richard was wearing his favorite charcoal gray suit and red tie.

Some of their closest friends and family arrived first, and receiving them was more difficult than she'd imagined. Only a few knew of their situation, and she felt guilty not saying something to the ones who didn't, but this was neither the time nor the place for such conversation.

After a difficult first hour, she stood with a wad of

tissues in her hand feeling grateful for her decision not to
wear mascara. The line slowed for a moment and Samantha
approached. She stood directly in front of Emily, their faces
almost touching.

"She's here," Samantha whispered, her eyes wide.

"Who's here?"

"The woman from the restaurant." Emily peeked around
Samantha. "Don't look now," Sam scolded.

Emily straightened. "Which one is she?"

Samantha turned her head slightly and gave a sideways
glace. "She's standing by the photos. Dark hair, little black
dress, you can't miss her. She's got to be the best-looking
woman in the room ... present company excluded, of
course."

Emily peeked again. A tall woman, who appeared to be
dressed for a night out on the town, stood near the easel,
talking with the man in front of her. A black designer dress
did an admirable job of showcasing her long, slender legs.

"You've got to be kidding," Emily said, looking back at
Sam. "*She's* the one you saw him with at the restaurant?"
She twisted the ring on her finger.

"I'm afraid so, Em."

The line was backing up, so Emily motioned for Sam to
move on.

Emily kept a close eye on the woman in the little black
dress. At least Richard had good taste. The thought offered
little consolation, and she began to cry. No one noticed.

The woman knelt in front of the casket and lingered
a little longer than most. When she stood, she flipped her
long brown hair over her shoulder, and Emily thought she
saw a tear. *Who is this woman?*

Emily's heart sped up as the little black dress approached.
Every drop of blood in her body seemed to race toward her

head. Her face felt hot and her ears pounded so loud she wouldn't be able to hear anything the woman had to say. Perhaps she didn't want to.

The woman stopped directly in front of her. "I'm sorry for your loss."

If she tries to hug me, I swear I'm going to punch her in the face.

Emily nodded, attempting to regain her composure, before she reluctantly took the woman's hand. "Thank you … ah …"

"My name is Carolyn Giordano. I own a restaurant here in town. Richard was doing some work for me. He was a good man."

Emily nodded, struggling to hide her contempt.

Carolyn turned to leave, then stopped. She flipped her damn hair again and looked back. "Please come down to the restaurant sometime," she said. "It's Adrianna's on Third Avenue. Bring your family. Dinner is on me."

Emily forced a smile. "Thank you."

She exhaled sharply as Carolyn walked away. The tears returned. Again, no one noticed.

∞∞∞∞

Emily was no stranger to loss. The loneliness and abandonment that followed it had defined her at an early age.

Emily Rose McKenna had been born the fifth of eight siblings into a large, middle-class, Irish-Catholic family. Her mother, who'd prayed for a daughter after having three boys, had tried unsuccessfully to encourage tomboy Samantha to embrace her feminine side. When Emily had arrived, she'd vowed not to let her follow the same path as her sister. So, while Sam played touch football with the boys in the empty lot on the corner, Emily read or played with the other girls in the neighborhood.

When she was seven years old, the family had traveled to Ontario Shores State Park and spent a week camping with her Uncle Mike and his family. On their final day, as they prepared to leave, Emily wandered off to gather wild flowers. While she searched in the nearby woods, both families left for home, each assuming Emily was in the other car. The McKennas had driven seventy miles before unpacking the cars in the driveway and discovering that Emily was missing.

Her family, unable to contact anyone at the park, had raced back to retrieve her. They found Emily sitting alone in the dark, shivering on the steps of their cabin. She'd been crying for hours. Everyone had apologized profusely, but that acute feeling of loneliness and abandonment had been a defining moment in her young life.

When Emily was a freshman in high school, her beloved Grandma McKenna died suddenly at the age of seventy-one. Emily had spent a great deal of time with Rose McKenna in her home next door. Rose loved to talk about growing up in Ireland, and Emily loved to listen. When she passed, Emily once again felt the sting of abandonment.

Emily's father was a police officer, as was his father and his father's father. Every McKenna offspring aspired to follow the family tradition, except Emily. For her, the occupational hazard was far too dangerous to ignore. While no McKenna she'd known had died in the line of duty, every morning when her father left for work, Emily prayed that he'd be home for dinner.

Her oldest brother, Tommy, had a reputation as a tough guy in high school and a soft spot in his heart for his younger sisters. Sam could take care of herself, but he saw it as his duty to protect little Emily. After he nearly broke the nose of a classmate whom he discovered kissing Emily at a high school dance, most of the other boys decided it was much safer to pursue girls who were a little more available.

College was a whole new world full of fresh faces and exciting opportunities, but more importantly, she was no longer Tommy McKenna's little sister. Her natural beauty made her the target of every horny guy on campus, and there were plenty. However, Emily McKenna was no easy mark. Most men were really after only one thing. She promised herself that her heart would belong to a man who wanted more. She knew he was out there somewhere.

∞∞∞

Later that night, after the funeral, Emily sat alone in her dining room, nursing a broken heart. The unanswered questions Richard had left behind gnawed at her. Samantha had helped her begin to piece the puzzle together, and she didn't like the picture that was taking shape.

The envelope containing Richard's personal effects sat unopened in front of her on the table. She didn't remember how it got there or even how she'd got home that night. She'd passed it many times during the week, but couldn't bring herself to touch it—seeing the contents might be too painful. But it was becoming increasingly difficult to resist the voice that seemed to beckon her from inside the envelope marked with his name. *What are you waiting for, Emily? He was your husband, for God's sake. You have to face this sooner or later.*

Emily finally gave in, but she wasn't about to attempt it alone. She enlisted the help of Jose Cuervo. After fetching the bottle from the liquor cabinet, she returned to her seat, poured herself a shot and set the bottle on the table. She brought the glass to her lips, closed her eyes and quickly swallowed the liquid courage. The warmth spread down her throat into her chest and slowly eased her tension. She straightened up, reached over and picked up the envelope.

She thought it would be heavier, as if what remained of a person's life after they died should be more substantial. Richard's legacy meant more to her than the contents of that envelope. Regardless of her feelings for him just before the accident, he was undeniably a significant part of her life, and she had a difficult time accepting that he was gone.

Emily took a deep breath, opened the envelope, and gently spilled its contents onto the table. She stared at them for a moment. Richard's wallet, his cell phone, his wedding ring, and a pair of sunglasses looked back at her. A single tear slid down her cheek, and she wiped it away. She would get through this tonight.

She touched each item, moving them a little as if they were slightly out of place. His wallet was the first thing she picked up. She opened it slowly and stared at the picture on his driver's license. He never liked that photo. She recalled how she'd teased him about it. *Didn't anybody ever tell you to close your mouth when you're getting your picture taken? It looks like you're trying to order food in a Chinese restaurant.* They had both laughed at her remark. She allowed herself to laugh again, but the laughter quickly turned to tears.

When she composed herself, she picked up Richard's cell phone and turned it on. A picture of the two of them from their first cruise together appeared on the screen—surprising that he hadn't changed it in all this time. It reminded her of one of the best times in her life. Holding back the tears, she scrolled through his contacts list. Many unfamiliar names rolled past; business associates, she assumed. Her heart stopped at Carolyn's name. She didn't want to believe it meant anything more than the others.

Emily turned off the phone, returned it to its place on the table, and surveyed the items. Strange how important they were to Richard one moment and how meaningless they were the next.

Unsure of what to do with his stuff, she picked up the envelope to return its contents. Something else remained inside—a folded piece of paper. She reached in and grasped the edge of the paper firmly between her thumb and forefinger. An uneasy feeling started in the pit of her stomach and spread outward in waves. She set the envelope down and hesitated before unfolding the paper.

It was a letter. A chill descended on her as she read the salutation: Dear Emily. She checked the signature—Carolyn Giordano. *The little black dress.* Her pulse quickened and her stomach twisted as she read the contents of the letter.

When she'd finished, she set it on the table, wiped her eyes, and tried to compose herself. It didn't work. She attempted to read it again, but could barely see through the wall of tears. She squeezed her eyes shut, as if that might magically make it all go away. It didn't. She shook her head in disbelief. This is it, she thought. The proof she hoped she would never find.

Emily poured herself another shot and slammed it, bringing the glass down hard on the table.

Chapter 18

M ichael awoke covered in sweat, his heart racing. He pressed the call button. The clock on the wall showed two a.m. Michael groaned. The night nurse stepped into the room.

"What's the problem?' she asked.

Michael shook his head. "I'm sorry, I think it was just a bad dream. I'm feeling better now." His heart rate slowed.

She nodded and checked his vitals. "Everything looks fine," she said. "Your heart rate spiked, but it's normal again. Would you like a cold compress for your forehead?"

"No thanks. I'm fine."

She left, and he lay back on his bed and stared into the darkness. It was only a dream, but it had felt so real, so … unnerving.

He'd been lying in a hospital bed—not much of a stretch there—but in a different room. The woman from the coffee machine sat in a chair beside his bed. He remembered her green eyes. Doctors and nurses rushed around him, and when he looked at the chair again, the woman had gone. The monitor flatlined and the squeal woke him.

Unnerved by his dream, he struggled to get comfortable. He assured himself that's all it was. He slept in fits and starts between the noises from the hallway that slipped in with the light underneath his door. During one of those intervals another dream played.

Students milled around in the quad, walking and talking or just sitting in the grass. The air felt warm as I sat on a bench, notebook on my lap and pen in my hand. I stared down at a blank paper until a breeze brought with it a hint of perfume. I raised my head and turned to locate its source.

A female student walked barefoot through the grass behind me. She smiled, and I recognized her as the woman from the coffee machine—younger, but definitely her. She had a beautiful smile that I hadn't totally appreciated when I'd met her in the hospital. And the greenest eyes I'd ever seen.

Michael bolted upright in his bed. "What the hell was that?" he said to an empty room.

He couldn't get the picture of her out of his head. He'd felt something similar when he'd learned about Michael's life. However, this was more cerebral, while the other was more of an organic *feel-it-in-your-bones* kind of thing. Was his memory returning? But it didn't make sense. He needed to talk to Arthur again. His sanity depended on it. But he had no way to contact him.

The next morning, after tossing and turning for the rest of the night, Michael walked around the hospital, not only for therapy but to find the green-eyed woman. Two days ago, she'd visited her daughter. Perhaps she'd be back.

He felt guilty about his sudden obsession with a total stranger. Arthur had made it clear that his wife, Emily, was the reason he'd returned, but he couldn't stop thinking about the encounter at the vending machines.

Michael stepped off the elevator and pushed through the big double doors beneath the *Maternity* sign. After scanning the names on the big white board across from the nurse's station, he realized he had nothing to work with. He didn't even have a name—not the woman, her daughter, or the baby.

"Can I help you, sir?"

He turned to find himself face-to-face with one of the maternity nurses. "Hi ... uh ... a friend of mine ... I mean ... her daughter had a baby a few days ago, and I ..."

Her eyes narrowed. "What's your friend's name?"

Busted! He looked down at his slippers. "Uh ... perhaps I should just give her a call."

"That would probably be the best thing," the nurse replied.

He parked himself on the bench across from the bank of elevators for a half-hour before deciding that sitting there in his pajamas wasn't the way he wanted her to see him again. What would he even say to her if she walked through the elevator doors? He would have to work on a contingency plan.

Several of Michael's friends stopped by to see him throughout the afternoon and evening. Apparently, Angie had been busy spreading the news of his recovery. As promised, Danielle announced them as they arrived, and Michael was grateful to at least give the impression that he remembered some of their names. His parents stopped by to sit with him during dinner.

After everyone had left, Danielle walked in with her hands behind her back and a sheepish grin on her face. She cleared her throat. "Good evening, Mr. Riordan."

"Hi, Danielle. Mr. Riordan is my father. You can call me Michael."

"Then, good evening ... Michael." She smiled a nervous little smile. "I have a favor to ask."

"Sure. What can I do for you?"

"I feel a little funny asking, but would you sign my book?"

What? Why would anyone want me to ...? Suddenly, he

remembered; Michael had written a novel.

"I'd love to." His smile put her at ease.

Danielle extended her arms, book in one hand and pen in the other. Michael took the book and flipped through the pages. *Impressive.* In college he'd aspired to do what Michael had already accomplished. Then it occurred to him that *he* was Michael and this was *his* book. But something about it didn't seem right, as if he were stealing credit for something he didn't actually do. It might not be a bad idea to find a copy and read it.

He flipped back to the title page and realized that he had no idea how Michael Riordan signed his name. He could probably go searching for Michael's—uh, *his*—wallet and study the signature on the driver's license, but how would that look to Danielle? He took the pen from her hand and wrote: *To Danielle, who took such good care of me,* and then scribbled *Michael Riordan.* He studied it for a moment and grinned. *From now on, that will be Michael Riordan's official signature.*

"Thank you so much, Mr. Rior … I mean, Michael."

"My pleasure, dear," he replied. "I'm going to miss you when I leave."

"Me, too." She smiled and waved her little wave as she left his room.

ᴏᴏᴏᴏᴏ

Two beds, a couple of small desks, and a dorm-sized refrigerator on the floor cluttered the small room. Gary sat on the edge of the bed across from me, hands clasped and elbows resting on his knees.

"Come on, man, you've got to help me out," he said. "I thought roommates were supposed to have each other's backs?"

"Forget it. No more blind dates."

"I need you." He almost whined. *"This sophomore's a tough nut to crack, and she won't have drinks with me unless we bring our roommates."*

I chuckled. Gary, a self-professed ladies' man, wanted to be alone with her. Apparently, she felt the need for a buffer. Smart girl. *"Have you even met this roommate?"*

"Of course."

"Does she have a name? Have you talked to her?"

"Well, not exactly."

"She doesn't have a name, exactly... or you haven't exactly talked to her?"

"Her name is Charlotte, and she did say hello to me once." He grinned. *"Don't worry. You're going to love her."*

Gary relentlessly continued his sales pitch, and we finally struck a deal. I agreed to meet Gary and the girls for drinks Friday night.

Bodies packed the campus pub when I arrived, and I pushed through the throng, hoping Gary had been there early enough to get a table. I made my way to the back of the room and saw Gary motioning me toward an empty seat.

Two women sat at the table with him. My stomach flipped. *"It's her!"* I said aloud.

It'd been little more than a whisper, insignificant in the noisy bar, but she looked in my direction when the words left my mouth. Our eyes met. I held her gaze, and for a moment, we were alone in the room. She smiled. Slowly, other people reappeared, and I wiped my palms on my jeans. When I reached the table, Gary stood.

"Hey buddy, glad you could make it."

Gary sat between the two girls and gestured at the blonde on his right, who looked bored. *"This is Charlotte Johnson."*

I nodded, forcing a smile.

"And this," Gary gestured toward the green-eyed mystery girl on his left, *"is Emily McKenna."*

The tough nut, I thought. At least now she had a name. Wait a minute. Emily?
That's when she leaned over and whispered in my ear. "That's right, Richard. My name is Emily."

"Holy shit!" Michael bolted upright in bed. "Emily?" Sweat covered him again and a chill ran down his spine. *Is it possible that ... ?*

∞∞∞∞

"Boy, am I glad to see you," Michael said when Arthur showed up Sunday morning, coffee and doughnuts in hand.

"How are you feeling today?" Arthur asked as he sat down.

Michael brought him up to speed on what had happened since his last visit. He described his recent dreams, surprising himself with how well he remembered every detail.

"At first, I just thought I was dreaming. You know, the random mixed-up stuff people usually see when they sleep. Most of the time, it doesn't seem to make much sense. But, this feels different now." He paused to study Arthur's reaction. "Oh yeah, the girl I keep seeing in my dreams ... I met her two days ago. Here in the hospital."

"I see."

Michael eyed him curiously for a moment. "Is that all you have to say? I have a chance meeting here in the hospital with a woman who begins showing up in my dreams. Last night she tells me her name is Emily, and all you can say is 'I see'? What exactly is it you see?"

Arthur inhaled slowly. "I believe these dreams are actually your memories coming back, and the woman you met here in the hospital was the catalyst. Often, seeing someone or something significant from your past helps the mind to connect with the memories."

"From my past? Are you trying to tell me that by some strange coincidence, Emily shows up here while I'm out walking around?"

"No."

"No? Then what *are* you saying?"

"Oh, I think it was Emily, but there was nothing *coincidental* about it."

"How's that?"

"You see, Michael, I have it on pretty good authority that everything happens for a reason. We may not understand the reason at the time or be aware of all the seemingly insignificant events that led up to it, but I assure you this didn't happen by chance."

Michael said nothing while he tried to wrap his head around what Arthur had just said. "So, what does this mean?" he finally asked. "Emily knows about me? She certainly didn't let on when we met the other day."

"No, not consciously. Unfortunately, this isn't the time or place for a detailed discussion of mind, body, and spirit. Suffice it to say, greater forces are at work in the universe, conspiring to ensure your success."

Michael leaned forward. "Greater forces?"

Arthur nodded. "We are continually given opportunities to realize our dreams. But these opportunities are often disguised as problems or even tragedy. It requires understanding and awareness."

"I have a feeling that's the difficult part."

"Nothing is difficult unless you think it is. Attitude is the key. I like to call it an attitude of gratitude. When you look at life's challenges as blessings rather than burdens, that's what they become."

Michael said nothing, eyes drifting.

"It all starts up here," Arthur added, tapping the side of his head.

Michael ran his hand through his hair. "Wow. I never thought of it like that."

"Yes, well, you're not alone."

∞∞∞∞

Doctor Howard came by the next morning wearing a Howdy Doody smile.

"I've got great news, Michael," he said. "I just signed your release papers. Someone from Ridgemont will be here in the morning to transport you to their facility. You've done surprisingly well in the week since you regained consciousness. Based on your progress so far, you could be home in another week or two."

"Thanks, Doc." Michael wouldn't admit it, but he was a little relieved not to be going home yet, wherever that was. While more of Richard's memories came back every day, there were many things he didn't know about Michael, such as where he lived or what he might find there. In the meantime, he hoped he could lean on Angie to help fill in some of the missing pieces.

Many people who suffered a trauma such as his had to rebuild one life; he had to rebuild two.

Chapter 19

Now that Michael felt better, the hospital food lost its appeal. Funny how not having eaten for a month lowers one's culinary standards for a while. He didn't finish tonight's mystery meat, and for the record, Jello is not a proper dessert. A big piece of pie with a side of ice cream—now that's dessert!

The cafeteria was nearly empty that evening when Michael wandered in around eight o'clock. He bought a cup of coffee and a slice of coconut cream pie. Still using his cane to get around, he balanced his coffee and dessert on the tray in his free hand. While a part of him hoped to run into Emily again, another part of him conceded that perhaps it would be better to wait until she could see him in street clothes.

The pie didn't disappoint, and he finished it quickly. While he sat staring into his cup, he had another flashback. They'd become more frequent over the past forty-eight hours, showing up unannounced, no longer limited to his dreams. The floodgates had opened. He didn't complain.

He let years of memories wash over him until Arthur sat on the chair he'd pulled up to the table.

"Hello, Michael," Arthur said with his usual smile. "Dining out, I see."

"You could say that." He pointed to his empty plate. "You should try the pie."

"I watched you as I walked over here. You couldn't take your eyes off your cup."

Michael took a sip of coffee and set the cup down

slowly. "Now I remember you. We met outside the homeless shelter."

"We did."

"I remember talking for a long time before we finally fell asleep. I also recall thinking that you were a big pain in the ass." He smiled.

"Well, as far as the pain," Arthur leaned over the table, "sometimes the truth hurts."

Michael looked at his cup and then back at Arthur. "It seems like such a long time ago."

"It was ... and it wasn't."

A strange answer from a strange man. Arthur often talked in riddles, as if challenging Michael to uncover the hidden wisdom on his own. He just needed to open his mind a little to find it.

"I was wondering about something," Michael said.

"Yes?"

"Whatever happened to the Blue Knight?"

"I'm not sure what you mean."

"My car."

"Yes. Well, your car was, as they say, totaled. You're lucky to be ..." He paused to laugh at himself. "I was going to say alive, but, well ..."

Michael didn't find it amusing. "That car was my favorite thing in the whole world."

"Really?" Arthur leaned back in his chair and folded his arms across his chest. "Then perhaps we should be going car shopping rather than chasing around after your soul mate."

"My soul mate?" Michael frowned. "I'm not even sure what that means."

"It means this is not the first lifetime you and Emily have shared. You are kindred spirits, traveling together through many incarnations, sharing an adventure. To borrow a phrase from your younger generation, you are BFFs ... *literally.*"

"How come I don't remember any of that?"

"You're not supposed to. Each new life is a fresh start, a clean slate, a new opportunity. We choose each one because of its potential for learning or balancing of karmic energy from past lives. More often than not, the two go hand-in-hand. If we remembered someone from a previous life, we could be prejudiced when we meet them again in the next."

"Karma?" He raised an eyebrow. "You mean like what goes around comes around?"

"Yes, that is the common perception and not altogether untrue, but it's more about experiential growth than moral reciprocity." He paused. "What I mean is, we experience both sides of a particular situation, not so much for retribution as for greater understanding. For example, the passive soul in one lifetime may become the aggressor in the next, the victim becomes the perpetrator. One gets to experience life from many different perspectives—different sexes, body types, health, intelligence, economic status, religions, nationalities. In the end, there must be balance."

"You mean to tell me that I've been a woman before?"

Arthur smiled.

"And Emily and I?"

"I'm afraid this is not the first time you've broken her heart."

"Really?"

"It's a pattern. One you have been unable to break out of, so you try again and again."

"You mean we're stuck because of me?"

"Let's just say the two of you had agreed to help each other. She's not going to bail on you just because it hasn't been going so well lately. It's called unconditional love."

"What can I do?"

"You're doing it," Arthur reminded him. "Perhaps you don't remember, but we had a conversation in the hospital shortly after you died. In fact, we talked about some of the same things we've been talking about here. You made up your mind that the cycle would end with this lifetime."

Arthur paused to rub his chin. "Ironic how you always seem to be able to come to that conclusion *after* you die."

"So what happened?" Michael asked.

"My job was to assist you with your transition, but you refused to go. You put up a pretty big stink, as I recall. You loved Emily very much and refused to leave until she knew the truth. I was moved by your devotion to her, so I interceded on your behalf."

Richard swallowed the last sip of coffee and set the cup on the table. "Who did you …?"

Arthur's eyes glanced upward as he tilted his head back. Richard nodded.

"You were offered a second chance, but there was a logistical problem. You were already dead. So, together, we came up with a plan."

"A Walk-in." Michael nodded. The past week had begun to make a little more sense.

"Yes. You couldn't come back the usual way. There wasn't enough time. This was the only way to get you back here and maintain a reasonable age differential. Fortunately, we found an appropriate donor."

"This wasn't a hostile takeover, was it?"

"Oh, no. It's always a mutual agreement."

Michael rubbed the back of his neck. "It feels like the old program has been uninstalled and the system is rebooting." He put his hands down on the table and smiled. "Now I'm just waiting for the rest of the memory to load." He leaned in, eyes wide. "So what's the rest of the plan?"

Arthur smiled. "You're going to have to figure that out on your own."

Michael stared at Arthur, feeling somewhat deflated. "But how am I—"

"Everything you need is right here." Arthur tapped the center of his chest. "You have an opportunity now to see things in a way that was previously not possible. You already have more information than most people—you know the reason why you're here. You've been given the gift of a new perspective and a chance to make different choices. What you do with it is up to you."

Michael leaned back in his seat. "No pressure there," he said wryly.

"I'll leave you with one last thought. Whether you think you will succeed or you think you will fail, you're right." He stood up and pushed in his chair, not waiting for any comment. "Goodnight, Michael."

Michael watched him leave and absently brought his cup up to his lips. When he realized it was empty, he quickly set it back down.

∞∞∞

Later that night he lay in bed and stared into the darkness. *Everything you need is right here,* Arthur had said. *You've been given a gift … what you do with it is up to you.* Richard had never thought with his heart. Emotions led to drama, and drama led to confrontation. Someone always got hurt.

To Richard Dunham, confrontation was like a hornet's nest—something to avoid if possible, and certainly not something to stir up intentionally. Over the years, he'd become adept at playing it safe. You'd never find him picking a fight or expressing a controversial opinion. No, he was content to just watch and listen, keeping his opinion—if he had one—to himself.

Richard grew up as an only child, living under strict rule. Alfred Dunham had little tolerance for the missteps of a child. Young Richard quickly realized that resistance was futile, and life was a lot easier when he kept his mouth shut and did what he was told. His mother had played good cop to his father's bad cop on the few occasions when he'd tested his boundaries. Eventually, he learned to play the game and keep his opinions to himself.

Despite his stern upbringing, or maybe because of it, Richard developed a good sense of humor. While it was certainly an endearing quality, it also became a defense mechanism, a handy tool to redirect attention from examining his true feelings.

Richard studied hard in school. *Eyes on the prize.* Good grades brought scholarships and the opportunity to attend a college whose academic standing was well above what his family would have otherwise been able to afford. He was focused—driven to succeed where his father had failed. That is, until that warm spring day in his junior year when the wheels suddenly came off the track. It was a day that would change his life forever.

∞∞∞∞∞

Michael tossed and turned in his bed, thinking about Emily and how meeting her had changed his life. He wanted to sleep, but his mind wasn't giving in to his fatigue. According to Arthur, they were destined to meet and live happily ever after, something they had been trying to do for many lifetimes, apparently without much success. He wished he could remember some of them and perhaps learn from his mistakes. *Is that too much to ask?*

Eventually, he drifted off to sleep. If he'd known what he would find there—the reason he wore a bracelet that read Michael Riordan—he would have called for the nurse and asked for a pot of coffee.

An alarm squealed—a flatline on the monitor. A woman jumped up from her bedside chair as two nurses rushed in and pushed her out of the way. Emily! A doctor followed on their heels shouting rapid-fire orders. They huddled around the bed. I couldn't see the patient. I didn't need to. Tears streamed down Emily's face and I felt her distress. But anger and frustration moved her, not grief. My heart sank.

"I can't watch this," she said and walked away. I followed her into the hall. She leaned back against the wall near the doorway and folded her arms across her chest.

"If you leave me now, Richard, I hope you go straight to hell." She spoke, but her lips never moved. I heard her thoughts! "Emily?"

She didn't respond.

"Emily, can you hear me?" The communication only worked one-way.

She wiped a tear defiantly, as if she wasn't about to waste any more of them on the man who gave her everything and then took it all away.

The flurry of activity in the room stopped. Then I heard it. We both heard it.

"Time of death, 11:43 pm."

Emily stood still for a moment, a blank expression on her face. She turned around and pounded the wall with her fist. "Damn it, Richard!" She rested her forehead against the wall. "You throw away twenty-four years of marriage, but that's not enough. No, you have to leave me here alone, broken, with no one to punish. You must really hate me, Richard." She hesitated. "Well, I hate you more."

I couldn't believe what I was hearing. I don't hate you, Emily. I love you. You are the only woman I've ever loved. Please, don't do this. I didn't mean to leave. It was an accident. I was on my way to see you, to tell you the truth. I know I should have done it sooner, but …

I looked away. But what? No buts … I was only thinking of myself. My modus operandi. I should have been thinking of us instead of just me. I'm so sorry. We should have had this conversation while I was alive. I want to go back. I want a second chance.

Emily stared straight ahead, looking right through me as the tears flowed freely. She hung her head and sobbed uncontrollably. I wanted desperately to console her. I put my arms around her but they passed right through.

A man's voice broke the silence. "It's pretty arrogant to believe we always have tomorrow, don't you think?"

I turned around. Arthur, wearing hospital scrubs, leaned against the opposite wall. "Arthur?"

"Hello, Richard."

"What are you doing here?"

"We need to talk."

"Please, just give me a minute." I turned back to Emily, but she was gone. I looked up and down the hall. It was empty. I peeked into the room. Emily stood by the side of the bed, alone and sobbing.

I needed to communicate to her that I was not the lifeless body lying on the bed before her. To tell her that my love for her was alive and well, even if I didn't appear to be. That I had never stopped loving her. She needs to know the truth.

Emily began to whisper something to the lifeless body on the bed. I moved closer to listen.

"I wish I could forgive you, Richard, but I can't. You betrayed me. You betrayed us. I thought we would love each other forever. I never expected this."

I looked into her eyes and saw equal parts of love and hate. What have I done? I had to look away.

"I never stopped loving you, Richard. Don't you see? That's why this hurts so much." She picked up the edge of the sheet and wiped her tear-stained cheeks. "I found out today that Lexi is pregnant. I wanted us to be able to share this new little angel together, like we did with Kayla. Damn it, Richard! You've ruined everything."

Emily laid her head on his chest. "You can't leave me like this. Not now!"

What we had was special. How could I have stood by and watched it fall apart? Maybe she's wrong about some things—I wasn't unfaithful—but in the end, I was responsible. It happened on my watch. Now, it was too late. She would never know the truth. The realization pierced my heart like a hot knife.

Michael sat upright, covered in sweat once again. A sliver of light from beneath the door was the only thing visible in an otherwise dark room.

He walked to the bathroom, flipped on the light, and splashed cold water on his face. Turning his head slowly from side to side, he studied his reflection in the mirror.

Michael's skin was a shade darker than Richard's, and the stubble on his face seemed to grow twice as fast. He tilted his head back and rubbed his chin. His dark brown hair showed signs of gray at the temples, and he wondered if the length—which was almost three inches longer than he was accustomed to—was the result of neglect, or perhaps indifference.

I could have done a lot worse. He wondered how Emily

would feel about this new package.

"So, what are you going to do now, handsome?" he said aloud to his reflection, trying to muster up some positive energy. He waited for an answer, but none came. After what he'd just witnessed, making everything right with Emily would require a Herculean effort. More than nine months had passed since that night in the hospital. Had Emily moved on, forgiven him even, or did she still harbor the same feelings?

I might have taken up residence in another man's body, but it's still me. They were still soul mates. Perhaps she would recognize that. They could still finish this life together. He needed to be the man Richard could've been. A single tear rolled down his cheek. He closed his eyes. *I need to make Emily love me again.*

Chapter 20

M ichael worked hard at Ridgemont, earning himself an early release. Angie had visited often. In an effort to stimulate his memory, she enlisted the help of some of his favorite foods. Each time she visited, she surprised him with something different—a cheese steak from Sal's, pizza from Angelo's, ice cream from Cold Stone, and pie and coffee from Maggie's Diner. Though he enjoyed the culinary tour of Michael's life, he was pretty sure most of those memories weren't coming back. He didn't know how to tell his sister.

He even survived a visit from Rhona. Fortunately, Angela had warned him about Rhona Williams and her no-holds-barred outlook on life. 'Go big or go home' was her motto. When she visited, she sashayed in with her tight skirt and four-inch heels and gave him a big squeeze. Michael wondered if she was as touchy-feely with all her clients. Perhaps she was interested in more than just his writing skills. Without the benefit of any previous experience with her, he would have to improvise.

"You look good, Michael."

"Thanks. I—"

"I'm a little disappointed, you know. I haven't heard from you in months."

Michael shrugged.

"How's the next book coming along? Please tell me you've been working on it."

"I'm sorry, but—"

"Michael. You've got to continue writing. You need to

keep the momentum going." Her eyes widened. "Wait. This is perfect. You're going to be laid up for a while. You can use this time to write. Take advantage of your situation."

"Yeah. This is perfect." Perhaps she'd like to trade places. He didn't think so.

Rhona smiled and shrugged. "You know what I mean."

Her enthusiasm, together with her five-foot-ten-inch frame were, at times, a bit intimidating. The intensity of her blue eyes had no off switch. She was well endowed and not at all shy about using it as the central accessory in her fashionable attire.

At some point during her monologue, she said something that gave Michael an idea that would serve multiple purposes, the first of which would be to get Rhona out of his room.

"I've got an idea for the next book," he announced, interrupting her.

She stopped talking and looked at him. "That's great. What is it?"

"I can't tell you yet. I need to develop it a little more."

"This is good news, Michael." She looked at her watch. "I'd better get going and let you get to work."

"Can you do me a favor before you go?" he asked.

"Absolutely. Whatever you want."

"Can you stop at the nurse's station on your way out and ask them to bring me a pad of paper and something to write with?"

"Of course, dear. I'll do it right now." She kissed him on the cheek and hurried out the door.

A few minutes later, a nurse came by with the requested items and set them on his tray. He thanked her, picked up the pen and paper, and wrote down everything he could remember about his previous life.

∞∞∞

Michael stood at the railing of the Overlook on a warm day in the middle of June. He'd completed two circuits of the pond and stopped to rest before continuing with the remainder of his workout. He'd built up his strength and walked without the aid of a cane since he left Ridgemont a month ago.

Summer would arrive in another week. The steady rain of the past two weeks had forced him to walk on the treadmills at the gym or in the mall with the senior crowd— not much chance of running into Emily there. He'd worked his way up to two miles per day and couldn't wait to move his therapy sessions back outside.

He looked over the pond with a singular focus—meeting Emily again. He'd thought about it every day since he left the hospital, but now the possibility of seeing her again and having a real conversation seemed imminent. He counted on her keeping up with her exercise routine, which included walking in the park two to three days per week. She'd have to show up sooner or later, and he was determined to be there when she did.

His many unanswered questions left him unprepared for their first real encounter. Would Emily know it was him? Would she feel some strange feeling, like déjà vu? Was there some sort of energy signature souls gave off that could be detected and recognized subconsciously by others? He wondered if she'd felt anything when they met briefly in the hospital. Would he be able to keep his secret, or would he spill his guts immediately? He had no similar experience to call upon.

Another more troubling thought crossed his mind, one he hadn't considered but would soon have to face. How much did Emily know about the accident? Would she recognize his name as the other person involved—the man who killed her husband? The fact that it hadn't been Michael's fault probably wouldn't matter much at that point.

He closed his eyes and tried to think. Arthur's voice spoke in the darkness. "Let me tell you a secret. Whether you think you will succeed or you think you will fail, you are right."

But Arthur. What if Emily—

"Life doesn't happen *to* you, it happens *through* you. Decide what it is you want and move fearlessly in that direction. Everyone comes into this world unaware, but not unequipped. Everything you need is inside you. Trust in it."

"Okay. I can do this," Michael said aloud.

He opened his eyes, half-expecting Arthur to be standing next to him, but he was alone. Michael rubbed the back of his neck and stared over the park in silence.

"It's showtime," the voice said.

What?

A dog barked behind him. Michael turned and smiled. His old friend Bogey stood near a tree barking in his direction. "Hey, Bogey ... come here, boy." As Michael bent down, he realized his mistake.

The hand holding the leash let go. Bogey ran to Michael and licked his face. Michael held him behind the ears and glanced at Emily. She stood frozen, her eyes wide as if she'd seen a ghost. His pulse quickened, and he couldn't look away.

"I'm sorry," he said as he stood up.

For a moment, she just stared at the two of them. "How did you know my dog's name?"

"I didn't ... I mean ... I had a dog that looked just like ... his name was Bogart. I used to call him Bogey for short."

Emily eyed him suspiciously but said nothing.

"You mean *his* name is Bogey, too?" Michael said, pointing at the dog. "Wow. What are the chances of—"

"He ran to you like you were old friends," Emily said, a bewildered look on her face.

"Yeah ... that was a little strange, wasn't it?" Michael shrugged.

"More than a little, I'd say." She still hadn't moved. "You mean to tell me your dog looked just like mine *and* had the same name?"

Michael reached down and picked up the end of the leash. "Same make and model. What are the chances? Right?"

He walked over to Emily and handed her the leash. Their hands touched. A subtle flash of electricity passed through him, and a lifetime of feelings bubbled to the surface, ready to erupt. Michael had grossly underestimated his emotional reaction to meeting her again, much less touching her. His heart was about to burst, and his frustration at trying to restrain it, to hold it together, was almost unbearable.

Michael studied the ground, and the silence turned awkward. When he finally looked up at Emily, it appeared as if she might cry. He wanted to wrap his arms around her and tell her everything would be all right. He wanted to comfort her the way Richard had done long ago. He needed to come clean, to tell her his secret. But he couldn't do that. Not yet, anyway.

He remembered Arthur's warning that no matter how *he* felt, or what *he* remembered, no one else would understand it coming from *Michael*. As far as everyone else was concerned, he was Michael, not Richard. If he didn't remember that, he could get himself into a lot of trouble.

"You're sad," he said.

"I'm fine." She watched Bogey with glassy eyes that

told him otherwise.

"Is there anything I can do?"

She paused. "No. Thank you. That's very kind of you, but there's really nothing you can do."

He didn't want her to leave yet. "Come on, try me, Em."

"What did you say?" she asked slowly, as she studied him through squinted eyes.

He'd slipped again. Damage control. "Uh ... what I was ... I was trying to say was ... try me, I *am* a good listener. A very good listener. Everyone tells me that."

"Oh." Her eyes still searched his.

Michael shifted his weight to his other foot and tried not to look too nervous. He quickly changed the subject. "So ... your dog's name is Bogey." He said and looked down at the dog again, "As in Humphrey Bogart?" He forced a smile, trying to determine if his recovery had been successful.

"Yes, he was named after the actor."

"Ah, you must be a *Casablanca* fan. That's my favorite."

"Well, yes, but it's my husband's dog. He named him."

"Oh, you're married."

She looked away. "I was. He passed away last year."

"I'm sorry to hear that." *You have no idea how sorry.*

"It was a car accident."

Michael didn't know what to say. Another awkward pause.

The warm breeze blew a few strands of hair across Emily's face. She pushed them back. "You look familiar."

He could see her mind turning and wanted to hide his face from her stare. "Yeah, I get that a lot," he said matter-of-factly, "I must have—"

"Oh, my God!"

His heart stopped. He wanted to run, but he couldn't move.

"You're Slim Jim." She smiled.

A wave of relief swept over him. He played dumb. "Slim Jim?"

Her eyes were wide. "Yes. At the hospital. I gave you money to buy a Slim Jim. Don't you remember?"

He rubbed his chin slowly. "I reckon you did."

They both laughed.

"You cut your hair," she said, looking him over. "You clean up nice."

"Thank you," he replied with a grin. "Your daughter had a baby. Boy or girl?"

"It was a boy. Tyler James."

Michael studied her. "I have a real hard time believing you could be a grandmother. Are you sure you don't just hang around vending machines buying snacks for strange men?"

She laughed. "Well, you were a little strange. But, you looked kind of cute standing there in your jammies."

"A present from my mom." He shoved his hands in his pockets and hung his head like a little boy. An awkward pause followed.

Emily spoke first. "I don't even know your real name."

"I'm sorry. My name is Michael. Michael Riordan." He nearly choked on the words as he thought about how normal that must sound to anyone he met, but how utterly ridiculous it sounded to him. He took a step closer and held out his hand, studying her face for signs of any further recognition.

She took his hand and replied in a soft voice, "It's nice to meet you, Michael. I'm Emily Dunham."

Eager to touch her again, Michael held her hand a bit too long. Emily gave him a look and he let go with a sheepish grin. That was smooth, he thought. *Don't get creepy or you'll scare her away.*

"I ... uh ... should probably get going," she said.

He made no attempt to hide his disappointment. "Maybe I'll run into you again sometime, huh?"

"Do you come here often?"

"Pretty much every day, weather permitting. Got a bum leg," he said as he patted his right leg. "Walking is good therapy."

"I walk here a lot myself," she replied. "Maybe I'll see you around."

You can bet on that, he thought. "I hope so."

Bogey watched him as Emily turned to walk away. She tugged on the leash and he barked before reluctantly following.

Michael couldn't move, replaying their conversation in his head. He prayed that he hadn't said the wrong things, hadn't scared her away. Finally, he turned and walked back to the railing. He watched the two of them below as they headed out of the park.

Memories of her flooded in—the big green eyes that he got lost in, the way she laughed at his jokes even when they weren't funny, the way she twirled her hair around her finger when she was nervous. He leaned over, resting his arms on the steel rail.

"I love you, Em," he whispered just before they walked out of sight.

Chapter 21

Michael returned home later that day with renewed hope. He'd crossed the first threshold, a milestone on his journey to redemption, and not just personal redemption but a validation of their love and their life together. Their love had meant a great deal to Emily, and he wanted her to be able to hold onto that whether she thought Richard was dead or alive.

That would be impossible if she believed he betrayed her with another woman. It was a capital offense, the mere suspicion of which was often enough to destroy a relationship. At the same time, he needed to break the cycle, as Arthur had put it.

On the way home, he stopped and bought himself a big steak in preparation for a celebratory dinner. He planned to teach Michael the proper way to grill a piece of beef. The absurdity of that thought caused him to laugh aloud in the grocery store. Embarrassed, he explained to the cashier that it was an inside joke, which only made him laugh harder. He also bought two bottles of Pinot, Emily's favorite, from the liquor store. Some reviewers described it as the most romantic of wines, and Emily would sometimes refer to it by its nickname—*sex in a glass*. He planned to open one bottle tonight and save the other to share with her sometime in the near future.

Michael had a little time before dinner, so he poured himself a glass of wine and headed for the living room. Apparently, *Michael* had made enough money from his book and his state pension to afford a nice house and a comfortable lifestyle. Spacious and well laid out, Michael's home had a modern look while maintaining the traditional charm of high ceilings, natural woodwork, and two stone fireplaces.

In the mood for some smooth jazz, he found a couple of Miles Davis CDs in Michael's collection. The stereo equipment was top of the line. He sank into a big leather recliner—undoubtedly, Michael's favorite chair—and closed his eyes. The music soothed his soul while he replayed the day's events. When he reached the part where he had touched Emily, he savored those few precious seconds. He would win her heart once more, or die—*again*—trying.

As he had done every day since Rhona's visit, he thought about his past in an effort to reconstruct the details of his life as Richard Dunham. At his request, Angie had brought him three spiral-bound notebooks, which he'd filled during the remainder of his stay at Ridgemont. When he returned home, he found Michael's laptop and transcribed all of his handwritten notes. The process of remembering and writing it all down had been therapeutic, offering insights into his former life that were available only from this new perspective.

At first, he'd merely tried to placate Rhona when he told her that he had an idea for the next book. But upon further examination, he discovered he had the basis of a compelling story. Over the past few weeks, the idea had grown on him and he'd constructed a detailed outline. It was such a bizarre tale that no one would believe he'd based it on a true story. No one, that is, except Emily. She would have to believe it. Richard was the only person who could have written it. If there ever came a time that he might need a real convincer, perhaps this next book could be his ace in the hole.

Shortly after his return home from rehab, Michael found a copy of the first book that the previous tenant—as he sometimes referred to the former Michael Riordan—had written. Angie had suggested he read it, hoping it might jog his memory. The few passages he'd stopped to examine while flipping through the pages had impressed him. He wondered from which part of the mind/body/spirit trinity that such writing skills emanated. Would he be able to pick up where Michael left off?

When the music stopped, he set about the task of preparing dinner. He couldn't wait to give the Jenn-Air downdraft cooktop a try. He had been lobbying for one of his own as part of their kitchen renovation. Like the rest of the house, Michael's kitchen was a well-thought-out mix of old and new. Modern stainless steel appliances were situated alongside painted cabinets and old-fashioned built-ins.

The food was delicious, but he hadn't gotten used to eating alone. His celebration lost steam as he remembered all the nights when a fine dinner such as this had included Emily sitting across the table. He poured another glass of wine.

After dinner, he threw everything in the sink and put on another CD. He sank into the recliner, where he eventually fell asleep.

∞∞∞∞

Michael awoke early the next morning as sunlight poured in through the open blinds. He pulled himself up from the leather chair, stumbled into the kitchen, and tapped his fingers on the counter as he watched the coffee slowly fill the glass carafe. He shot a sideways glance at the sink full of dirty dishes, dismissing them until he had finished at least his first cup. When the coffeemaker signaled the end of the cycle, he poured a cup of coffee and headed for the study to write.

Michael picked up his laptop from the desk and looked around. In his previous life, his office had been setup for efficiency; this room was designed for comfort. The oak desk was large and uncluttered with a view of the back yard. Two upholstered chairs sat facing a stone fireplace, a wall of built-in bookshelves behind them.

Spending time inside on such a beautiful day was not an option. Michael let himself out the French doors and sat on the deck.

Around ten o'clock, he remembered that Angie had planned to visit in the afternoon, and he hadn't cleaned the house much since his return from the hospital. He decided to take a shower, wash the dishes, and give the place the once-over before she arrived.

∞∞∞∞

"Hello," Angie called from the kitchen, arriving earlier than expected.

"In here." Michael shoved two newspapers under the sofa then adjusted the cushions.

"I didn't have lunch yet. Got anything to eat?"

"There's not much, but you can help yourself to whatever you can find."

"Michael! Get in here," she called a few seconds later.

"What's the matter?" He hurried to the kitchen.

"What the hell is this?" She stood in front of the open refrigerator holding a half-empty bottle of wine.

He shrugged. "What does it look like? A bottle of wine. And a pretty good one at that."

"What is it doing in your refrigerator?"

"I had some last night with dinner. Do you want a glass?"

"Have you lost your mind?"

He grinned. "That's what they tell me."

Angie glared at him.

"What ...?"

"You're an alcoholic, Michael." She shook the bottle. "You shouldn't be anywhere near this stuff."

"An alcoholic?"

She walked over to the sink and poured the contents of the bottle down the drain.

"Hey!" Michael protested.

"Seriously, Michael?" She glared at him again. "Were you planning to finish this?"

After what I've been through, I should have finished both bottles last night. He said nothing.

"You better hand over the other one, too," she called over her shoulder.

"Come on, Ang. You don't understand."

"No, *you* don't understand. Give me that bottle before I come over there and—"

"Okay!" He reluctantly retrieved the unopened bottle from the fridge and handed it to her. This was new territory for him, but clearly, he shouldn't take it lightly. She emptied the second bottle and threw them both in the recycle bin under the sink.

Angie turned around, tears in her eyes. Her voice softened. "Damn it, Michael. You were doing so well. What happened?"

"I guess I forgot." It was a stupid thing to say, but it was all he could think of.

She took his right hand, retrieved something from her

pocket, and set it gently in his palm. "Did you forget this, too?" she asked.

He turned the bronze coin with the number two embossed in the middle between his fingers. A two-year sobriety coin.

He looked up at her. "Is this yours?"

She nodded. "You have one just like it. We got them together. You really don't remember?"

He shook his head slowly, "I'm sorry, Ang." Her shoulders sagged, the disappointment evident in her eyes. He put his arms around her, still holding her coin in his hand, while she sobbed on his chest. When her tears subsided, he pulled back and kissed her forehead.

"I'll do better now. I promise." He returned the coin.

"You worked so hard. Then I watched you throw it all away after the first accident. It scared me, Michael." Her eyes began to fill up, and she looked away. "I can't watch you do that again."

"Things are different now."

"Really? How?"

He wanted to tell her, but he couldn't find the right words.

"Yeah, things are different, all right. You had another accident. This time, you almost died. You wake up from a three-week coma to find you've lost your memory. You *forget* you're an alcoholic. That's sooo much better."

Michael frowned and opened his mouth, but no words came out.

She sat on one of the kitchen chairs. "I just don't understand how anyone could forget something like that."

"I'll let you in on a secret," he said, looking around as if to make sure no one else was listening. "I didn't recognize Mom and Dad the first time they came to visit me in the hospital. But you have to promise not to tell Mom … it would kill her … not to mention, make a liar out of me."

Angie hesitated before forcing a smile as she wiped away a final tear that clung to her chin. "Your secret's safe with me." She sighed.

Michael and his sister spent the next two hours talking at the kitchen table. At first, Angie described their strained relationship during Michael's dark period between the two accidents. It was difficult to hear and caused him some concern. He silently wondered if the problem would continue, given Michael's new circumstances. He decided to proceed with caution.

Angie displayed a great deal of compassion for her older brother. He could see why they'd been close. He'd grown fond of her in the short time he'd known her. Fortunately, their conversation took a turn for the better, and they reminisced about happier times. Well, Angie was reminiscing. Michael was learning a great deal about the man whose shoes—and life—he'd stepped into.

Before Angie left, she helped him locate his coin. He set it on the desk in his study.

"No, Michael. It doesn't work that way." She picked up the coin and handed it to him. "You have to carry it with you."

"I spend a lot of time in here. This is where I write."

"I don't care. You need to have it with you wherever you go."

"It doesn't mean anything now, does it?" He stared at the coin in his open palm. "I'm starting over."

"It means you did it once. You can do it again." She gently closed his fingers around the coin. "Come back to the meetings and earn another one."

He nodded and slipped the coin in his pocket.

When she left, Michael dropped the coin in a desk drawer and headed to the park for his daily workout, hoping to bump into Emily again. Angie didn't understand. He didn't need any tokens. Those were Michael's demons, not his. If there was even a chance that he would see Emily, he couldn't risk creating a situation that might arouse her suspicion—or worse, scare her away.

Chapter 22

Emily was not at the park that afternoon. In fact, Michael wouldn't see her for another week. During that time, he walked every day, alternating mornings and afternoons, hoping their paths would cross. It wasn't stalking, he reasoned, because he didn't follow her around. He simply planned to be there one day when she showed up.

Fate, if there was such a thing, smiled on him on the first day of summer when he spotted Emily parking her car outside the front gate. He waited and approached as she entered the park.

"Emily," Michael called. He started toward her, then slowed his pace so he wouldn't look too eager.

Her eyes widened when she saw him, and she waved.

"You remembered," Michael said.

"Of course. You're the dog whisperer."

Michael grinned. "Where's Bogey today?"

"He's home. Most of the time, I come here alone."

Emily wore blue running shorts and a new pair of Nikes. Michael struggled to keep from staring at her shapely legs. They agreed to walk together and set off for the trail.

His heart pounded as his brain cycled through memories of when they dated. The novelty of a new relationship excited him, even as he enjoyed the comfort of an old friend. Their conversation quickly settled into a familiar rhythm, and his confidence grew. He had done this once before. Whatever negative feelings she might still have for Richard had nothing to do with Michael. He can be just as charming and resourceful as he was when he won her heart twenty-five years ago.

After four laps around the pond, they walked to the front gate.

"Let's do this again," Michael said.

"I'd like that." She flashed those green eyes and a quick smile. "I'm usually here around the same time on Monday, Wednesday, and Friday."

"Good to know."

"Then, I guess I'll see you when I see you," Emily said as she walked away.

Michael grinned. "Not if I see you first."

Emily stopped, turned around, and studied him through squinted eyes. It was something Richard and Emily used to say. Michael wanted to reach out, grab the words, and pull them back into his mouth. He shrugged, then waved before Emily walked to her car.

He saw her two more times the next week, and neither mentioned their previous parting remarks. On Thursday, another perfect summer day, Michael decided to make an unscheduled visit to the park to sit near the water and enjoy the warm air and sunshine.

Emily showed up thirty minutes later and sat on the bench beside him, an iPod strapped to her arm.

"I didn't expect to see you here today," Michael said.

She pulled out her ear buds. "I could say the same thing."

Emily wore her hair up, something she did when she hadn't had time to wash it. Emily's was a natural beauty, no need for primping.

"You here to walk?" he asked.

She stood up in her green tank top and white shorts and placed her hands on her hips. "Who wants to know?"

"Let's do it."

She started off ahead of him, and he stopped for a moment to watch. She was still the most beautiful woman on the planet. Michael caught up with her and they walked in silence for a few minutes before he noticed her watching him.

"Something has been bothering me lately," she said with a little frown.

He swallowed, hoping she couldn't sense his apprehension. "What is it?"

"It's your name. It sounded familiar, but I couldn't remember where I had heard it ... until now."

For a moment, Michael couldn't breathe, let alone speak.

"You're an author, aren't you?"

He exhaled. "Guilty as charged."

"I work for Pendulum Publishing," she said, smiling.

He raised an eyebrow. "Have you read my book?"

"I have."

He waited for her to elaborate, but she didn't. "Well?"

"I liked it very much." She smiled.

It suddenly occurred to him that he knew virtually nothing about the book that he ... uh ... *Michael*, had written. If she started asking questions, he was in trouble. *Note to self: Read your book.* "I'm working on another one."

"Really? What's it about?"

He looked at her with a sly grin. "I could tell you, but then I'd have to kill you."

"That wouldn't be wise. My boyfriend Phillip is the Assistant District Attorney."

Michael stopped while Emily continued to walk.

After a few steps, she turned around. "What? You weren't really planning to kill me ... were you?"

"Your *boyfriend*?"

"I know. It sounds so ... high school. I—"

"No, I mean, you're seeing someone?"

She cocked her head and frowned. "Yes. Is that a problem?"

You bet it is! "No ... no," he caught up to her, "it's just that you never mentioned him before."

"It's nothing serious at this point. I met him at a fundraiser and he asked me to dinner. I refused at first, but he was persistent. Evidently, he's used to getting what he wants."

"And that doesn't concern you a little?"

"Well, maybe a little, but he's friends with my brother, Tommy, so I finally agreed. We've been seeing each other now for about a month."

"You're dating a lawyer?" He noticed her twirling a few strands of her hair around her finger, something she did when she was nervous. "It was so cold last winter," he said to break the awkward silence, "that I saw a lawyer with his hands in his *own* pockets."

"Michael! That's not very nice." She gently slapped his shoulder. "You don't really know anything about him."

Their eyes met, and she studied him.

"And I was beginning to think you were borderline charming," she said.

He looked away so she wouldn't see him smile. "I'm sorry. I just don't want to see you get hurt."

"So, you think lawyers are incapable of having an honest relationship?"

They stopped at a bench, and Michael sat without answering.

Emily remained standing and put her hands on her hips. "Oh my God, Michael. You're jealous."

He looked up at her. "No. I'm not ... jealous," he said

and looked down at his feet. "Well, maybe a little."

She eyed him suspiciously as she sat down. "I didn't see that coming."

He shrugged. "Surprise."

Neither said anything for a moment. He thought he saw a faint smile play on her lips. "Not your type, huh?" he asked.

"No ... it's just that ... I don't know. I thought maybe you were gay."

He looked at her and blinked, unsure he heard her correctly. "Gay?"

She shrugged. "Well, you're clean-cut, you don't seem to be after what most guys I meet are after, and except for the lawyer joke, you've been very polite." She smiled again.

"Maybe I'm just a nice, relatively polite ... heterosexual guy." He straightened his back and puffed up his chest. "There *are* still a few of us left."

"I'm sorry, Michael. I hope I haven't hurt your feelings. You're a friend that I like spending time with. Maybe we can just leave it at that for now."

Michael took a deep breath and tried to hide his disappointment for fear of jeopardizing his mission.

Gay? She thought I was gay? As setbacks go, it was a small one. After all, he was pretty sure that clean-cut, borderline charming, straight guys were in demand these days.

Finally, he stood and grinned down at her. "What do you say we go over to my place and catch some reruns of *Project Runway?"*

They both laughed.

ooooo

Michael tapped his fingers against the steering wheel to a Van Halen tune on his way home from the park. The Honda

Accord and its 4-cylinder automatic bored him. After driving the Blue Knight, it was like driving a lawn mower.

He drove on autopilot thinking about Emily. She just wanted to be friends and happened to be dating arguably the most eligible bachelor in town. But she was, and perhaps still is, his wife. He wanted to stop pretending and tell her the truth.

He decided he had to tell someone.

Helena Cruz, a respected intuitive and energy healer, owned the Springfield Wellness Spa and had been a client and good friend of Richard's. He never really understood what she did or how she did it, but she was good at it. If there was a chance that anyone would be open to his story, he bet it would be Helena.

Michael parked his car outside the spa. Exotic flowers, which he thought could only grow in the tropics, appeared to thrive in the neatly trimmed gardens that lined the gravel path leading up to the front door. He'd never been inside the front of the building before. He'd always parked in the lot out back and only gone as far as Helena's office. This was different. He opened the door and stepped across the threshold into another world.

Soothing music and exotic incense and oils drifted through the air in a warm welcome. He introduced himself to the receptionist, a plump, older woman wearing an Indian caftan, who directed him to the waiting area.

A plush, oriental rug cushioned his steps as Michael made his way across the room and sank into one of the over-stuffed chairs. Warm, muted colors and soft lighting had been skillfully orchestrated to create an intimate setting. He sat back and surrendered to the peaceful surroundings until a pair of large, ornate bookshelves in the corner of the room drew his attention and ignited his curiosity. He extracted himself from his comfortable seat to take a closer look.

An eclectic mix of merchandise, some of which he recognized and others he did not, adorned the shelves. Silk scarves in unusual colors and patterns hung from an antique brass rack that stood next to the shelves. He stopped to feel the smooth fabric between his thumb and forefinger. On one of the adjacent shelves, he found an impressive array of handmade jewelry in all shapes and sizes, ranging in style from understated to extreme.

Further along, dozens of tiny bottles of oils with strange names like Melaleuca and Patchouli filled a shelf labeled essential oils. How essential can they be? He wondered. He'd never heard of most of them and had no idea how they would be used.

Was he missing out on something? Perhaps there were other worlds to explore beyond the boundaries of his limited imagination. Compared to other events, this seemed relatively minor, but it was a mind-opening experience nevertheless.

"You don't know what you don't know," a voice said— or did it? He turned around but found himself alone.

On another shelf, he discovered two dozen trays of crystals and gemstones—some polished and smooth while others had a rough, natural appearance. Little printed labels contained words such as Carnelian, Lapis Lazuli, and Moonstone. Michael had no idea such things even existed.

Little silver cans of gourmet teas, each one tied with a different color ribbon, filled another shelf. He imagined exotic places where such beverages as Ruby Slipper, Emperor's Bliss, and Eve's Temptation might be consumed.

He picked up a can marked China White and wondered if perhaps it contained something more potent than tea.

"Can I help you?"

Still holding the can, Michael turned around to see Helena's warm smile. "I'll bet this one is a real trip." He held up the can so she could read the label.

"That depends. Are you with the DEA?"

He laughed. She had a quick wit. He liked that. Helena's shiny, raven hair fell to the middle of her back, but her most striking feature was her iridescent blue eyes that gave her an exotic look.

"I'm sorry, I couldn't help it," she said. "I'm Helena Cruz."

"Michael Riordan."

She studied him for a moment. "Have we met before?"

Yes, but I was wearing a different body. "Not exactly."

She tilted her head and paused for a moment, then led him through an arched doorway and into her office. She stopped beside a smooth, burled maple desk and motioned to one of two upholstered chairs that faced it. She sat in the high-back leather chair on the other side.

"So what can I do for you, Michael?"

"You knew a man named Richard Dunham."

"Yes, I did. Are you a friend of his?"

Michael smiled. "You could say that."

Helena waited for him to continue.

"What if I told you ... that I am Richard Dunham?"

She paused briefly while she studied him. "Stranger things have happened."

"They have?"

"In my line of work, I see a lot of what you might call strange things. I believe that anything is possible." She folded her arms and leaned over her desk. "I recognized something familiar about you when we met. Perhaps it was your aura."

"My aura?" Michael had heard the word before, but he

wasn't sure what it meant.

"Yes." Helena smiled. "It's like an energy signature. More precisely, a subtle energy field that extends outward into the space around your body. It's associated with various personality traits, as well as thoughts and feelings. We sometimes see it depicted in religious art as a halo."

"You're saying I have a halo?" He grinned.

Helena laughed. "I'm saying everyone does. Some people can see it more readily than others. I happen to be one of those people."

"So it's like a spiritual fingerprint?"

"Yes and no. It's unique like a fingerprint, but fingerprints are tied to a particular body. A spirit can inhabit different bodies throughout its journey. The fingerprints change, but not the aura."

He nodded.

"So, tell me more," she said. "I'm dying to hear why you think you're Richard Dunham."

Helena's encouraging smile put him at ease, so he told his story without holding anything back. It felt good to be able to tell it to someone he was reasonably sure wouldn't think he'd lost his mind. When he'd finished, Helena asked him a few questions only Richard would be able to answer. He did.

Helena got up, walked around the desk, and sat in the chair next to him. "This is incredible." She stared into his eyes. "It really is you, isn't it?"

"In the flesh." He grinned. "Just not mine."

Helena continued to study him without a word.

"Well?" he finally asked.

"How can I help?"

"I don't know." He sighed. "I guess for now I just needed someone to listen and understand."

"Done and done. What's next?" She smiled.

"It's Emily. She's the reason I came back. Unfortunately, Richard was already six feet under, so ..." Michael forced a smile as he pointed to himself with both thumbs. "This is what I got."

"Have you seen her yet?"

"I met her in the park a couple times, and we've reconnected as friends. But I don't know how to tell her the truth."

"Well, I wouldn't just blurt it out like you did with me," she said, "unless you want a restraining order."

"What do you think I should do?"

Helena smiled. "First, let me ask you something. What happened with Richard and Emily?"

Michael snorted. "Richard was a jackass." It was somehow easier to say, and perhaps to see, from where he now sat—as if he was talking about someone else.

Helena struggled to hold back a smile. "I'm sorry, Michael. Why do you say that?"

"He was constantly chasing things that he thought would make him happy. Turns out, there was always something more he wanted."

"Was Richard unhappy?"

Michael shifted uncomfortably in his seat. "He thought so. But it was more like ungrateful. He wanted something more, to be someone else."

Helena's voice softened. "Why do you think that was?"

"I don't know," Michael said as he met her gaze. "Truth is, he had everything he needed."

She stared at him without speaking.

"I guess he lacked the proper focus. There just wasn't enough time for everything."

"We all have the same amount of time," she replied. "It's

our choice what we do with it."

Eyes drifting, Michael said nothing.

Helena touched his shoulder and their eyes met. "As far as what to do, I think you should listen to your heart. You said it yourself, you have everything you need."

"But I'm not Richard any more."

She smiled. "Be careful what you wish for."

"A little late for that. So, what can I do now?"

She put her hand on his knee. "I'm afraid you're going to have to work that out on your own."

They sat silently for a moment.

Helena stood, walked around the desk and opened the top drawer. "I have something for you." She retrieved a small object, returned to her seat, and held it out in front of her. Richard offered his hand, and in his palm, she set a small polished stone with irregular stripes ranging in color from honey to dark brown. Its smooth surface felt cool against his skin.

"Thank you. What's it for?"

"It's Tiger Eye. It promotes insight and clear thinking. Keep it close. I have a feeling you are going to need it."

"A feeling?"

Helena made eye contact and held it. "Do you trust me?"

He couldn't look away. "Yes ... yes I do."

Chapter 23

Phillip held her chair and Emily sat. She had never been to the bar in the front of *Autour du Monde*, let alone seated for dinner. Phillip, on the other hand, knew the maître d' and was accustomed to getting the best table in the house, even on short notice.

The sommelier looked on as Phillip swirled and tasted the wine. He approved and the waiter filled their glasses.

"To fine food and beautiful company." He raised his glass.

Emily smiled as she touched his glass with hers then brought it to her lips. If the food was as good as the wine, she was in for a treat. The view across the table wasn't too bad, either.

Phillip had a classic Mediterranean look about him, presumably from his mother's side of the family. His closely cropped black hair provided a striking contrast with hazel eyes that appeared more gray than brown. He wore a custom tailored suit that hung flawlessly from his broad shoulders, and she guessed that his shirt cost more than her entire ensemble.

Heads turned and people whispered when he walked into a room. At times, Emily felt a little self-conscious being with him, if not intimidated by his station in the community. However, that had been more than offset by his generosity and striking good looks. It felt a little like living a fairy tale, and she was sure she could get used to the celebrity.

Phillip Morgan, however, born to a prominent

Springfield family, grew up knowing the benefits of privilege and was no stranger to the limelight. His father, the Honorable Bartholomew Morgan, pushed him to be the best at everything, grooming him to take his seat on the bench someday.

Presently the Assistant District Attorney for the City of Springfield, Phillip was something of a local hero and the popular choice for DA in the upcoming election. It was all part of the plan; stepping stones to the Governor's office. Phillip had all the right cards and played them as he'd been taught.

Looking across the table at Phillip Morgan in *Autour du Monde* was like a dream—the glamour of being with someone rich and powerful who could give you everything you wanted—and Emily was getting caught up in it. Part of her screamed for a reality check, while another part of her—the part that was in control at the moment—told her to enjoy the ride. After all, how often does an opportunity like this come along?

The beef bourguignon was to die for, and after their flaming desserts had been extinguished and consumed, Phillip ordered another drink. Emily studied him as he spoke to the waiter. While she missed Richard's sense of humor, Phillip's sense of style and knowledge of everyone and everything in Springfield impressed her. But what impressed her most was that he deliberately left his cell phone in the car. Little things like that could win a girl's heart.

"Let's take a walk," Phillip said when they left the restaurant. "It's a beautiful night, and Armory Square is only a few blocks away."

At the heart of the recent downtown renaissance, Armory Square boasted a collection of up-scale shops, eateries, and night clubs. Phillip informed the valet that they would return in an hour, and they headed off in that direction.

The two walked silently for almost a block. Emily noticed Phillip glancing at her every few seconds.

"What's on your mind?" she asked, keeping an eye on the sidewalk.

"There's something that's been troubling me."

"Don't be shy, Phillip. Tell me what it is."

"I've been informed that you've been seen on a regular basis in the park with another man."

She hesitated before looking up at him. "And why does that trouble you?"

Phillip held her gaze. "I thought we were ... *together.*"

Emily looked away. She had been enjoying her time with Phillip, but until now, neither one had broached the subject of exclusivity.

"What does this other man mean to you?" he asked.

"His name is Michael, and he's just a friend."

"Hmmm. I don't like it," he said, as if he had a say in who she spent time with.

The part of her that had taken a backseat at the restaurant screamed inside. "Are you concerned about me or about your campaign?"

"How do you think it would look if the soon-to-be District Attorney, the man responsible for controlling crime in Springfield, couldn't control his own woman?"

Emily looked at him incredulously. "First of all, I'm not *your* woman. And second, you can't control me like some kind of pet monkey."

Phillip wrinkled his brow as if this was a revelation.

She stopped walking. "You were *informed?*"

Phillip turned around.

"Are you spying on me?"

He took a step toward her. "Emily, darling, I didn't mean to upset you ... and no, I'm not spying on you," he

said calmly. "The fact is, I'm a very public figure, and I—
we—have to be sensitive to the image we project. With the
election only a few months away, we have to be on our best
behavior."

"So, what are you saying?"

"I'm saying that, at least for the time being, I would
appreciate it if you weren't seen with this friend of yours
in public."

"I'm not going to stop seeing Michael," she declared.
"God, Phillip, you make it sound like I'm doing something
wrong. He's my walking partner. We walk."

They continued in silence. "I'm getting tired," Emily
said after a while. "I'd like to go home now." For someone
who was supposedly so intelligent, Phillip had found a way
to ruin an otherwise perfect evening.

∞∞∞∞∞

At eleven o'clock the next morning, Emily's doorbell rang.
She opened it and nearly burst out laughing. It appeared as
if a huge bunch of flowers had walked up to her doorstep.
The large arrangement concealed the delivery person from
the waist up. She asked him to carry them inside and set
them on the dining room table, hoping it would support the
weight. He let himself out as she opened the card:

I noticed these in a shop window. They were stunning.
They reminded me of you. Please forgive my insensitivity.
Phillip.

She leaned over and inhaled slowly. *God, they smell beautiful.*
She had to give Phillip kudos. If you're going to act like a jerk
once in a while, knowing how to apologize is important.

Chapter 24

Three weeks passed and, other than his meetings with Emily in the park, Michael spent most of his time working on the new book. He found the writing process difficult. It dredged up painful memories of what he had lost—what he had let slip through his fingers. At the time, it had seemed like too much work to maintain their relationship. Now, he spent considerably more time and energy trying to get it back.

Michael continued to see Emily. Occasionally, she brought Bogey and the three of them walked together like old times. Michael and Emily talked easily about anything and everything. Before long, they finished each other's sentences like an old married couple. When they talked about Richard, Michael impressed Emily with his perceptive insights.

"Good morning, Emily." Michael approached the Overlook railing with one hand behind his back.

Emily leaned on the railing, staring at the reflection of the low clouds in the gray pond. She turned at the sound of his voice and smiled unconvincingly. Today, July eighteenth, was Richard and Emily's wedding anniversary. Ironically, this one he remembered but wasn't at liberty to acknowledge.

"I brought you something." He pulled his hand from behind his back and held a single red rose between them.

Emily looked from the rose to Michael, then began to cry.

"That's not the reaction I was hoping for ..."

"I'm sorry," she said as she swiped at the tears rolling down her cheeks.

"What's the matter, Em?" he asked in a soft voice. "Did something happen?"

"No." She took the rose, closed her eyes and smelled it. Michael waited. "Today is my wedding anniversary," she said in a trembling voice. "It would have been number twenty-five. I can't make up my mind whether I'm sad or angry—whether I miss him or wish I'd killed him myself."

Her words felt like a dagger in his heart.

Michael put his arms around her. Emily buried her face in his chest and sobbed. He said nothing, just held her for the first time in over a year. Tears welled in his own eyes. He didn't want to let go. *Ever.*

They stood for a few moments in silence. Emily raised her head enough to see the wet spot her tears had left on Michael's shirt. She pulled back just enough to wipe it with her free hand, as if that might remove it. "I'm sorry."

"Don't be." He looked into her eyes and could have sworn something transpired between them at that moment. It happened in an instant—maybe only a fraction of an instant. A recognition ... an awareness. He wondered if she felt it.

"Let's get some coffee," he suggested. "We could talk about it ... or not. It's up to you."

"Okay. I don't want to stay here any longer."

"I'll buy you breakfast if you're feeling up to it."

Emily nodded.

"Come on." He slipped his arm around her, and they left the Overlook together.

ooooooo

Michael and Emily sat in silence during the drive to Maggie's Diner. When they arrived, Michael held the door open for Emily and followed her inside. The building looked like an old railroad car, long and narrow, with a counter along one side and retro-style booths along the other. The food was great and, in his opinion, they made the best coffee in town.

A waitress behind the counter greeted them and told them to sit wherever they liked. Richard chose a booth at the end of the row. A handful of customers remained after the breakfast rush, and he nodded politely to a couple as he passed their booth. A folded newspaper sat on the table and he moved it out of the way as they both slid into their seats.

"Are you hungry?" he asked.

"I think I'll just have coffee."

A waitress came over and remembered Michael. They talked for a minute before he handed her the paper and ordered two coffees.

"You must be a regular here," Emily said to Michael when the waitress left.

He grinned and rested his arm on the table. "When you taste the coffee, you'll see why."

Emily touched the back of his hand. "Thank you for doing this."

"You looked like you could use a distraction."

"This is exactly what I needed," she said as their coffee arrived. "You're very perceptive."

He added a splash of cream and stirred, tapping the spoon on the edge of the cup when he was finished. "Nothing like drowning your sorrow in a good cup of coffee."

"I'm sure there are those who would say alcohol works better."

"Perhaps, but I think I'll just stick with coffee for now." He smiled.

Emily studied him. "Are you sure you're not gay?" she asked. "You seem to be more in touch with your feelings than most men I meet."

In touch with my feelings? I've never heard that one before. If you only knew who you were talking to ...

He straightened up and looked into her eyes. "I assure you, I'm as straight as they come."

She nodded, then let the conversation drop.

"The part about the feelings," he said, "my wife would have disagreed. She once told me she didn't think I had any."

"Perhaps she didn't know you as well as she thought."

"Perhaps," he said, taking another sip of his coffee to hide his smile. He decided to stop before he said anything that might get him in trouble later on.

"So ... you're married?" she asked, glancing at his ring finger.

"I was," he admitted. "She died in an accident six years ago."

"I'm sorry to hear that. I know how hard that can be."

He studied her expression. "I think you would have liked her."

"What was her name?"

"Emily," he said without thinking. He didn't realize his mistake until he saw the strange look on her face.

"Did I say Emily?" he shrugged, forcing a smile. "You're Emily ... I knew that. Her name was Jessica."

A flicker of a smile appeared on Emily's face before her expression fell.

Michael sighed. "When I found you crying in the park, you were thinking about your husband."

"Yes," she admitted. "Did I tell you that today would have been our twenty-fifth anniversary?" The tears returned and she looked away.

"You mentioned it." The bell above the door jingled. He looked up. Two policemen entered. One he recognized as Tommy McKenna.

Tommy walked in like he owned the place and started flirting with the waitress behind the counter. Michael watched him from the corner of his eye. His partner looked around the room. Neither of them sat down. Fortunately, Emily's back was facing them.

Michael moved a little closer to the window, hoping Emily's body might block Tommy's view if he happened to look their way. He didn't want to take the chance that Tommy knew Michael Riordan.

Tommy said something to his partner, patted him on the shoulder, and walked toward their table. Emily was still crying. This wasn't going to go well.

"Hey, Sis," he said when he reached their table. He glanced at Michael before looking at his sister. "What's wrong?"

At first, Emily didn't answer.

Please say something, Michael thought, looking down at the black-and-white-checkered tile floor.

"I'm okay," she finally replied, wiping a tear before looking up at him.

"Is this guy bothering you?" Tommy looked sideways at Michael, and then back to Emily.

"No," she said. "He's a friend."

"You're sure you're okay?"

"Yes, Tommy. You can go now," she said calmly.

"I'll be right over there at the counter." His eyes became little slits as he looked directly at Michael. "If you need anything, just holler."

"I said I was okay."

Tommy turned and walked back to the counter, said something to his partner, and they sat down.

Michael stretched out both arms and laid them across the table. Emily studied him for a moment and placed her hands in his.

"I'm sorry that you have to go through something like this. I know it's not easy," he said.

"Thank you. Richard and I used to go up to the Overlook," she said looking down at their hands. "I guess that's why I was there today." She hesitated for a moment before looking up at him. "I'm glad you showed up when you did."

"Me, too," he said. "It must be a sad place for you now."

"I can handle the sadness," she said as her expression hardened. "I wish that's all it was."

"I don't understand."

She let go of his hands to wipe another tear. "I found out after he died that he had been unfaithful. I had suspected it, but I didn't want to believe it unless I found proof."

He hated himself for what she was going through— what he had put her through. She deserved to know the truth.

"What kind of proof?" he asked.

"What?"

"You said you had proof. What was it?"

"He lied to me," she said as she twisted a few strands of hair around her finger. "I hate lies."

Michael avoided her stare. He had been lying to everyone, including Emily. He wondered how she would feel when she learned the truth. Perhaps he had waited too long. He stole a glance at the counter where Tommy was eating.

"My sister saw them having dinner together one night."

"What?" Michael realized he hadn't been paying attention. "Did you say your sister saw them?"

Emily nodded. "He was supposed to be working."

That must be what Samantha wanted me to tell her.

Emily continued. "Then after he died, I found a letter from the woman he was seen with. She claimed they were having an affair and Richard was buying her expensive gifts with money from our savings. When he bought plane tickets for them to go away together, she backed out. She said she didn't want to be a home wrecker—even paid back all the money he had spent."

She stopped to take a deep breath.

He remembered reading that letter at Carolyn's house before shoving it in his pocket—no doubt where it had been found. Despite the tension, he couldn't help laughing. "That's quite a story."

She looked at him like he had just spit in her cup. "It's not funny, Michael."

"I'm sorry, but I think it is." He sat back in his seat. "Well, maybe not funny, but it's pretty bizarre, wouldn't you say?"

She scrutinized him, her expression unreadable.

"C'mon, Emily. What kind of woman accepts expensive gifts and then when she starts to have second thoughts—*if* she has second thoughts—pays back the money? To the guy's wife? What did she do ... mail you a check?"

"No." The muscles in her face tightened. "She gave it to Richard and he put it back in our account."

"How do you know that?"

"She said so in the letter."

The fry cook called out to the waitress and Michael turned his head. He took a sip of coffee before looking back. "So, she just mailed you a letter?"

"No, it was with Richard's personal effects from the hospital."

"So he had this letter on him when he died? How do you suppose that happened?"

Emily stared at her cup, turning it nervously in her hands.

"You want to know what I think happened?" Michael asked. He pushed his cup aside and leaned forward, not waiting for her to answer. "I think poor Richard may have gotten himself into some sort of trouble that involved the woman who wrote the letter. Financial trouble, perhaps. He got in over his head, and he panicked. You said yourself that he was different just before the accident—distant, distracted. You thought it was because of another woman, but what if he was trying to figure out how to break the news to you?"

"What about the money?" she asked.

He studied her for a moment, trying to gauge her reaction to his story so far. "This woman ... does she have a name?"

"Carolyn."

"Okay. Perhaps this Carolyn likes Richard. Perhaps she's got money and offers him a way out of this mess. By now, Richard is desperate and takes her money, but she's expecting some sort of payback, if you know what I mean."

Emily rolled her eyes and took another sip of coffee as he continued.

"What if *he's* the one who has second thoughts? Perhaps he realizes it would be better to tell you than to end up in Carolyn's debt and do something that would really hurt you. Maybe she shows him the letter—tries to blackmail him. What if he's on his way over to your place to come clean when he has the accident?"

Emily remained silent for a moment, and he could see the wheels turning. It felt good to get a chance to explain, even if it was disguised as a hypothetical story. For now, he just needed to open the door a crack.

He raised his eyebrows. "Well?"

"That was also quite a story," she said. "Where do you come up with this stuff?"

"Uh ..." He wanted to tell her, but with Tommy watching them, this wasn't the time or the place. "I'm a writer. It's what I do," he replied with a smile.

"How do you explain what Samantha saw at the restaurant?" she asked.

"That ..." He paused to rub his chin. "I'm sure there must be a logical explanation. Do you think Samantha could have just misread the whole thing?"

"I doubt it. Sam's a cop. She's pretty good at sizing up a situation."

"Things aren't always as they appear." He bit his lip to keep from smiling. "What did Richard have to say about it?"

She looked out the dirty window at the cars passing by. "I never got the chance to ask him," she sighed.

"Tried and convicted without an opportunity to tell his side of the story?"

"I don't think I like what you're insinuating," she said as she turned to face him again. "I'm not the bad guy here."

"All I'm saying is that—"

"Just let me deal with this my way."

"I'm sorry, but I can't do that."

"Excuse me?"

"I like you, Emily, and I don't want to see you wasting any more time beating yourself up. He's gone. You have to let it go."

Emily crossed her arms on the edge of the table and leaned toward him. "I don't need *you*, or anyone else for that matter, telling me what to think or how to behave."

Michael hesitated. His eyes met hers. He had seen that look before and knew enough to proceed with caution. He took another sip of coffee as he considered his next move.

"I'm sorry if I upset you, Emily. That wasn't my intention."

She leaned back in her seat.

"I'd like to share something with you that I've learned recently," he said. "To be honest with you, I resisted it at first. What I know now is this ... forgiveness is not for the other person. It's for you."

Emily looked out the window again. She sat silently, as if studying the cars passing by in the street. After a few moments, she turned toward him.

"Did *you* forgive whoever it was that hurt you?"

He swallowed through the lump in his throat. "Yes," he said softly, "I did, and it set me free. I only hope someday she can do the same."

"And if she doesn't?"

"I'm afraid it will continue to eat her up inside. She's locked in a prison of her own making and she doesn't know she holds the only key. All anyone else can do is to show her that she has it, but *she* must put it in the lock and turn it."

"It seems a little late for that."

"It's never too late," he replied.

Emily looked past him, absently twirling a few strands of her hair around her finger.

Michael noticed Tommy and his partner get up to leave. He made eye contact, and Tommy gestured, pointing first with two fingers at his own eyes and then with his index finger at Michael. *I'm watching you. Message received.* Michael quickly looked back at Emily, hoping that she hadn't noticed his distraction.

This is not good, he thought as he tried to conceal his growing anxiety. Not good at all.

Chapter 25

Michael returned home from breakfast with an uneasy feeling that continued to gnaw at him as he climbed the stairs to his front porch. Tommy McKenna had him rattled. He stood on the porch for a moment, remembering the first time he met Emily's big brother.

Emily had brought Richard home one weekend to meet the family shortly after they began dating. Overall, they were not a very welcoming bunch, but Tommy appeared to be the watchdog. He sat in the corner of the room like a pit bull, showing his teeth. But it wasn't just the teeth that were frightening; it was the long, low growl that let you know he meant business. Richard had heard stories over the years of how Tommy would run off Emily's boyfriends—some with threats and others with actual bodily harm—before any of them got too close.

Now he appeared to be doing it again, but this time he was a pit bull wearing a gun and carrying a badge. It presented a far more dangerous scenario.

Michael removed the contents of the mailbox and fumbled in his pocket for his key. He looked up and down the street and took another deep breath of fresh air before stepping inside. He closed the door behind him, deposited his keys in their normal spot on the half table in the hallway, and flipped through the mail. It appeared to be the usual stuff, deserving only a cursory glance until one piece caught his attention. The return address indicated it was from his friends, Ben and Michelle, whom he hadn't seen for some time.

Wait a minute! He turned the envelope back over and reread the address. For a moment, he questioned who and where he was. Ben and Michelle were *Richard and Emily's* friends. He tore open the envelope and found a wedding invitation. Evidently, they knew Michael Riordan well enough to invite him to their wedding. He set the rest of the mail on the table, walked to the fridge, and placed the invitation underneath one of the magnets. An uneasy feeling came over him, and he pulled back the corner to expose the salutation. It read, "Michael Riordan and Guest."

Dammit, he thought, realizing that Emily's invitation would most likely be addressed the same way. She would be there, but she probably wouldn't be alone. Unless … Prince Phillip is too busy, or perhaps too pretentious, to attend some middle-class wedding reception. He suddenly had a reason to smile. Given their history with the couple, Emily wouldn't miss this. She would go alone if need be. This might be the opportunity he'd been looking for.

Michael found himself thinking of when he … uh, Richard … proposed to Emily. He would never forget that day. Okay, maybe temporarily, but it was back now.

He had landed a good job as a computer systems analyst right out of college. Determined not to move back in with his parents, he'd rented a small apartment in Springfield.

Emily, who was finishing her senior year, spent many weekends curled up next to him on the sofa, watching old movies. Richard was a Humphrey Bogart fan and soon Emily shared his enthusiasm. *Casablanca,* in which Bogey shared the screen with Ingrid Bergman, soon became a favorite.

They lost count of how many times they'd watched the 1942 film full of romance and intrigue. They'd even memorized many of the lines and sometimes found themselves spontaneously acting out entire scenes. Coincidentally, Bogart's name in that particular film was Richard. Everyone in Casablanca knew him as Rick and Emily called him that sometimes.

He closed his eyes and returned to 1987 again.

Shortly after Emily had graduated, Richard invited her over on a Saturday evening for dinner and a movie. He had learned his way around the kitchen, and the two often preferred a quiet dinner at home over a night on the town.

They finished eating and moved to the sofa. The movie didn't start for another half-hour, so they sat and talked. Richard felt as if someone or something had sucked all the air out of his apartment. His mouth became dry and the sofa felt like a cactus. He shifted uncomfortably several times before going into the kitchen to get a drink of water.

"Can I tell you a story, Rick?" Emily asked when he returned. Her words came from a scene in *Casablanca*. Perhaps she sensed his restlessness and hoped a little distraction would calm him down. He sat next to her and played along.

"Does it have a wow finish?" he replied.

"I don't know the finish yet."

"Go on. Tell it. Maybe one will come to you as you go along."

In the scene, Bogey had been drinking, and Richard thought about pouring himself a tall one. Emily did, in fact, have a story to tell, but she had no idea that this time the wow finish would be provided by the man sitting next to her. Richard closed his eyes and took a calming breath as he retrieved the small velvet-covered box that had been burning a hole in his pocket all evening. He opened it and held it out in front of her.

"Here's looking at you, kid," he said in character, then

added his own words. "For the rest of my life."

At first, she just stared at him, but the look in those big, green eyes told him he'd made the right decision. "Will you marry me?" he asked, anxious to hear the word.

"Yes."

That was the word.

Michael shook his head and returned to the present. He pulled the invitation off the fridge. August 25th. He had about five weeks to prepare—haircut, new suit, perhaps a dance lesson or two. Michael Riordan better not have two left feet. He had to look his best and bring his A-game. It was time to take this relationship to the next level, and Ben and Michelle's wedding would be the perfect place to start.

Chapter 26

M ichael fumbled with his tie. He knew how to tie a necktie—he could tie one in his sleep—but today was the big day. Although he hadn't seen Emily as often in the past few weeks, their relationship seemed to be moving along nicely. The fact that she was dating a giant of a man, a pillar of the community, a veritable Prince Charming, wasn't going to discourage him any longer. He could be charming, too. After all, Emily married *him* all those years ago. Okay, maybe his charm has been in hibernation for a while, but it was about to be awakened. David would eventually do battle with Goliath and everyone knows how that turned out.

With a renewed sense of purpose, he put the finishing touches on his necktie and looked at his reflection. Pleased with what he saw, he grabbed his jacket from the bed and headed out the door.

Michael arrived at the reception early and sat at the bar. He had not talked to Emily in almost a week and wondered if she had been avoiding him. He ordered a club soda and glanced at the door.

Michael had left the church service after sitting in back and watching as much of the ceremony as he could. Emily sat about halfway between himself and the altar. She was alone. He couldn't see her face, but he knew when she was crying.

He looked past the rows of bottles arranged in front of a large mirror along the back of the bar and studied his reflection. Even after four months, he still found it strange to see another man's face staring back at him. He hoped someday he would get used to it. It didn't seem likely.

"Michael?" a familiar voice called from over his right shoulder.

He turned, Emily stood alone by his side. He smiled as the scent of her perfume brought back memories from another life. It made him dizzy and, for a moment, unable to think straight. *Say something.*

"What are you doing here?" she asked.

"Of all the gin joints in all the towns in all the world, you walk into mine," he replied as coolly as he could with his best Humphrey Bogart voice.

Emily laughed and set her purse on the bar. "I came to Casablanca for a wedding. I didn't expect to find *you* here."

She remembered. Okay, relax. He took a deep breath. *This is Emily, the woman you lived with for twenty-four years, not some blind date.* Michael ordered her a glass of wine, and she sat on the stool next to him. She appeared genuinely happy to see him. Perhaps, she hadn't been avoiding him, after all.

When her drink arrived, she took a sip and looked at him curiously. "My favorite. How did you know?"

He shrugged. "Lucky guess."

Emily smiled. "So, what are you doing here?"

"Same as you, I imagine."

"Right … the wedding," her voice trailed off, and she took a sip of wine. "Are you a friend of the bride or groom?"

"Both, actually."

"Really?" Her eyes widened. "So am I."

He changed the subject, not wanting to get tripped up discussing their past relationships with the newlyweds. "I haven't seen you in the park lately …"

"Michael." She looked down at her glass. "You know I—"

"Yeah, I know." He didn't try to hide his disappointment. "But, hey, we're just two good friends who happened to meet at a wedding reception, right? Where's the harm in that?"

"There isn't any." She smiled and raised her glass. He brought his up to meet hers and they both took a drink.

"You clean up nice," he said, looking her up and down.

"Excuse me?"

"Uh … what I meant was … you know … I've only seen you in the park, and … it's just that you look fantastic."

She smiled, but said nothing.

Real smooth, he thought. "I'm sorry, I haven't done this in a while…"

"What … talk?" she asked with a grin.

"Talk to a beautiful woman." He held her gaze.

Emily blushed before looking away. "Thank you, Michael. You're sweet. I was going to say the same about you."

"That I'm a beautiful woman?" He looked down at his clothes and smoothed his tie with his hand. "That wasn't exactly the look I was going for."

Emily laughed, and he looked up at her, remembering how he loved to make her laugh. He missed that. He laughed along with her.

"I didn't see you at the church. Are you here alone?" she asked.

"As a matter of fact, I am. And you? Where's *Victor*?"

She smiled momentarily before her expression fell. She looked back at the glass of wine in front of her. "That was Richard's favorite movie," she said without looking up. "I couldn't even tell you how many times we watched it together."

"I'm sorry. No more *Casablanca* talk."

She put her hand on his arm. "I'll be fine," she said, looking at him with those eyes.

Michael met her gaze, holding it as long as he could before he had to look away.

"He probably doesn't deserve it, but I still miss him from time to time." She took another drink as a silence descended upon them.

"So, you didn't answer my question," he said.

"Which question was that?"

"You're obviously here alone. Where is Prince Charming?"

"If you're referring to Phillip, he had a previous engagement." She paused. "He's very important, you know."

There was something like sarcasm, or perhaps even disdain, in her voice. *What's this? A tiny crack in the Prince's armor?*

Before he could say anything, a voice on the PA informed them that the wedding party had arrived and asked the guests to take their seats as quickly as possible.

Michael stood and looked at Emily.

"But I don't have a proper date," she teased.

He bent his arm at the elbow and offered it to her. "Perhaps I can be of service."

She hopped off her stool and took his arm. Emily smiled. "Sounds like a plan."

Michael couldn't imagine how the day could be going any better.

They ate dinner and talked like old friends. In Michael's eyes, Emily was the only other person in the room. It seemed like a lifetime ago, and perhaps it was, but he was falling in love with her all over again. He studied her and noticed that she really hadn't changed much in twenty-five years. Sure, tiny laugh lines had begun to appear at the corners of her eyes and strands of gray threaded her dark hair along her hairline, but it only made her more attractive—much like the taste of a fine wine that improves with age.

The band began to play an old Eagles tune—*The Best of My Love*—that had been one of their favorites, and without thinking, he asked her to dance. She agreed, and they walked onto the dance floor. Neither one spoke as he held her in his arms, swaying to the music. Halfway through the love song, he sensed the lyrics were making her feel a little awkward.

"This is one of my favorite songs," he said. "I hope it isn't making you uncomfortable."

"No ... I'm fine."

Clearly, she wasn't. He began to second guess his snap decision.

Whenever they'd danced to this song in the past, he'd always stolen a kiss at the end. The thought crossed his mind. Perhaps the only thing holding him back was the image of her running for the parking lot if he did. He had to keep reminding himself that, while he was holding the woman with whom he had spent most of his life, Emily was in the arms of a virtual stranger. Nothing could have prepared him for this.

The music faded and their movement slowed. They looked into each other's eyes. This is where he belonged. Time stood still. Many of the other guests moved toward their seats, but Michael and Emily held each other's gaze. Their heads moved a little closer, eyes still locked. Suddenly, the music began again with an upbeat tempo, and their moment vanished. Emily glanced away and then back. They silently agreed to return to their seats as more couples approached the dance floor.

Michael sat down while Emily excused herself and picked up her purse. He watched as she headed off to find the ladies' room. After a couple of deep breaths to restore his normal heart rate, he stood slowly and walked over to the bar.

Emily returned shortly after he sat down again. She thanked him for the glass of wine and continued on as if nothing had happened. Soon Michael found himself relaxing and having the best time he had had since ... well, he couldn't remember. The band had taken a break and Emily was laughing at one of Michael's jokes when he noticed a man in an expensive suit walking toward them. He stopped behind Emily and put his hands on her shoulders.

Emily looked up at him. "Phillip," she said, an element of surprise in her voice. "I thought you weren't going to be able to make it." She shot a nervous glance at Michael, then back at Phillip.

"Hello, darling," he said and leaned over to kiss her on the cheek.

Michael looked away. When he turned back, she looked as if she had been caught doing something wrong. We were just sitting here when he walked in, he thought. Does Phil have her on that short a leash?

Phillip straightened up. "I ducked out early. I knew you would be the most beautiful woman here." He looked down at Michael. "I couldn't risk one of the other guests stealing you away."

Michael forced a smile. *Great! Rich AND charming. I think I'm going to be sick.*

The man took a step toward Michael and extended his hand. "Phillip Morgan, Assistant District Attorney."

Assistant Jackass is more like it, he thought as he stood and reluctantly shook the man's hand. "Michael Riordan."

"Michael Riordan ..." Phillip looked at Emily as he repeated the name. "That sounds familiar." He looked back at Michael. "What do you do?"

"I'm a writer."

"I mean for a living."

"So do I," Michael said as calmly as he could.

"Hmmm ... anything I might have read?"

"I don't know. Can you read?"

Phillip's arrogant eyes narrowed.

"Just kidding, Phil." Michael grinned. "I've only written one book. It's called *Chance of a Lifetime*, and it's about this writer who meets a pretty girl at a wedding while her boyfriend is out playing golf."

Phillip frowned. He opened his mouth to speak, but before he could say anything, Michael pointed at him and grinned.

"Got you again." Phillip looked like a stuffed shirt while Emily tried to conceal a nervous smile.

"Actually, it's the story of a young man who questions the meaning of life after a serious injury shatters his dreams. But I imagine you're more of the murder mystery or courtroom drama type."

"Frankly, I don't have time to read *fiction*," Phillip said, as if he was somehow better than the rest of them.

"That's a shame," Michael replied. "Anyway, I should probably leave you two alone." He looked at Emily and nodded his head. "I had a wonderful time. Thank you for the dance."

Emily's eyes widened, and she flashed a quick smile. Michael turned and headed for the bar, not waiting for Phil's reaction.

The first glass of Scotch went down too easily, and he sat with his back against the bar and ordered another. Emily and *Prince Phillip* sat at the table talking, and he would have given anything to listen in on their conversation. He wondered how many times she'd seen him and how serious it was. He watched Emily steal a glance in his direction every now and then.

Michael knew who Phillip Morgan was. Anyone in Springfield who owned a television or read a newspaper knew him. He appeared to be on a fast track to the DA's office and took advantage of every opportunity to get his face in front of potential voters. Now it looked as if he were on a fast track to get into Emily's pants. That is, if he hadn't been there already. The thought made his blood boil. He turned around and ordered another drink, unable to watch any longer.

After a few minutes, he set his empty glass on the bar and stood, planning to go to their table and give that pompous ass a piece of his mind. He'd only taken a couple of steps when he saw them stand and walk toward the dance floor. He turned and headed for the men's room.

When he returned, he ordered another drink and looked for the couple on the dance floor. They weren't hard to find. Phil must have noticed all the video cameras because he was hamming it up. *This guy was too much.* Emily floated around the dance floor with Fred Astaire in an Armani suit. She appeared to be enjoying herself.

He took another drink and scolded himself for his behavior. *Way to go, Michael. That was charming. Don't let him get to you.* He decided he'd seen enough. He finished his drink, pulled out his wallet, and dropped a couple of bills on the bar.

Michael, who was in no condition to drive, made it home safely in spite of himself. The evening had gone well until that jackass Morgan showed up. He kicked off his shoes and fell onto the sofa. Five minutes later, the doorbell rang. *Who the hell could that be?*

"Nobody's home," he called.

The bell rang again.

You've got to be kidding. "I'm coming," he grumbled.

When he reached the door, the bell rang again. He looked through the peephole. Tommy. He hesitated before opening the door.

Tommy's eyes widened when he saw him. "You?"

"What do you want?" Michael asked abruptly.

"I was told to deliver a message. A very good friend of mine did not ... appreciate ... your wise-ass remarks in front of his girl this evening."

HIS girl? "So he sent one of his goons over here to scare me off?"

Tommy jabbed his index finger hard into Michael's chest. It pushed him backward into the room. He followed him in. "That's right, tough guy."

Michael, still a little shaky from the alcohol, struggled to regain his balance.

"I had a feeling you were trouble when I saw you at the diner," Tommy growled. "Consider this your second warning."

Tommy was a couple of inches taller than Michael and outweighed him by thirty pounds, most of which appeared to be muscle. Nevertheless, Michael straightened up and stood his ground.

"Emily is a friend of mine," he said.

"Not any more." Both men stared at each other. "*Comprende?*"

Michael pointed toward the door. "Get the hell out of my house."

"Or what ... you'll call the police?" Tommy snickered.

"Get out."

Slowly, Tommy turned to leave. He stopped when he reached the front porch. "You don't want me to have to come back here," he said.

Michael locked the door behind him and exhaled sharply. I never did like you very much, he thought, but I always gave you the benefit of the doubt—one of Springfield's finest, my ass. Turns out you're nothing but a two-bit thug. He watched through the peephole as Tommy drove away.

Michael walked toward the kitchen, stopped at his desk and placed one hand on the edge for support. He noticed the two-year coin sitting there. He picked it up, looked at it briefly, and threw it across the room.

Note to self: Buy a bottle of Scotch.

Chapter 27

M ichael dragged himself out of bed the next morning, reminded of what can happen when one consumes too much alcohol. The few times Richard had overdone it in his lifetime didn't prepare him for what he felt at the moment. His brain seemed to have expanded overnight, mercilessly pushing against the inside of his skull. He debated whether to crawl back to bed or to split open his head and relieve the pressure. However, even with his diminished powers of reasoning, he decided on a third option, which was both quicker than the first and less lethal than the second.

Michael rummaged through the bathroom medicine cabinet and found a single ibuprofen tablet. This, of course, was unacceptable. Despite having slept in his clothes, he headed to the drug store to restock his medicine cabinet.

After raising a few eyebrows in the checkout line, Michael returned to his car with a bottle of water and a pharmacy-in-a-bag. He reached into the plastic sack and pulled out the first three bottles he touched. He swallowed a couple of pills from each and washed them down with the water.

Next, he stopped for a mega-dose of caffeine. When he pulled into Maggie's, he scanned the parking lot for Tommy's cruiser. The coast was clear. Inside, he ordered a large coffee after getting a whiff of the greasy, but otherwise tasty, breakfast fare. Breakfast was out of the question. Keeping the pills down was difficult enough without throwing a few slices of bacon into the mix.

Michael felt a little better by the time he parked his car in his driveway and walked to the front door. He slipped his key into the deadbolt and found it unlocked. *That's odd. I always lock the door.* However, given the way he left this morning, he couldn't be sure. He did a quick scan up and down the street and, after finding nothing out of the ordinary, pushed the door open a few inches. He paused to listen. Nothing.

Tommy McKenna had him on edge after their last meeting, and he hoped the thug hadn't paid him another visit. The thought sobered him and, as he slowly opened the door, he silently berated himself for not moving one of the baseball bats he'd found in the basement up to the hall closet.

He left the door ajar and crept silently into the living room, his senses on full alert. In the middle of the room, he stopped and looked around. Nothing seemed out of place. The clock ticked on the mantle. He realized he'd been holding his breath and exhaled slowly.

A rustle in the kitchen sent a chill through his body. *You've got to be kidding. There really is someone in here?* His hand shook as he reached for the fireplace poker from the brass stand on the hearth. He raised the makeshift weapon and examined it, wondering if he could really hit someone with it. He hoped he wouldn't have to find out.

He stood next to the kitchen door with his back against the dining room wall and listened again. Nothing. He rested his head against the wall and tried to slow his runaway heart. The hammering was so loud he feared it might give away his position. Holding the weapon in front of himself, he thrust his head around the corner and pulled it back quickly like he'd seen the detectives do on television. Before his brain could fully process what he had seen, Angie, who was sitting at the kitchen table with a cup of coffee and a magazine, jumped up from her chair.

"Michael?" she called. "Is that you?"

Michael exhaled before he stepped into the kitchen. Angie held a rolled up magazine in front of her like a sword.

"You scared the shit out of me," she said, lowering her paper weapon. She looked at the fireplace tool in his hand. "What the hell are you doing?"

Michael's heart was still pounding. "*I* scared *you*?" he blurted. "You're the one who's not supposed to be here." He set the poker down on the edge of the table and walked to the sink to get a drink of water.

"You look like hell," she said.

"I didn't sleep well, but thanks for noticing."

Angie sat down. "So what were you going to do with that thing?"

He finished drinking, set the glass down in the sink, and turned to face her. "I'm not sure, but I think I was going to crack your skull with it."

"God, Michael, what has gotten into you?"

"What are you doing here?"

"My car's in the shop down on Culver. I didn't want to sit in a dirty waiting room for two hours, so I grabbed a magazine and walked over here." She raised her cup. "And the coffee here is better," she said with a forced a smile.

Michael poured himself a cup from the pot that Angie had made. He pulled out the chair across from her and sat. "You're getting your car fixed ... on Sunday? Who's open on Sunday?"

"Just about everybody." She shook her head. "You've really got to get out more."

"I get out."

"Really? So, what is it you've been doing with yourself?"

She took a sip of coffee. "I mean, besides scaring the crap out of innocent women."

Michael rolled his head from side to side, relaxing the tension in his neck, and leaned back in his chair. "Did I tell you I met someone?"

She raised an eyebrow. "You mean a woman?"

"No, I mean an alien. He landed in the backyard last night."

She pushed her glasses down and glared at him over the rims.

"Of course, a woman," he declared. "I'm not gay."

She shook her head and laughed. "I didn't think you were. It's just that you haven't had a date or even mentioned a woman since ... I can't even remember."

"Yeah, well—"

"Does she have a name?"

"Actually, she does."

Angie leaned forward. "Well? Is it a secret, or are you going to tell me what it is?" Before he could answer, she asked, "What ... is she someone famous?"

"No, but her boyfriend is," he grumbled.

"She has a boyfriend?"

"Phillip Morgan," he replied, studying her reaction.

"You're kidding," she snorted. "Good luck with *that*."

"Seriously, Ang? You're not helping."

"He's a catch, Michael. Even if she was crazy enough to let him go, that's got to be a hard act to follow."

"Still not helping."

"I'm sorry," she said, trying to conceal her amusement. "So, are you going to tell me her name or not?"

"Emily ... her name is Emily."

"How did you two meet?"

We met at the campus pub twenty-seven years ago.

"Michael?"

He realized he'd been staring at his ring finger. He looked up. "I'm sorry. We met in the park. It was a few months ago when I was doing my therapy."

"What about the Phillip thing? How long has that been going on?"

"I think it started shortly before I met her."

"Bummer."

"Yeah, I really like her, Ang."

"Then don't give up. Some things are meant to be, no matter how ridiculously unlikely it may look in the beginning." She snickered before turning serious. "Look. You've beaten greater odds than this. You just have to keep the faith, bro."

"You're right." He stood and picked up the poker.

"So what's with the Rambo act?" Angie asked, motioning toward the weapon in his hand. "I've never seen you like this."

"It's nothing. I thought you might have been ..." His voice trailed off as he thought twice about what he was going to say.

Angie narrowed her eyes. "Michael? Who did you think I was?"

"Forget it. It's nothing. I'm going to go get changed." He left the room before she could say another word.

∞∞∞∞

Tommy McKenna sat in his police cruiser outside Maggie's Diner while his partner Jason went inside to order a couple of breakfast sandwiches and coffee to go. Tommy did all the driving—and all the thinking as far as he was concerned—while Jason, who had been on the force only two years, made most of the food runs. Occasionally, Tommy would offer to order the food if a pretty young waitress was inside. He favored three local eateries and tried to keep track of who was working each shift. He'd never been considered the sharpest knife in the drawer, but he paid attention to details when it came to women.

Tommy was busy checking the onboard computer installed on the cruiser's console, taking care of some unofficial business. When he looked up, he saw Jason sitting at the counter talking with the waitress. He tapped *R-i-o-r-d-a-n* on the keyboard, and pressed the Enter key.

He'd visited Riordan a few nights ago at Phillip's request. The fact that he'd been ordered off the property did not sit well, but he had to be careful when he was in uniform on unofficial business. He'd heard the name Michael Riordan before, but he couldn't quite put his finger on where or when. It was familiar, but not in a good way.

Apparently, Phillip had a similar reaction when he met Michael at the wedding. Great minds think alike, Tommy reasoned. When Phillip asked him to run Riordan's name through the criminal database, Tommy told him he'd already done so and came up with no warrants or criminal record. He tried to stay one step ahead of his friend. After all, Tommy knew he was every bit as smart as Phillip. He just didn't get the breaks his friend had gotten. Unlike Phillip, he wasn't born with a silver spoon in his mouth. Money changes everything.

Not deterred by Tommy's report, Phillip had asked him to check into motor vehicle accident and missing persons reports for the last two years. It wasn't the first time Tommy had done background checks, or even some after-hours surveillance. Hell, he'd been doing as much with Emily's boyfriends since high school, but now he had the resources of the Springfield Police Department at his disposal. The fact that his orders came from the ADA made it all the more justifiable.

Phillip Morgan had recently set his sights on Emily after they met at a fundraiser, and whatever Phillip wanted, he generally got. Tommy was okay with Phillip dating his sister, which was a good thing for him because the man didn't like taking no for an answer. When such misunderstandings arose, things had a way of working themselves out in Phillip's favor. More often than not, that *way* involved Officer Thomas McKenna. The two had been good friends since they met when Tommy was in the Academy and Phil was in Law School. Now, Phillip would employ him from time to time whenever his considerable powers of persuasion weren't sufficient. Some things required a little muscle.

He got a hit. *One record found for Riordan, Michael J.* He pressed Enter and the requested data filled the screen.

"Son of a bitch!" he said aloud.

Michael Riordan, white male, fifty years old, had been involved in a fatal accident last year that killed one Richard Dunham. There were copies of both of their driver's licenses. It was him, all right. But why was he sniffing around the victim's widow?

Tommy rubbed his chin as he attempted to organize the facts and determine how the pieces of this puzzle might fit together. *OK, what have we got here? We've got one Michael Riordan involved in a fatal car accident. The report says he was not at fault. Then, less than a year later, he's making time with the victim's widow. Why? Is he a stalker? Is he running a con? Is he after the insurance money?* He pulled a small spiral-bound notebook from his shirt pocket and made a few notes. *No way this is just a coincidence!* Something didn't smell right and he would follow his nose until he found it. He always did.

Jason set the cardboard tray with two cups of coffee on the roof and opened the passenger door. Tommy slipped the notebook back into his pocket. Jason tossed the bag in and handed him one of the cups before he sat down and closed the door.

Jason looked at the computer and then to Tommy. "What're you doing?" he asked.

"Nothing. Just thinking," Tommy replied as he tapped the Escape key to clear the screen. He opened his coffee and took a sip. He would get to the bottom of this Riordan thing, but it would have to wait. He couldn't risk telling some wet-behind-the-ears rookie about his system. It'd been working too well up to this point.

The two officers sat in the idling car and ate in relative silence. Jason made several attempts to start up a conversation, but Tommy was otherwise preoccupied.

"C'mon, man, something's eatin' you. What is it?" Jason asked.

Tommy considered avoiding his question again, but didn't want to raise any suspicion. "If you must know, I was thinking about this hot little number I met last night," he lied with a devious grin.

Jason looked at him in awe. Tommy was something of a legend around the station house with no shortage of incredible stories surrounding the man's romantic escapades, most of which had been corroborated by one or more of his fellow officers.

At fifty-three, Tommy looked ten years younger. He worked in the gym every other day and could keep up with anyone on the force in terms of strength and endurance. His sandy blond hair, clear blue eyes, and chiseled features were enough to make just about any woman in Springfield take a second look—and the uniform didn't hurt.

"Did you—"

"Jason! A gentleman doesn't kiss and tell," he said, feigning a degree of modesty and integrity.

"I wasn't asking about kissing." The rookie grinned.

"Let's just say, I rocked her world." He gave his partner a big wink and took another bite of his sandwich.

"Wow," Jason whispered like a teenager.

Kids, Tommy thought. They're so easily amused.

Chapter 28

After breakfast Sunday morning, Michael headed to the park as he'd done three times that week, hoping to find Emily. Each time, he'd left disappointed. He felt as if she'd been avoiding him, and he didn't understand why.

He may have crossed the line at Maggie's. He'd clearly upset her a couple of times, but reassured himself his intentions were noble. Everything he'd said to her was more to comfort her than to clear his name.

That was over a month ago. It didn't make sense. He believed their connection at Ben and Michelle's wedding had been a turning point in their relationship. The energy between them when he held her on that dance floor had been unmistakable. He'd seen it in her eyes. The eyes don't lie. Perhaps she'd changed her schedule. Shit happens, he reminded himself. There had to be some other reason why he hadn't seen her.

Other than being a little too warm for his personal taste, it was a beautiful day, one that shouldn't be wasted worrying—least of all about something that may or may not be true. He took a couple of deep breaths and watched one of the ducks circle the pond and come in for a perfect landing, skidding across the water for a few feet before stopping with a final flap of its wings. From his seat on one of the wooden benches, he had a great view of the pond and its inhabitants, as well as the steady stream of people who filled the park on weekends.

With a half-mile long trail around the pond, Franklin

Park was a Mecca for dog walkers. At any given time, it contained as many dogs as it did people. In his past life, he and Bogey walked among them, but now he just observed the rituals. Some dogs walked their owners, while others stopped every two or three feet to sniff out some invisible nugget as their owners stood patiently at the edge of the trail. He couldn't help wondering if either activity might still be considered walking the dog.

Whether walking or not, the activity was a form of social networking. Everyone seemed to know each other, and when someone new showed up, the dog owners quickly welcomed them into the club. Michael found it all quite amusing. He wondered what aliens would think if they landed in the park and observed the activity. Who would they assume was the more intelligent life form, the one leading the way or the one following behind picking up the poop?

"Hey," a voice called from over his shoulder.

Michael turned and smiled when he saw Emily approaching. "Hey, yourself. Where've you been hiding lately?"

"I've been pretty busy," she said awkwardly, her smile only a flicker. Lying wasn't one of her strong suits.

"I thought maybe it was something I said."

She sat next to him. He waited for her to respond, but she didn't. "Do you want to walk?" he asked.

"No. I can't."

"Em?"

Instead of answering, she reached into her purse and held out an envelope. "Here, this is for you."

He took it and flipped it over. "Can I open it now?"

"No." She placed her hand on his. "Not now." She smiled, but it seemed forced, as if there were something she wasn't telling him. She glanced in the direction of her car.

"You're not leaving, are you?" he asked as she stood.

"I have to go," she whispered and walked away.

Michael looked at the envelope in his hands and then back at Emily as she disappeared through the front gate. He had a bad feeling about the contents. Beads of sweat formed on his brow. Was it the midday sun, or the way Emily had rushed off?

He took a deep breath, opened the envelope, and pulled out a card with a picture of a sunset over the ocean. He flipped it open.

Dear Michael,

Just a note to say thank you for being such a good friend. I have enjoyed our walks in the park and our conversations. You have a wonderful sense of humor, as well as an interesting outlook on life. Your words in the coffee shop that day have helped me more than you know. For that, I am grateful.

However, Phillip is not happy with our relationship. I think he sees you as a threat. I assured him he has nothing to worry about, but he has asked me to stop meeting with you. You've made it clear you don't care for the man, but I do, and for now, I am going to honor his wishes. I hope you understand. I will always remember you as one of my best friends.

Emily

Michael's heart fell as he set the card on the bench. *Best friends? Is that all you think we are? Friends? I can't accept that, Emily. We're more than friends, and I'm going to prove it.* He had underestimated Phillip Morgan, and now the man was turning into a major problem. Michael hadn't anticipated such stiff resistance, but he wasn't going down without a fight.

He slipped the card back into the envelope and left the park. When he climbed into his car, his heart beat at its normal rate, but his mind still raced. He threw the card onto the passenger seat and sat for a few minutes, thinking.

"Shit!" He pounded the steering wheel with both fists before hitting the turn signal and checking the side mirror. He waited for a car to pass, but it pulled up alongside and slowed to a stop, blocking him in. Tommy.

He wore plain clothes and presumably drove his own car—like he had nothing better to do on his day off. He stared silently at Michael, whose heart was about to jump out of his chest onto the seat next to him. Nevertheless, Michael refused to look away. He would not be intimidated. Finally, Tommy made his *I'm watching you* gesture and drove off.

Michael started to breathe again.

Chapter 29

Michael sat on his deck, a bottle of beer on the table next to him. The full moon illuminated his surroundings with an eerie silver light. After writing all afternoon, he'd reviewed his work until it became too difficult to see. He set the manuscript down and took another pull on the beer. His thoughts turned again to Emily and *The Card*. After reading *The Card*, as he now called it, he understood why she'd stopped coming to the park: Phillip Morgan.

Is that what Emily really wanted or what Phillip wanted for her? Something was wrong. Emily was too stubborn to let anyone tell her what to do with her life.

"Hi, Ang," Michael said when he noticed his sister climbing the stairs.

She reached the top step and stopped dead in her tracks. "What the hell is that?" she asked, pointing to the bottle.

Shit! Michael glanced at it and then back at his sister.

"Dammit, Michael!"

He pointed to the empty chair across the table. "Please, Ang, just sit down. We need to talk."

"Not with this thing here." She picked up the bottle between her thumb and forefinger, holding it away from her body like it was toxic waste. In one fluid motion, she heaved it over the railing into the backyard.

"Fine." Michael sighed.

Angela sat. "So what is it you wanted to talk about?" She set her keys on the table and leaned back in her chair.

He hesitated. "Remember the day you broke into my house and—"

"I have a key, Michael," she reminded him as she folded her arms across her chest.

"Okay, but remember when you asked me who I thought was in the house?"

"I remember you avoided the question and ducked out of the room."

"I thought it might be Emily's brother, Tommy."

She looked at him curiously. "But why would—"

"He threatened me the night of the wedding. He's working for Phillip Morgan and he warned me to stay away from Emily."

Her eyes grew wide. "Seriously? What are you going to do?"

"Do?" he said a little too loudly. He lowered his voice. "Nothing. He's a cop."

"You've got to at least tell her, Michael."

"But he's her brother. And it's not the first time he's done something like this," he said, opening the door to the real reason for this conversation.

"How do you know that?"

"Because he did it to me once before ... twenty-seven years ago."

She stared slack-jawed. "What? How is that even possible?"

"I'm not who I appear to be."

"You *have* been acting pretty strange since the accident, but I just figured—"

"Yeah, you figured I got my bell rung a little too hard and needed some time to recover." He paused. "It's a little more complicated than that."

"What do you mean?"

"I mean your brother died in that accident."

She let out a nervous laugh. "Come on, Michael, you're starting to creep me out."

"I'm sorry, Angie, but I need your help. I can't do this alone any more. I have to tell someone."

"Tell someone what?"

A dog barked in the yard next door. Michael glanced toward the sound.

"What is it, Michael?"

He leaned closer. "Do you know what a *Walk-in* is?"

Her eyes narrowed. "You mean like when you don't have an appointment?"

"No." He shook his head. "More like ... *Heaven Can Wait*."

"The movie?"

"Yes. After Warren Beatty dies, his soul comes back and trades places with another who wants to leave. He's given the chance to continue his life in the body of someone else." He took a deep breath. "Michael is my someone else."

"Are you drunk?" she snorted. "God, Michael. What the hell is wrong with you?"

Their eyes locked. Michael remained silent.

"That's impossible." Angela stood. She placed both hands on the edge of the table. "If that were true, then who were ... I mean are ... *shit!* I don't know what I mean."

"My name was Richard Dunham."

Angie blinked, as if unsure she heard him correctly. "You mean the jerk who caused your first accident?"

"I wouldn't have put it that way, but yes." He studied her reaction.

"This is crazy, Michael. Stop it." She walked over to the railing as if to put some distance between them. "How many beers have you had tonight?"

Michael didn't answer.

"I don't believe any of this," she said, turning to face him.

"I know it sounds crazy, but it's true. Why would I make something like this up?"

She stared at him without speaking.

"You said it yourself. I've been acting strange since the accident. Now you know why."

She turned around and looked over the backyard. "And Michael?"

"I'm sorry, Ang, but he's gone." He stood and walked to the railing. In the moonlight, her expression was unreadable. "I would have told you sooner, but I didn't know how."

Tears began to fall and she wiped them several times before looking at him. "I guess that would explain some things ... like *forgetting* you were an alcoholic. People don't forget things like that."

"I don't imagine they do. I did lose my memory for a while. All of it. I didn't know who I was, where I was, or how I got there until Richard's memories started to come back."

She closed her eyes. He waited. "So what's this have to do with Tommy?" she asked.

"Emily is my wife."

Her eyes widened. "You've got to be kidding."

"I wish I was." His voice sounded flat. "I wish this was all some big joke, and I could go back to the way things were before I ... before the accident."

"That makes two of us," she whispered.

A silence descended upon them. Her tears glistened in the moonlight.

"Michael wasn't just my brother. He was my best friend," she finally said as she wiped her cheeks. "Now he's gone because of you. How do you expect me to feel?"

"I was hoping you would understand." He touched her arm just above the elbow. "I need an ally, someone I can talk to. Someone I can be honest with."

"Honest?" She pulled her arm away and let the word hang there for a moment. "I don't know Mi ..." she hesitated, apparently having trouble saying his name. "I don't know if I can do that."

"Look, I understand this is difficult, but please don't shut me out. It's a lot to process, so just—"

"It sure is." She walked back to the table and picked up her keys. "I have to go."

"Angie ..."

"Goodbye," she said without looking back.

Michael opened his mouth to speak, but decided against it. *This is a fine mess you've gotten yourself into this time.* He had just scared away the only friend he had left. No one even knew he was alive. The only person he hadn't alienated yet was Arthur, whom he had no way of contacting.

While sitting alone and feeling sorry for himself, it occurred to him that this must have been how Emily had felt. The fear of abandonment had gripped her since childhood. He'd seen it in her eyes on occasion. He tried to imagine what it would have taken, in the face of such a fear, to push him away like she did.

Could I have been so oblivious that I didn't see what I was doing to her? He wondered what her reaction would have been if she'd been the one on his deck tonight instead of Angela.

∞∞∞∞

Michael spent the next ten days at home finishing his

manuscript. He hadn't heard from Angela, and that bothered him. Maybe it was for the best. She would have gotten over the pizza boxes, Chinese food containers, and empty Doritos bags strewn about the house, perhaps even helped him clean up. But the empty beer bottles, they would have set her off again. She didn't get it. He could handle the alcohol. *I'm not Michael.* Now that she knew that, he would probably never see her again.

Friday evening, he cleared the sofa in the living room and fell into a deep sleep. The doorbell rang. He sat up, disoriented. The bell rang again, and he feared that Tommy was back for another round.

He stumbled to the door and put his eye to the peephole as the bell rang a third time. He straightened up and rubbed his eyes, then took a deep breath and looked again. Angela.

His muscles relaxed, and he opened the door. Angie stepped inside without a word. She looked around with fire in her eyes, so he kept his distance. When she finally looked up at him, he saw disappointment and perhaps a little fear.

"You look like hell," Angie said. "Is this how it's going to be?"

"I've been writing."

"Really? Are you sure you haven't just been holed up in here feeling sorry for yourself? I've seen this before, you know."

"I'm finished."

"Finished acting like a drunken hermit, I hope."

"Finished writing the second book."

"Was it worth it?"

"You don't understand."

"Can I read it? Will that help me understand?"

"Yes," he motioned for her to sit. "But you must read it with an open mind. It's based on a true story. Richard's story. Well, most of it's true. I had to improvise in a few places."

"What about the ending?"

"It's written," he said. "Wishful thinking, perhaps, but it's written."

"And how does it turn out?"

"You're going to have to read it."

"So where is it?"

He shrugged. "It's here somewhere." He stood up and looked around.

Angela watched him for a moment before lifting a pizza box from the coffee table, exposing a stack of paper held together by a binder clip. "Is this it?"

He turned to look at her. "That's it."

She picked it up and put it on her lap. "Now, what?"

"Read it if you like, just get it out of my sight. I'm not sure what I'm going to do with it, but right now, I don't want it here."

Chapter 30

Despite their current situation, Michael called Emily on Saturday morning to ask her to lunch. They had not had any contact since *The Card*, and he needed to hear it with his own ears. In his opinion, ending a relationship with a piece of paper was cowardly. The Emily he knew was no coward. He needed to see her, to look into her eyes as she said the words. A part of him held onto the hope that he could change her mind, so he was pleasantly surprised, even encouraged, when she accepted his invitation.

With Tommy acting as his enforcer, Phillip had a virtual restraining order against him, so Michael decided that a trip out of town was a wise choice. They talked during the thirty minute drive to Riverside, but not with the same easy give-and-take to which they'd become accustomed. Emily remained guarded, hesitant to stray from simple, benign small talk. While the specter of Phillip Morgan loomed large in the cabin of Michael's car, he sensed there was more to her recent withdrawal.

"We're here," he said as they pulled into the parking lot of the Riverside Grill. Situated along the scenic Algonquin River, the Grill had an outside dining area that overlooked the valley. Now mid-September, the leaves had begun to change, adding splashes of orange and gold to the panorama.

"This is nice," she said, her voice quiet. "Hopefully, the food is as good as the view."

They picked up their orders and headed for the tables outside. After eating in silence for a few minutes, Emily spoke, her gaze still fixed on the landscape before her.

"Richard talked about coming up here," she said. "He had an old, I guess you'd call it *classic*, car he used to love to drive up Route 7. He would stop somewhere for breakfast. It might have been this place. He never took me."

"I'm sure he regrets that," Michael said, as he took a bite of his sandwich. "What kind of car was it?"

"A 1968 Mustang. It needed a lot of work when he bought it, but he was pretty good with cars. He did most of the work himself." She sighed.

"You didn't like the car?"

"Oh, I liked it, it's just that ..." Her voice trailed off.

Michael waited. "It's just that, what?"

She stopped eating and looked at him. "Sometimes, I think he loved that car more than he loved me." Emily paused, holding his gaze.

Michael waited as long as he could before looking away.

"There were nights when he would be out in the garage making love to that damn car while I was lying in bed alone," she said, her eyes fixed on the horizon once again.

Michael's chest tightened as he pictured her alone in their bed waiting for him. At the same time, he was somewhat encouraged that she was confiding in him again.

Michael set his sandwich down and swallowed hard. "I didn't know you felt like that."

She stopped eating and looked at him. "What?"

"I mean ... I ... I just meant women in general." He frowned. "Frankly, I've been guilty of the same thing. I never thought of how my wife felt ... until now. I guess it's one of those moments. I forget what they call them."

"An *aha moment*," she offered, her voice flat.

"Yeah, that's it."

"So, why are men so insensitive to such things?" she

asked just before he looked away.

"Hmmm. Loaded question." He took a deep breath. "I think men and women are just wired differently."

"That sounds like a cop-out."

"Perhaps it is. Perhaps we aren't willing to admit that we often let insignificant, material things get in the way of the more important things in life. In my experience, women are more likely to value the things you can't put a price on, such as love and family. My wife was one of those women."

Emily studied him for a moment. "Good answer."

"Unfortunately, it appears I learned that lesson too late."

"Too late for what?" she asked.

"Too late to make a difference, I guess." He watched her eat the last french fry. When she'd finished, she turned to him.

"Weren't you the one who told me that it's never too late?" Their eyes locked, and he couldn't look away. Emily picked up her napkin and wiped the corner of her mouth. She raised her eyebrows impatiently.

"Yeah, I guess I was," he finally admitted. "So, let me ask you something."

Emily shifted uncomfortably as if she regretted not ending the conversation when she had the chance.

"Why is it suddenly too late for us?" he asked.

She twirled a few strands of hair around her index finger and avoided his stare. "Michael, I ... I told you ... I like you, but you know I'm seeing Phillip," she said without looking up.

"How's that working out for you?" He waited for a response, which didn't come.

She stood, gathered their empty plates, and walked away.

"Emily." He followed her.

She deposited everything in the trash barrel, then turned to face him.

"I'm sorry," he said. "But when we're not together, I find myself missing you. I feel a connection between us. I think I'd miss you even if we'd never met."

She stood motionless in front of him and held his gaze.

"I want to see more of you, not less," he moved a little closer. "I think you know that, but you choose to push me away."

Emily lowered her head. "Michael, don't."

Michael brought his hand up under her chin and gently lifted her head.

She didn't resist, but she avoided his gaze. A few strands of hair blew across her face, and he brushed them back. Finally, she surrendered and looked into his eyes. Warmth surged in his chest and he leaned in, hoping she would reciprocate. He could feel her breath on his upper lip.

At the last second, Emily turned her head. She hesitated for an instant then turned back to meet his lips. His mind let go of everything else. He could have stayed in that moment forever.

She pulled back and studied him, searching for something.

"Emily?" he whispered.

She didn't respond and appeared to struggle with her thoughts for a moment before lowering her head. They stood together—forehead to forehead—eyes closed, hearing only their breathing.

Emily began to shake her head from side to side. She pulled back, eyes still looking down. "I can't."

"What?"

She raised her head, but her eyes darted back and forth, avoiding his. "We have to go." She turned and walked toward the parking lot.

Michael watched her for a moment before following. "Emily," he called.

She stopped, and he closed the distance between them. "Emily, please."

She turned around, biting her lip to hold back tears.

"You have to be honest with yourself, Emily. I know you felt it."

Her eyes were wide as she stared at him. She did not respond.

"Tell me you didn't feel something powerful— something you can't explain. Make me believe that, and I will disappear. I won't bother you again."

She covered her mouth with her hand. He watched her as she turned and hurried toward the car. He couldn't push her for fear that he would drive her away forever.

It was a quiet ride home.

∞∞∞∞∞

"Another Saturday night, and I ain't got nobody ... " Ain't that the truth, he thought as he turned off the radio and pulled into his driveway. He had dropped Emily off hours ago and had been driving around ever since. Emily hadn't looked at him the entire ride home, staring silently out the window. If she thanked him when he dropped her off, that was the extent of their conversation.

He second-guessed opening up to her like he did, but it had been five months since his return as Michael Riordan. Given her reaction today, he wasn't holding out much hope for when, or if, he told her the truth.

Michael grabbed a bottle of Scotch from behind the cereal boxes where he had stashed it a few days ago to hide it from Angela's judgmental eyes. She still had a problem with him having a drink now and then. He set it down on the counter, realizing he had become one of those sorry souls who hid booze around the house. Perhaps Angie was right.

Michael sat down in his chair in the living room. He found an empty glass on the end table, one of the benefits of not yet having cleaned the house. He picked it up, blew into it, and decided it was clean enough. After pouring himself a drink, he opened his laptop and began to read what he had written.

He looked for answers from his past, but grew more distracted with each whiff of the smoky liquid in his glass. It had an earthy quality, like wet leaves burning, or perhaps a smoldering campfire. It stirred up unfamiliar memories. Vague recollections of someone else's life became intertwined with his own thoughts. He tried to dismiss the idea that the real Michael Riordan had somehow returned in an attempt to regain control. He didn't recall Arthur ever mentioning such a scenario. Could he be running out of time? Did the physical body somehow retain some of Michael's memories? Something in his DNA?

As the evening wore on, Michael lost count of how many times he refilled his glass. It's a small glass, he told himself. His frustration grew with every word he read, as well as the memories that didn't belong, each one relentlessly vying for his attention. Finally, he reached some sort of alcohol-induced breaking point and threw his laptop across the room. It smashed against the fireplace.

He stared at the pieces on the floor. The release felt good, but he hadn't yet killed the beast. He closed his eyes, wishing it was all over and wanting desperately to feel the peace he felt immediately after his accident. When he opened them again, he noticed movement by the fireplace, and he squinted to get a better look. The words—his words—rose in bizarre animation from the broken machine. They moved slowly at first, gaining momentum as they climbed. He rubbed his eyes.

Soon, thousands of them formed a cloud that spun like a tornado. It was a whirling dervish with arms and legs protruding from the spinning mass, reaching for him, trying to pull him in. The beast would consume him, judging him for the sins of his past. He couldn't let that happen. He squeezed his eyes shut. When he opened them again, it was gone.

His story had become a living, breathing thing—a monster he had resurrected, word by word, cloaked in emotion. It was the story of his life, a life that had somehow spun out of control. He could have stopped it, but he didn't. Arthur had told him life was about choices, and he continued to make them, each one worse than the last. It had to stop.

A small amount of liquid remained in the bottom of his glass, and he knocked it to the floor with the back of his hand. He pulled himself up from his seat, walked over to the fireplace, and picked up what was left of his laptop. He closed it as best he could and tucked it under his arm. Michael grabbed his keys and left the house in a hurry.

∞∞∞∞

When he returned an hour later, he saw Angela's car parked in his driveway. *Seriously, Ang? I just want to be left alone tonight.* Right now, the last thing he needed was another lecture from his sister. He found her sitting on the sofa, watching television. The room had been cleaned.

"Where have you been?" she asked calmly.

"Out."

She turned off the TV. "Have you been drinking?"

"Nope." He followed her glaring eyes to the bottle he left on the end table. "Uh … not in the last hour, anyway," he said as he flopped down in the chair across from her. "If you must know, I was at Franklin Park. I went up to the Overlook and threw my laptop into the pond."

Angela sat up straight. "Michael! You didn't." It was the first time she had used his name since the night on his deck.

"It felt good," he said, nodding his head. "Made a bigger splash than I expected."

"What about your book? You have a backup, right?"

"Of course I do. It's on a flash drive," he assured her. "That splash wasn't nearly as big."

"Michael! What the hell is wrong with you?" Angie stood up. "I came over here to tell you how good your story is. Bizarre, but good. I was rooting for the poor bastard. Yeah, he screwed up, but he learned an important lesson, and I wanted to see him win back the love of his life."

"You were rooting for him, huh?"

She paced back and forth in front of him, then stopped. "If it's supposed to be you, I'm having a hard time making the connection."

Michael said nothing. A few seconds passed.

"You've got to tell this story," Angie pleaded, standing directly in front of him. "I think it can help people."

"Help them commit suicide, maybe."

She said nothing, and in the silence, he grew uncomfortable.

He looked up at her. "I just can't do it any more, Ang."

"What about Emily?"

He looked away. "What about her?"

"What's going on between the two of you?"

"Nothing," he snorted. "Well, that's not entirely true.

I kissed her."

"What?"

"Yeah, just before she ran away."

"Maybe you need to work on your kissing skills," she said as she sat down.

"Funny, Ang. But I don't think that's the problem. I think she felt the same thing I did, and it scared her." He shook his head slowly. "After I go up against her brother Tommy and that douchebag Morgan, Emily plays the I-just-want-to-be-friends card. That was bad enough. Now, I think I may have chased her away for good. I don't know how much more of this I can take."

"You need to tell her."

"Really? You think she's going to believe me? You think anyone is going to believe me? I'm a freak. I'm starting to think—"

"So, you're giving up? That doesn't sound like the maniac who almost cracked my head open with a fireplace poker."

"That was adrenaline."

"Man up, Michael." Her expression was dead serious. "You've got to tell her."

Michael felt the weight of her stare. She was right. But how?

Chapter 31

M ichael stood on Lexi's front porch. When Emily had agreed to see him, she asked to be picked up at her daughter's house. She was staying there for a few days while her kitchen was being renovated. He wondered if she would be jetting off to Ireland any time soon.

Emily had sounded surprised when he called. It had been four days since their lunch in Riverside, and he couldn't tell if she expected to hear from him sooner or never again. He told her there was something important that they needed to discuss, regardless of which way their relationship was headed. She agreed, adding that she had something to say, as well.

Michael reached for the doorbell, then stopped halfway. It had been over a year since he'd seen Lexi or been inside her house. He had a grandson living there whom he'd never met.

Michael rang the bell and waited on the front porch. Emily smiled politely as she let him in. He looked around the large foyer, remembering the weekends he'd spent helping Lexi and her husband refurbish the hundred-year-old Victorian home. Emily had been by his side much of the time. They had always worked well together.

He chuckled when he recalled the paintbrush fight they'd had the day Lexi left them alone to finish painting the dining room. At least one of the window frames still held telltale signs of their playful skirmish.

Their eyes met for a moment, and he smiled and

shrugged before Lexi appeared from the living room.

"Alexis, this is my friend, Michael." She gestured toward Lexi. "My daughter, Alexis."

"Nice to meet you." Michael looked at his beautiful daughter, and his heart turned a somersault. Lexi smiled.

"That's Kayla," Emily continued, pointing to the living room, "and Tyler's asleep. He's almost five months old."

"I'm sorry I missed him," Michael said.

Emily appeared to be in good spirits. He couldn't tell if she'd loosened up a bit or if it was an acting job worthy of an Academy Award.

"I just need a few minutes with Lexi before we leave," Emily said.

"Take your time."

Michael stood in the foyer as Emily followed Lexi into the kitchen. He looked into the living room where Kayla sat watching television. She hadn't noticed him come in.

"Hello," he said.

Her face lit up when she saw him. "Hi, Grampa," she said as she stood up and ran toward him.

Michael shot a quick glance toward the kitchen to see if anyone had overheard them. When Kayla reached him, he squatted down and held out his hand, afraid of how a big hug might appear to the women if they happened to walk in.

"Hello, Little Miss Sunshine." He shook her small hand.

"Let's go play," she said.

He stood and held out his finger. Kayla wrapped her hand around it and pulled him toward the corner of the living room. Looking back at the kitchen again, he saw Emily watching them, a strange look on her face. He smiled, holding up his free hand, fingers spread wide.

"Five minutes," he said.

Emily stared for a moment and nodded.

"Sit down, Grampa," Kayla said when they reached the appropriate spot.

He obliged, shooting another quick glance in the direction of the kitchen. He sat cross-legged on the floor, intrigued by the fact that she had called him "Grampa."

After all of the introductions had been made, he asked her, "Do you remember who I am?"

"Grampa."

His knee began to ache and he shifted his weight.

"How come you didn't come over for a long time?" she asked.

He cleared his throat. "It's not because I didn't want to, Sweetie. I had to go away for a while."

"To heaven?"

He hesitated with an answer.

"Gramma said you went to heaven."

"Well, we know that Grammas are always right, don't we?"

"Yup."

"Five minutes are up," Emily called from the dining room.

"Be right there." He looked at Kayla. "Grampa has to go now."

"Bye," she said, busy mixing up something on her little stove.

"I'd like to come back and play again sometime."

"Okay."

Michael stood up slowly and watched Kayla for a moment before leaving the room. The two women met him in the hall.

Lexi walked into the living room. "Put your things away, honey. It's time for bed."

Emily studied Michael, and then gave a quick nod. "We'd better go."

Outside, she asked, "So, where are you taking me?"

"I figured we'd go to Winslow's. We can get a booth in the back where no one will see us."

"You sounded a little mysterious on the phone." She watched him. "There's something we need to talk about?"

"Let's wait until we get there."

"I don't like surprises, Michael." She twirled a lock of hair around her finger.

"I know," he said. "Just promise to keep an open mind tonight."

"Like that's supposed to make me feel better?"

Michael felt her stare but kept his eyes on the rear view mirror as he backed out of the driveway.

ooooo

Tommy McKenna climbed the porch steps, the soft crunch of leather from his uniform echoing his progress. He pressed the doorbell and waited with his arms folded across his chest.

"Hi, Uncle Tommy," Lexi said when she opened the door, clearly surprised by his impromptu visit.

"Hey, Lex. Can I come in?"

"Sure." She stepped aside and let him pass.

Tommy looked around the room for a moment. He didn't get to see much of his niece or her family. Their visits were usually limited to the Fourth of July, Christmas, and perhaps the occasional meeting at her grandparents' house. He could sense her apprehension.

"What are you doing here?" she asked politely.

"I understand that your mom's been staying with you."

"She's having some work done at her house, so she'll be here for a few days."

"That's real nice of you." He smiled. "Is she here now?"

"No, she went out."

"Hmmm ... maybe you can help me." He unbuttoned his shirt pocket and pulled out a photograph and handed it to her. "Have you seen this man?"

She studied it for only a second or two before looking up at him with wide eyes. "His name is Michael. He was just here."

Tommy took a deep breath as he retrieved the photo and slipped it back into his pocket. "How long ago?"

"About ten minutes. He picked Mom up and they left."

"Do you know where they went?"

"No," she replied then cleared her throat. "Is she in some kind of danger?"

Tommy put his hand on her shoulder. "She'll be fine." *As soon as I run that low-life friend of hers out of town.* He put his burly arms around her and gave her a hug. "Your Uncle Tommy would never let anything bad happen to his little sister. You know that."

Lexi nodded.

"Are you sure she didn't say anything about where they were going?" he asked as he released her and took a step backward.

"I think they were going out for a drink. She said she wouldn't be late."

"That's good, Lex. Thanks."

"She's known him for a while," she added. "I heard his name before, but this is the first time I met him."

"He's not a criminal or anything like that," Tommy assured her. *At least as far as I can tell at the moment.* "I just want to talk to him."

Lexi relaxed a bit. "What should I tell her when she gets back?"

"Nothing." His expression became serious. "You have to promise me you won't say anything to her about our little talk tonight."

"Why?"

"I know your mom. No sense getting her all worked up over nothing."

"But—"

"Please, Lex. It's important. You need to trust me."

She had no reason not to. Lexi smiled an uneasy smile. "Okay."

Tommy reassured her there was no need to worry as she closed the door behind him. When he reached the sidewalk, he pulled out his cell phone and hit redial.

"They're out together," he said into the phone. "About fifteen minutes ago. I don't know, but it sounds like they went to a bar ..." The call ended abruptly. Tommy pocketed the phone and slid into the driver's seat of the police cruiser.

"Everything okay?" Jason asked.

"Yeah, sure," he replied, distracted.

"What's going on?"

Tommy glared at him, but quickly softened his expression. "Nothing's going on ... it's personal." He put the car in gear and pulled away from the curb. "We might have to make another quick stop."

"You're the driver."

Chapter 32

M ichael chose a booth in the back corner at Winslow's. He brought Emily there hoping that a little alcohol might soften the blow. He ordered two glasses of wine. *In vino veritas*. No smoky memories, just the truth.

They chatted for a short time, mostly small talk, until Emily was nearly finished with her first drink. She watched impatiently as Michael ordered her another.

"Well?" she finally asked as her eyes searched his.

Michael had been stalling, unsure how or where to begin.

"I thought you had something to tell me," she said. "Isn't that why we're here?"

"Yes, of course." He wiped his hands on his thighs. He felt the Tiger Eye in his pocket and it had a slightly calming effect. *Now would be a good time for some clear thinking.*

"What's going on, Michael?"

"It's just that ... okay, you have to remember that everything I am about to say is the truth, no matter how bizarre it may sound. I would never lie to you, Emily."

"Just say it, Michael." She picked up her glass.

"Don't you think it was a little odd that I knew your dog's name and your favorite wine?" he asked, pointing to her glass as she set it down. "Our conversations have been so easy and we seem to have so much in common, like we've known each other forever. Have you noticed?"

She pushed away from the table, as if the extra few inches between them offered some additional protection.

"Have you been stalking me? Please tell me you're not some psycho serial killer." A touch of fear flashed in her eyes as they darted around the room.

"Absolutely not," he assured her. "But we've known each other for much longer than you might think."

"What do you mean? How?"

He had an idea. "Do you remember the show *The Ghost Whisperer?*

She tilted her head. "Sure, but why—?"

"Do you believe the things that happened on the show are possible?"

"I suppose so," she said slowly. "I guess if I didn't, I wouldn't have watched it."

"Good point. Do you remember when Melinda's husband Jim died?"

"Yes." She frowned.

"Okay, do you remember the episode shortly after that where Jim's spirit didn't want to leave Melinda, so he walked into Sam's body right after a car accident?"

"Yes, Melinda was upset. She wanted him to move on."

"Okay, not so much that part. I'm talking about the whole *walk-in* thing." He stopped to take a drink, trying to act casual. "Do you think that sort of thing ever happens ... I mean, in real life?"

"Well," she hesitated, "I don't know anyone who's done it, but I guess it's possible."

He took another drink. "What if you did? Know someone, that is?"

"Michael, I'm pretty sure you didn't bring me here to discuss a TV show. What's going on?"

How do I do this? How do tell her I'm really the soul of her dead husband who just happens to have taken up residence in another man's body? And how do I explain hanging out with her for four months without ever mentioning it?

"Michael?"

No answer.

"Earth to Michael ..."

"Hmmm?" His head gave a little jerk and his eyes met hers.

"Where were you? We were talking and you just left, zoned right out. What's the matter with you? Why are we here?"

"I'm sorry, I just—"

Emily's phone rang and Michael stopped talking. He welcomed the momentary interruption. She pulled the phone from her purse, and stared at the screen as it rang again. "I'm sorry," she said. "I should take this."

Michael nodded.

"Hello," she said into her phone. "What? No, I don't remember." Her eyes met Michael's as he watched her. "You're kidding." She looked away. "But I'm not dressed for ... okay, fine." She slipped the phone back into her purse and took a big gulp of wine.

"Is everything ok?"

"No. I have to go," she said, mildly annoyed.

"Now?" he asked a little too loudly. He took a deep breath. "Please don't leave," he said calmly. "I'm not finished."

"I'm sorry, Michael."

"At least let me drive you home."

"Phillip's out front."

Michael blinked. "What?"

"I know, right?" She twirled her hair around her finger.

"How did he know where you were?"

"He just does." She sighed and stood.

Michael looked up, confused.

"I'm sorry."

Michael forced a smile and watched her walk away.

He sat alone in the empty booth, feeling as if every eye in the room rested on him. He replayed the conversation in his head and his frustration grew—frustration with himself for not being able to tell her the truth and frustration with Prince *Freakin'* Phillip who seemed to have Emily wrapped around his gold-plated little finger.

Michael slammed his fist on the table, and everyone looked at him. A waitress came over to his table, but he continued to stare at the empty seat where Emily had sat only a moment ago.

"Excuse me," the waitress said as she pointed to his glass. "Can I get you another?"

"I'm sorry, what?"

"Would you like another drink?" she asked.

It's hard enough to keep from walking over to the bar, but when the bar walks over to you ...

"I can come back," she said and turned to leave.

"I'll have a Scotch. Neat."

She picked up the empty glass and walked away.

Mentally, Richard and Michael were trading punches. Michael had just landed a hard jab. Now it was Richard's turn. The way he felt right now, he wouldn't stop at one drink, and that scared him. He dialed Angie's number. Voicemail.

"It's Michael. I'm at Winslow's. How soon can you get here?" He ended the call and set the phone on the table.

A few minutes later, his drink arrived. He paid the waitress and studied the glass in front of him. It was so close, he could smell it. The smoky memories returned, and he shuddered. He looked at the door. Nothing.

Slowly, his hands moved together to cradle the glass.

Richard was on the ropes. Michael was in control again. He turned the glass around in his hands. It felt good. It was the only thing in the room—until Tommy slid into the seat across from him.

"You know something, Riordan? You're getting to be a major pain in my ass." He was in uniform. Probably just got a call from Phillip.

Michael looked around the room and then at Tommy. "For once, why don't you try to mind your own goddamn business. I'm sure you've got more important things to—"

"You're making this my business," he snarled.

"Oh, yeah? What if I told you I'm really Richard, walking around in someone else's body? Emily is my wife, and I have every right to talk to her."

Tommy's eyes narrowed, and he showed his pit bull teeth. "I think you and I should go for a little walk."

"I kind of like it in here. Maybe another time." The words came out without thinking. He barely heard them above the hammering in his chest.

"I wasn't asking." His teeth seemed to grow by the minute.

"Michael," a voice called from ten feet away. It was Angie. She stopped at the end of his table and looked first at Tommy, then to Michael.

"Hi, Angie." He attempted to smile, but it was only a flicker. "This is Emily's brother, Tommy." He sent an S.O.S. signal with his eyes.

"Hello," she said, glancing at Tommy. He nodded as she turned toward Michael. "The others will be here in a couple minutes."

"That's great," he said, following her lead and feeling a little braver now. "Tommy was just leaving." He looked across the table and raised his eyebrows impatiently.

Leather squeaked as Tommy slid out of the seat without a word and stood next to Angela. He glared down at her for a moment before walking away. Michael watched him go, waiting for the now-familiar gesture. Tommy stopped to flash it just before he walked out the door. Michael tried to steel himself, but a chill ran down his spine. He shook it off and turned to Angie as she slid into the seat across from him.

"Thanks. You may have just saved my life."

She pointed to the glass in front of him. "How many have you had?"

He nodded his head toward the glass on the table.

"That's your first? Did you drink any yet?"

"My first Scotch," he said. "I haven't touched it."

She motioned for the waitress to come over and asked her to remove the glass. The waitress looked at Michael.

"Well?" Angie said to Michael with a firm voice.

He didn't bother to respond, nodding to the waitress who removed the glass and walked away.

"Thank you," Angie said.

"I wasn't sure you'd come."

"I almost didn't," she admitted. "But I couldn't let you fall down that hole again, no matter who you are."

Michael remained silent, but his eyes thanked her.

She put her elbows on the table and leaned in. "So, what happened? Why are you here?"

"I came here with Emily," he said, looking down at the empty table where his drink had been.

She watched him, waiting for him to continue. "And?"

"It didn't go so well."

"What did you say?"

"I tried to tell her the truth, but I didn't get very far."

"Why not?"

"Prince Phillip came by and collected her. He says 'jump' and she asks 'how high?' I don't get it. It's not like her."

Angie slumped down in her seat and stared at the edge of the table.

"What's the matter, Ang?"

She hesitated. "About the other night ..."

"It's okay."

"No, it's not," she insisted. "I'm sorry. It's not the kind of thing you hear every day. Whether I believe you or not, when I look at you, I see my brother." She swiped at a tear sliding down her cheek. "I still don't understand it."

"Angie, I—"

She straightened up. "Michael was never the same after Jessica died. We needed each other. We found strength in being together, but Michael never fully recovered."

"He's recovered now. Don't you see? He wanted to leave so he could be with Jessica—just like I wanted to return to be with Emily."

She held his gaze. "Even if you're right, where does that leave me?"

"A part of him never left." He tapped his chest. "Part of him is sitting right here. You still get to see him whenever you want." He forced a smile, hoping she would reciprocate. She did not.

"I know it's not the same," he continued, "but believe it or not, your friendship means a lot to me. I care about you. You're the sister I never had. Perhaps we can still help each other."

Angie looked away for a moment and then back at Michael. "So, what do we do now?"

"I'm not sure." He sighed. "But I don't want to stay here."

She stood up. "Come on, I'll walk you out."

He hesitated momentarily as a sobering thought crossed his mind. Did Tommy really leave, or is he waiting outside? When he stood up, Angie took his arm and they walked out together.

At Angie's car, he hugged her, kissed her forehead, and watched her drive away before heading toward his car. It was a moonless night. The air was still—almost too still—as if the wind held its breath in morbid anticipation. Fortunately, he had parked near the door, so the area around his car was fairly well lit. He could see the red and blue neon light of the beer sign reflected in his car window thirty feet away.

A door closed somewhere in the darkness behind him. He picked up his pace as he heard footsteps on the asphalt, each one louder than the last. Less than ten feet remained between himself and the relative safety of his car. He pressed the button on his key and watched the car's lights flash. In one fluid motion, he slipped inside and locked the door. He exhaled when a tall stranger in jeans and cowboy boots walked past and disappeared into the bar.

This Tommy thing is getting out of hand, he thought. He wasn't about to run away, but he wasn't going to be looking over his shoulder for the rest of his life, either.

Chapter 33

When Emily stepped outside of Winslow's, she saw Phillip's shiny black Town Car idling at the edge of the parking lot. She stopped to look back at the door she'd just walked through and thought of Michael sitting alone in the booth. He hadn't finished telling her what was on his mind, and she had never started. *What the hell am I doing?*

Emily found herself standing at the edge of two worlds, suddenly torn between two very different men. She imagined most women in her shoes would hold onto a man like Phillip with both hands. She wasn't most women. He was rich and charming—a real catch—but when she was with him, she felt like another one of his possessions. She thought she could get used to it, but so far it hadn't happened.

Michael was different. What he may have lacked in financial status and social graces, he made up for with sincerity, or at least that's what she thought at first. A recent discovery led her to believe he may have been hiding some things about his past. Nevertheless, he was charming in his own way, but there was something about him she couldn't explain—a strange sensation that drew her to him whenever he was around. She felt it when they first met in the hospital. When they kissed a few days ago, it was so powerful that it frightened her. She couldn't yet find the words to describe it—like she had known him all her life— but that was impossible. She tried to fight the feelings, but had so far been unsuccessful in eliminating them altogether.

Reluctantly, she continued to walk toward the waiting car. As she approached, a door opened and Phillip's driver stepped out. He reached for the back door handle, but Emily got there first.

"I can get it myself," she said and let herself in.

Phillip was on the phone. He ended the call as she sat down. She felt her pulse quicken and took a deep breath.

"My dear, did you forget our plans tonight?" His voice was calm, but condescending.

Emily raised her chin. "We didn't have plans tonight."

He smiled. "You caught me. I apologize, but I warned you to stay away from that Riordan character."

His charming little smile wasn't so charming at the moment. "You lied to me."

"Apparently, my dear, *you've* been lying to *me*. I thought we had an agreement."

"That's right, *you* thought. You never asked me what I thought."

He opened his mouth, but no words came out.

"You don't really care what I think, do you?"

"I've learned to trust my instincts," he said, "and I have a bad feeling about Michael Riordan."

"He's been very good to me."

"And I haven't?"

"He's different."

"He's dangerous," Phillip said, raising his voice. "Aren't you a little worried about—"

She cut him off. She hadn't seen him upset before, and she didn't care for it. "At the moment, I'm a little more worried about you than I am about Michael."

Phillip frowned and rubbed his chin. "Did he tell you he was married?"

"He told me his wife died in an accident a few years ago."

"Is that what he called it?"

"So, you've been checking up on him?" she asked, crossing her arms in front of her chest. "Have you been spying on *him*, too?"

"I never *spied* on anyone," he said, the edge gone from his voice. "I care about you, Emily. What's wrong with making sure you're safe?"

The perfect gentleman facade crumbled before her eyes. "I don't think you care about anyone but yourself."

"Emily, I'm only—"

"I think you better take me home. Right now." She was calm, but firm.

Phillip didn't argue. He motioned to the driver, who made a wide U-turn and sped off in the opposite direction. Five minutes later, the car reached its destination.

"Here we are," Phillip announced as they pulled up in front of Lexi's house.

Emily opened the door and stepped outside.

"Goodnight, Emily."

She closed the door without a word.

Phillip took out his phone as the car drove off. "Do it," he said when the call connected. "And don't forget to follow up in a couple of days."

∞∞∞∞∞

Lexi was still awake when Phillip dropped Emily off. It felt a little like role reversal—the anxious child waiting for the parent to return home safely. Emily poked her head into the living room as Lexi turned off the television.

"Goodnight, honey."

Lexi stood up. "Mom, wait." She walked toward the doorway. "Are you all right?"

"I'm fine."

Lexi stood in the hall studying her mother. "You look upset."

"It's nothing."

"He didn't hurt you, did he?"

"What?" *Where did that come from?* "Who didn't hurt me?"

"Michael."

Emily frowned. "Why would you think that?"

"Well ... you left with him ... and ... and then you came back looking like something bad happened."

"No, dear. I'm upset with Phillip."

"When did you see Phillip?"

Emily hesitated, not wanting to admit what she had done to Michael, but she saw the confusion in her daughter's eyes. "Michael and I went to Winslow's. We were talking when Phillip called from the parking lot, and I left with him." She sighed. "Phillip seems hell-bent on keeping us apart. For all his money and power and good looks, I think he's jealous."

Lexi said nothing.

"I just want to go to bed," Emily said as she kissed Lexi on the cheek and headed upstairs to the guest room.

Emily closed the door and leaned her back against it, thinking about what Phillip had said. The room was dark except for the glow of the digital clock on the table near the bed. She only had two glasses of wine. She could have used a couple more.

She flopped down on the bed and stared at the ceiling. *Damn you, Phillip!* Her Prince Charming was turning back into a frog. He appeared to be stepping up his campaign against Michael, and she became aware of a side of him that frightened her. Sure, Michael had deceived her as well, but he was somehow different. No matter how hard she tried to convince herself that she should end it, she couldn't stop thinking about him. *Am I being naive? Reckless? Or have I foolishly fallen in love?* The latter would most likely be a mistake.

Emily had, in fact, ended it with Michael, but like Phillip, he didn't want to take no for an answer. She had known Michael now for five months, but how much did she really know about him? What else might he be hiding? What was it that he tried to tell her tonight?

She picked up her phone and dialed Michael's number, but canceled the call before it connected. Maybe she didn't want to know. Emily tossed and turned for the next half-hour. She dialed Michael again, but changed her mind once more. *Look at me! I don't know what the hell I'm doing any more.* She couldn't trust any of the men in her life, and that was unacceptable.

ooooo

Emily awoke the next morning to a knock on the bedroom door. It was a few minutes before eight, but it felt like she had just closed her eyes. She silently regretted her decision to go in to the office rather than work from home until the kitchen was finished. She had to be there in an hour.

"Come in," she called.

The door flew open. Kayla ran toward her and jumped up on the bed. "Mornin', Gramma," she chirped. Her smile was infectious, and Emily couldn't help but respond in-kind.

"Good morning, sweetheart."

Kayla looked around the room. "Where's Grampa?"

She had not asked about Richard for months. Emily sat cross-legged on the bed and motioned for her granddaughter to sit in her lap. Kayla responded immediately.

"Remember, honey?" Emily whispered. "Grampa's in heaven." The jury was still out as far as she was concerned, but it was what she had told Kayla.

"He's back. He was here yesterday." It wasn't a question.

"You saw him? Where?"

"Here. He was with you, Gramma."

Why was she suddenly talking like this? "No, Kayla, that was Gramma's friend, Michael. Remember?" *You probably won't be seeing him again, either.*

Kayla shook her head from side to side. "No, Gramma. It was Grampa. He called me Little Miss Sunshine," she explained with a very serious look. "Grampa is the only one who calls me that."

Emily's head spun. She propped up the pillows behind her and leaned back.

"Gramma, are you okay?" Kayla asked, her innocent eyes searching.

"Yes, honey, I'm fine." She leaned forward and cradled her in her arms.

"Is Grampa coming back?"

She squeezed Little Miss Sunshine. "I don't know, honey. I don't know."

∞∞∞∞

Emily made it to work with three minutes to spare. The weekly staff meeting was uneventful, at least the parts Emily could remember. When the meeting broke up, she walked into her boss's office. He was on the phone. She sat and watched him across the messy desk.

"What can I do for you, Emily?" he asked after he hung up.

"I can't stay here today, Scott," she said. "I don't feel well."

"I thought you looked a little tired in the meeting. Is everything all right?"

"I don't know."

"You realize we're swamped right now. I just received a half-dozen new manuscripts from upstairs." He dropped his hand on a tall stack of papers on the corner of his desk.

"C'mon, Scott, I really feel like crap. I need to go home and sleep."

"You do that. Go home and sleep it off, and you can get started on one of these in the morning."

"I might not be coming in tomorrow, either."

Scott's expression fell. "What's wrong, Emily?"

"It's ... complicated."

"Do you want to talk about it?"

"Thanks, Scott, but I can't. Not now."

"Okay. But, can you do me a favor?"

Emily shrugged.

"Please, just take one of these home with you," he said with a tentative smile. "Who knows? You might be looking for something to read while you're recovering."

"Scott ..."

"Please, Emily?"

She sighed. "Okay, what have you got?"

He tapped the pile. "Pick one."

She stood up and walked to the corner of his desk, in no mood to make decisions. Hopefully, one of the titles would jump out at her. She picked up the first one. *Nope.* The second one was mildly interesting. *Keep going.* Something grabbed her attention when she picked up the third one, but it wasn't the title. The author's name was Michael Riordan.

Chapter 34

Michael found himself in the park again a few days later, not at all sure why he was there. For all the wonderful memories it held in his past life, and for a while in this one, it had taken on a darker, more desperate feel. Was he torturing himself or perhaps waiting for a miracle? He wondered if they were mutually exclusive.

After two laps around the pond, he stopped near the clubhouse for a drink of water. He thought he heard someone call his name as he bent over the fountain. He lifted his head and looked around, but quickly dismissed the idea that he had been the intended mark. As he continued his walk, he heard it again.

A familiar figure stared at him from one of the Chess tables. Michael walked in his direction, squinting for a better look. "Arthur. What are you doing here?"

"Hello, Michael. I'm playing Chess, of course."

Michael glanced at the empty seat across from him.

"Please," Arthur said, motioning for him to sit down.

Michael obliged. He leaned against the edge of the stone table and watched Arthur line up the blue and silver pieces on opposite ends of the board between them. "Boy, am I glad to see you again."

Arthur smiled. "I had a feeling you would be."

"Something's not right."

"How so?"

"It's really strange when a life you never had flashes before your eyes."

Arthur nodded as though deep in thought.

"Michael was the alcoholic, not me. But lately it seems like I'm the one with the problem. I'm hiding bottles and getting wasted way too often." He looked up at the sky and raked his fingers through his hair. "Do you want to know what the worst part is?"

Arthur stopped moving the pieces and looked at Michael.

"When I drink, I start having these memories that ... they're not mine." He frowned. "Sometimes, it feels as if Michael has come back to reclaim his property."

Instead of responding, Arthur rubbed his chin.

"Can he do that?"

"I've never heard of it. You know, some things are held in cellular memory and remain with the body. They never leave."

"Does that mean I'm an alcoholic?"

"I don't know. Are you?"

Michael wasn't sure how to answer. He watched Arthur continue to shuffle pieces around the board. "Tell me, Arthur. What am I doing wrong?" he finally asked.

"Who said you're doing anything wrong?"

"Look around. Things haven't exactly been going as planned."

"So, what have you learned?"

Michael looked away and didn't answer.

"Chess is perhaps the only game in which there is no element of chance," Arthur said, picking up one of the pieces in front of him and examining it. "Life is a kind of Chess game, wouldn't you say?"

"Not really. Have you forgotten that my life was cut short by a terrible accident?"

Arthur moved another piece. "An accident?"

"What would you call it?" The jury was still out on the whole accident/coincidence thing.

Arthur kept moving pieces around the board. "As I've told you, there are no accidents. You've been given a second chance, my friend. Isn't that what you wanted?"

"Yes, it is. I admit I messed up. I didn't appreciate what I had until I lost it. Now I'd give anything to get it back."

Arthur looked at him and smiled. "So, you *have* learned something."

Michael gave him a wary glance, but he knew the old man was right.

Arthur moved another piece. "You see, the universe is in a constant state of change—it's always moving forward. Each new situation we're faced with is a lesson prepared for our benefit. It's always positive, whether we see it that way in the moment or not."

Michael watched in silence.

"Every choice we make leads us to the next one. It's called evolution. Sometimes, our choices seem to take us backward instead of forward. But every choice is designed to teach us something."

Michael sighed. "Everything started out well enough, but now ... now it seems no matter what I do, Emily keeps pushing me away."

"Isn't that what Emily said about Richard?"

Neither spoke for a couple of minutes.

"It seems like I keep making the wrong choices," Michael said when the silence grew uncomfortable.

Arthur stopped to look at Michael. "There are no wrong choices," he said. "Each and every one moves us along a path to greater understanding of ourselves. We must not judge them, but be open to the lessons they bring. Everything in your life has led you to where you are right now."

"And where is that, exactly?"

"You're always precisely where you're supposed to be."

Michael made a tent with his hands and held it against his lips as he thought for a moment. "It certainly doesn't feel like it."

"That's where a little faith comes in handy."

"Faith in what?"

"Faith in yourself."

"I thought we were only supposed to have faith in God?"

Arthur chuckled. "Where do you think he lives? In a drafty old church somewhere? No, my friend," he said, tapping his chest, "he lives right here."

Michael said nothing, eyes drifting.

"Listen to your heart," Arthur continued. "You have always had everything you need. I am only here to remind you."

"Believe me, Arthur. I'm trying."

"Remember this. It is always darkest before the dawn. Do not be fooled by the darkness. It is merely the absence of light. Follow your heart, for it will light the way."

Arthur resumed his game and Michael watched him silently. He had just captured one of the pieces—a knight—and held it up between them. Michael took the piece and studied it, turning it between his thumb and forefinger.

"That move is called a gambit," Arthur explained. "The objective is to sacrifice the knight—the one you are holding—for a greater advantage. You see, in Chess, as in life, having the most pieces, or *material* as they are called, doesn't always provide the greatest advantage. Sometimes, it's better to sacrifice some of your *material* for a higher purpose. It can be a very effective strategy."

Michael set the piece down. "I'm not sure I understand."

Arthur smiled. "Soon you will understand the meaning

of all of this."

"But, how will I know when—"

"You will know."

Michael studied Arthur's face, waiting for him to add something more.

Arthur stood up. "I'm sorry, my friend, but I must be going." He began to gather the pieces and put them in a drawstring pouch.

"Don't go yet," Michael pleaded.

"My work here is done."

"What? Wait a minute. What do I do now?"

"I've told you everything you need to know. Look into your heart and you will find the answer. You know what you want. Keep moving in that direction. You are the only one who can stop you."

Michael stood and watched him drop the last piece in the bag and pull the string. "Will I see you again?"

"Perhaps. I'm never very far away."

A strange answer. "Can I drive you somewhere?"

"No, thank you." He smiled. "I rather enjoy the journey."

Michael was curious now. "You're sure? It's no trouble."

"Goodbye, Michael." Arthur turned and walked away.

Michael watched him leave. The jury came back with its verdict. There was no way that meeting was a coincidence.

∞∞∞∞

Michael awoke early the next morning. On his way home from the park the night before, Rhona had called. While Rhona always seemed excited about something, this time he sensed more than her usual effervescence. She wouldn't give up the reason over the phone, so he agreed to meet her at the office in the morning.

On his way downtown, he stopped at Maggie's for breakfast. Once again, Maggie didn't disappoint. He left a generous tip for the waitress and paid the check at the counter. When he stepped outside, he saw Tommy's police cruiser in the street, signal on, waiting to turn into Maggie's parking lot. *Son of a bitch!*

Michael walked quickly to his car and got in, hoping he hadn't been spotted. He hunkered down in his seat, afraid to start the car and draw any attention to himself. This is ridiculous, he thought. The man isn't just a psychopath ... he's a psychopath with a gun and a badge. It would have to stop soon, but he had a feeling it wasn't going to be pretty.

Michael watched as Tommy parked the car, relieved to see both men enter the building. As soon as they were inside, he started his car and merged with the traffic heading east on the boulevard. The more distance he put between himself and Tommy McKenna, the better he felt.

Michael arrived at Rhona's office a little early and was greeted with a big smile and an even bigger hug.

"How's my favorite writer?" she said when she finally released him. He sat in one of the two chairs facing her desk—a big desk, a power desk. He expected nothing less. A framed poster on the wall showed a hang glider stepping off a cliff above the words 'You only live once.' He shook his head.

"If you're talking about me, I'm doing as well as can be expected, I guess."

"I just had to tell you in person," Rhona said, all smiles. "You've really outdone yourself."

He raised an eyebrow. "I have?"

"Come on, Sweetie, don't be so modest." She leaned across the desk, her eyes like two blue lasers. "The new book. I love it. Couldn't put it down."

Michael tilted his head and stared, unsure that he had

heard her correctly. "You read it?" He straightened in his seat. "When ... how did you do that?"

Rhona drew back. He waited.

"I'm not sure what you mean, Michael. Your sister dropped it off last week. I read it as soon as I got my hot little hands on it."

"My sister," he said under his breath. "Angela gave it to you?" His voice rose.

She wrinkled her nose as if she'd just smelled something awful.

"What did she say?" Michael lowered his head, closed his eyes, and pinched the bridge of his nose. "I mean, when she dropped it off."

Rhona shifted nervously in her chair. "She said you were busy working on another project, but you wanted me to have the manuscript ASAP. I didn't—"

"Damn it, Rhona." He slumped back in his seat.

"I'm sorry, Michael."

Suddenly, it hit him. One of those aha moments, as Emily liked to call them. He had been paddling against the current all this time. His arms were getting tired. Arthur had tried to convince him that everything happens for a reason, and the sooner he stopped resisting and agreed to just go with the flow, the happier he would be.

Michael leaned his head back and closed his eyes. "I need to turn this boat around."

"What?"

He realized he had said it out loud and opened his eyes. "Nothing." He sighed.

Rhona chewed her bottom lip.

"It's okay, Rhona. You didn't do anything wrong." His expression softened. "I'm glad you liked it."

"Good." Relief washed over her face and she offered a tentative smile. "I sent it to a couple publishers."

Chapter 35

T housands of raindrops danced in the street, illuminated momentarily by the headlights of an approaching vehicle. Michael waited for it to pass before returning his gaze to the second story window—the guest room where Emily was staying.

He'd been sitting in his car for about an hour, strategically parked across the street with an unobstructed view of Lexi's house. It felt like a stakeout. Actually, it felt a little creepier than that. It wasn't the first time he'd sat in the very same spot. There had been two others. Okay, three, but who's counting?

The light in her room was on when he arrived, and he imagined her reading in bed. She favored mysteries and romances, and he wondered which one she might be involved in tonight. He recalled the many nights that he'd come to bed and found her asleep, a book teetering in her hands or lying face down on her chest. He would gently extract it and kiss her forehead before turning out the light. He glanced at his phone—just before eleven. If she fell asleep now, who would turn out the light?

He had no plans other than to sit and stare at her window. The sliver of light that escaped from between the curtains offered a measure of comfort. He liked to know where she was and that she was safe. He certainly didn't approve of her spending time with Phillip. The man could not be trusted. For that matter, he didn't like her spending time with anyone but himself. His goal was to find a way to make that happen. The sooner, the better.

About eleven-thirty, the inside of his car lit up as another vehicle pulled to a stop behind his. When he saw the light bar on the roof, his throat closed. *You've got to be kidding. Talk about stalkers. How does he do it?* Tommy seemed to know where Michael was at any given moment. The man was relentless.

Michael tried to slow the sudden increase in his heart rate by taking a few deep breaths as he waited for Tommy to get out of the cruiser. He thought about starting the car and making a run for it, but his Honda didn't stand a chance against the cruiser's big V-8. He watched in his rear view mirror as the door opened. Then he saw the ponytail as the officer closed the door and walked toward his car.

After he exhaled, another equally disturbing thought crossed his mind. *Samantha.* He squinted against the headlights in his mirror, trying to get a better look. If he had to choose, he would rather face Sam and her verbal abuse than Tommy, who tended to be more physical. Either way, Emily would find out.

The flashlight beam shined in on him as he rolled down his window. The first thing he noticed as his eyes moved up to meet the officer's was a shiny gold plate pinned to her chest that read GONZALEZ. Their eyes met and he noticed she looked tougher than Samantha, if that was possible. Relief washed over him nevertheless.

"License and registration, please," she said mechanically. The rain had all but stopped.

He retrieved the requested items and handed them to her. She turned the flashlight to her hand and studied them for a moment. Michael waited.

"What are you doing out here tonight, Mr. Riordan?"

"I was driving home from dinner when I began to feel sick. I had to pull over."

"I drove by here forty-five minutes ago. You were in the same spot."

"I must have dozed off after the cramps subsided," he responded without hesitation. "If you ever go to Adrianna's, don't order the fish." He smiled tentatively.

Gonzalez did not reciprocate. "Wait here," she said and walked back to the cruiser.

She reappeared at his window a few minutes later. "In the future, try not to sit in your car too long in a residential neighborhood."

"I didn't think there was a law against that."

"There isn't," she admitted, "but some folks tend to get nervous when they see strangers sitting in cars in front of their homes. They're funny like that."

"I understand. I'll be more considerate."

"Do you feel well enough to drive home now?" She was less mechanical, her voice softer.

"Yes, ma'am. I'm feeling much better."

"Then I suggest you do that." She handed him his papers.

He thanked her and threw them on the passenger seat.

"Mr. Riordan?"

"Yes?" He turned in her direction, avoiding eye contact at first.

"Next time, get the prime rib." She flashed a smile before walking away.

Michael nodded, anxious to leave the scene. Gonzalez had called in his information, or at least ran it through her computer, when she had gone back to her car. It was standard procedure. If Tommy was working a shift tonight, he would somehow get wind of it and show up soon.

Michael didn't take the time to roll up his window. As soon as Gonzalez took the first step toward the cruiser, he turned the key in the ignition. The engine attempted to turn over a couple of times, but wouldn't start. Gonzalez stopped to watch him, hand on her hip.

If I was driving The Blue Knight, this wouldn't be happening. He tried it again. She took a step in his direction as the car failed to start. He pumped the accelerator and turned the key. This time the engine fired up, and he revved it a couple of times. When he noticed Officer Gonzalez in his side mirror heading back to her car, he stepped on the accelerator and drove away. He had just dodged a bullet and was content to go directly home. No more covert ops.

∞∞∞∞∞

The next morning Michael poured a bowl of cereal and sat down in the living room to eat. The Tiger Eye that Helena had given him sat on the end table next to his chair. He picked it up and turned it around in his fingers, marveling at the intricate lines and swirls. He set the stone down, looked around the messy room, and thought about giving it a good cleaning. Taking a few minutes to pick up the empty glasses and old newspapers would help, but it seemed like too much work to do a thorough cleaning. He favored more enjoyable, or perhaps less strenuous, activities. Besides, he was the only one who had to look at the room, and it was good enough for him.

As soon as the last thought crossed his mind, he remembered something Arthur had said that night in the shelter. "Perhaps Emily wanted more." He remembered the conversation as if it were yesterday. They'd been discussing Richard and Emily's relationship, and he'd just told Arthur he was content with the way things were. It was a fair statement, if by *content* he meant stuck in a rut and too tired or lazy to work his way out. Looking back at it now, it certainly didn't sound like a recipe for a healthy relationship.

He looked around the room again. Emily wouldn't stand for this. Whether a dirty room or a struggling relationship, she wouldn't let things slide, look the other way, or otherwise throw in the towel. He admired her tenacity, but at the same time, he realized he had resisted her repeated attempts to do something about their situation.

How had he grown so complacent, so willing to believe Emily would always be there? Did he think that, given enough time, she would eventually come around to his way of thinking? Was he really that arrogant, as Arthur had put it? He clearly had a different perspective now.

After giving his situation some serious thought, Michael pulled himself off his chair, gathered some cleaning supplies from the kitchen, and went to work. Not only did he pick up anything that didn't belong, he dusted, vacuumed, and put everything back in its proper place. When he'd finished, he stood back and smiled. He'd done a good job, one he knew would make Emily proud.

Michael didn't stop there. After giving the entire house a much-needed cleaning on the inside, he directed his focus outside. The sun shone and the temperature hovered in that comfortable range between summer heat and the crispness of autumn in the northeast. The height of the grass embarrassed him, so cutting it was first on the list. He would have preferred to sit on his John Deere rather than push Michael's little mower around. Nevertheless, he made short work of the yard, then trimmed the edges and swept up.

After putting all the equipment away, he sat on the edge of the hammock in the backyard, kicked off his shoes, and swung his legs onto the canvas. The big hammock swayed gently from side to side in a relaxing rhythm. There was plenty of room for Emily by his side.

The air had cooled, but the sun felt warm on his skin, and Michael drifted off to sleep. The low, hoarse call of a crow in a nearby tree startled him awake two hours later. Feeling refreshed, he considered going for a drive. He'd been so busy cleaning that he'd forgotten to stop for lunch. Acutely aware of the consequences of his oversight, he decided that a pulled pork sandwich from the Riverside Grill might be just what he needed.

Michael drove north on Route 7, honoring the posted speed limit. The green of summer had given way to vibrant red, orange, and gold. The scenery didn't disappoint, and once inside the Grill, neither did the food. On the drive back, he dialed Emily's number, not sure what he would say if she answered. It didn't matter. He listened to her voicemail message before he hung up. Perhaps he just wanted to hear her voice.

He pulled into his driveway and stopped for a moment to admire the well-trimmed yard before turning off the car. He strolled up the walk, satisfied with his work. When he reached the front porch, he noticed a large envelope holding the lid of his mailbox open. He turned the envelope over and rubbed the back of his neck.

Two oak rocking chairs sat on the porch. He chose the closest one and lowered himself onto the seat. It moved back and forth gently as he examined the envelope—no postage and no return address. Clearly, it had been hand-delivered, and he had a pretty good idea by whom. His heart pounded as he turned the envelope over and slid his finger along the underside of the flap.

Michael pulled out a manila folder, letting the envelope

fall to the floor. The words Springfield Police Department were printed on the front, wrapped around an official-looking seal. His name had been handwritten on the tab. He opened it and found a police report inside with both of his names all over it. His scanned a detailed account of the accident that killed Richard Dunham and sent Michael Riordan to the hospital. He exhaled when he realized that he had been holding his breath.

At first, it hardly felt real, reading a written account of his own death. He studied it for a few minutes, unaware of most of the details. His own memory was sketchy after his car had stopped rolling and everything went black. Apparently, he'd still been breathing when they'd loaded him into the back of an ambulance. He'd *expired* in the hospital two hours later. The accident had been Richard's fault. Failure to obey a stop sign.

Before closing the folder, he noticed a yellow Post-it note stuck to the inside cover. *I know who you are, Riordan. Whatever game you've been playing is over. Pack your bags and move on, or Emily gets a copy.* His stomach suddenly felt like it was warming up for a gymnastics meet.

Beads of sweat formed on his forehead in spite of the cool evening breeze. He slipped two fingers inside his collar and tugged at it to keep from choking. Dusk had arrived by the time Michael got up from his chair. He walked inside and set the folder on the table near the door. He hadn't seen this coming. He'd been out-played. *Checkmate.*

Chapter 36

Michael paced around his living room. With time running out, he decided to take his chances and tell Emily everything. He needed to see her, and it had to be tonight.

Tommy was still a problem, always showing up at the worst possible time, as if he somehow knew Michael's every move. He had to find a way to get to Emily's without being pulled over. He didn't want to think about what that crazy bastard might have planned for their next meeting.

As Michael reached for his keys, he considered driving to Angie's on the way and switching cars. *Try to relax. You're being paranoid again.*

He opened the door to leave, but what he saw on his front porch stopped him in his tracks. Tommy McKenna, arms crossed as if he had been waiting for him, blocked his path. He wore street clothes. Not a good sign.

"What the hell are you doing here?" Michael asked.

"Just came by to see what my old friend Michael Riordan was up to," Tommy replied, leaning against the door frame.

"I was just leaving." He didn't have time for this.

"I can see that," Tommy replied, grinning like it was funny.

Michael took a step forward in an attempt to get around him, but Tommy cut him off.

"Where you headed?"

"I'm going out."

"Meeting someone?"

Tommy stood about three inches taller than he did. Michael looked up at him impatiently. "That's none of your damn business."

"It is if that someone is my little sister ... don't you think?"

"She's a big girl, don't *you* think? She certainly doesn't need you looking after her."

"That's where you're wrong, tough guy," he replied and thrust an index finger toward Michael's chest. Michael slapped his hand away before it reached its target. He wouldn't let him get away with that move twice.

Tommy looked surprised by the quick response, but it didn't last long. Before Michael could react, Tommy pushed his chest. Michael rocked back on his heels and took a couple of steps backward to keep from falling down. Unfortunately, the baseball bat had never made it up to the hall closet.

"What do you want?" Michael demanded when he regained his balance.

"I just wanted to make sure you got my little going away present."

They were standing inside the front door, and Michael unconsciously glanced at the folder sitting on the table next to him. Tommy's eyes followed.

"Does Emily know?" Michael asked.

"I guess that's going to be up to you, isn't it?" Tommy said as he looked past Michael into the living room. "Where's all the boxes? I thought you'd be in here packing up your shit."

The thought of being run out of town sent Michael's stomach into a spin. *That's not going to happen.*

"I gotta tell you, Riordan," Tommy shook his head slowly. "I'm a little disappointed."

"Well, get used to it," Michael said. "I'm not going anywhere."

Tommy's eyes grew wild for a second before a grin slowly spread across his lips. "Hmmm," he said, rubbing his chin. "Maybe that's not such a bad thing, after all. It just means I'm going to finally get to mess you up."

Michael knew he had to do something quickly, or that's most likely what would happen. While he considered his options, a car pulled up to the curb out front and Tommy turned his head to take a look. Michael felt the keys in his hand and made a fist, sliding his car key between his fingers. With Tommy distracted, Michael lunged for his throat, leading with the key.

He had hesitated a fraction of a second, and it cost him. Tommy turned around quickly and deflected the attack. Grabbing Michael by the neck with his right hand, he pushed him up against the wall. Their faces were inches apart, and Michael could smell the alcohol on Tommy's breath.

"I thought you were smarter than that, Riordan," he said through clenched teeth.

Michael tried to speak, but nothing came out.

"Tommy!" a voice called from the open doorway.

Tommy's head spun around. "Emily! What the hell are you doing here?" He held his grip on Michael's neck.

"I told you not to hurt him."

Still pinned against the wall, unable to speak, Michael's eyes moved to find Emily's, unsure of what he had just heard.

"Let him go."

Tommy loosened his grip on Michael's neck, closing his fist around his shirt collar. "No," he protested. "The guy jumped me. He's dangerous, Emily. That's what I've been trying to tell you."

She looked at Michael, her expression unreadable. Michael was unable, or perhaps unwilling, to believe that she was somehow involved in Tommy's recent activities. He swallowed hard, but said nothing.

"Get in here." Tommy grabbed Emily by the arm and pulled her inside. Still holding on to Michael, he closed the door behind her.

Tommy's cell phone rang, and he motioned with his free hand for Emily to go into the living room, pushing Michael in behind her. He retrieved the phone from his pocket and held it to his ear.

"No, I'm here now," he said into the phone, "but we have a problem." He paused. "But I'm—" He pulled the phone away from his ear and looked at it as if the other party had hung up mid-sentence.

Emily stopped in the middle of the room. She stood with her hands on her hips and glared at Tommy as he walked in. "What do you think you're doing?"

Tommy looked at the two of them, but said nothing. Michael rubbed his neck and straightened his collar.

"You need to go now, Tommy. I can handle this," Emily said.

"I can't do that, Sis."

Michael watched her argue with her brother, not sure why she was there.

"Emily, tell me what's going on," Michael pleaded. "You owe me at least that much."

"She doesn't owe you anything," Tommy snarled.

Michael continued to look at Emily, ignoring the remark. "Emily?"

"I'm not sure that I do," she said, holding his gaze. Her expression was hard, but he noticed a small crack—a trace of uncertainty in her eyes.

"So, it's been you the whole time?" he asked before his throat tightened.

"No. Not at first," she admitted. "The problem was that I started to fall for you."

"That was a problem?"

"Not for me. For Phillip."

"Yeah, me, too," Tommy said, before shrinking a little under Emily's glare. Michael was still unsure of Emily's role in all this, but he began to question which one of the two was in charge.

"After the wedding, Tommy told me about your involvement in the accident," she continued. "At first, I didn't believe it. I assumed Phillip put him up to it." She looked away again for a moment before facing him. "You pissed him off, Michael. That's not something people do without consequences."

"Was that the reason for the card? You didn't want to piss him off?"

She avoided his accusation. "When I realized it was a sham, that our relationship was a lie, I had to put an end to it. It broke my heart, but I just couldn't go down that road again."

"But it wasn't a sham. Everything I felt was real. I think you felt it, too."

Tommy rolled his eyes as he pretended to play an invisible violin.

Michael ignored him and continued, "I planned to tell you about the accident, but the longer I waited, the more concerned I became that it would scare you away."

"Do you really think I want to be with a man who is afraid to tell me the truth?" she asked. Her hands were on her hips. "I did that once. It didn't turn out so well."

Michael's instincts had been correct. Their relationship had been moving forward. Now he realized it had only been a matter of time before the dominoes began to fall. It had been built on a lie. He lost her once before. Apparently, he hadn't learned his lesson the first time.

"You're right. I should have told you," he admitted.

"Would you have done anything differently?"

"It doesn't matter. I deserved to know the truth."

He glanced at Tommy, who stood like a tag team wrestler impatiently awaiting his turn to enter the ring. When Michael looked back at Emily, she pulled something from the large purse that hung over her shoulder.

"While we're on the subject of full disclosure," she said, "what do you have to say about this?"

Chapter 37

E mily held his manuscript in her hand, waiting for an explanation. Michael stared at it before meeting her gaze, unsure where to begin or what to say. He looked for something that might indicate her emotional response to what was on those pages, but found nothing.

"What's that?" Tommy asked.

Emily ignored him. "Well, Michael?"

He raked his fingers through his hair, looked at Tommy, and back to Emily. He suddenly felt naked, the harsh light of truth exposing his flaws. He squirmed a little as he thought of her reading his words.

Perhaps it was a book that was never meant to be published, but needed to be written. It was personal, a journey that was more important than the final destination.

A riches-to-rags story, he didn't let it end there. He created a better ending, which might offer hope to others who had lost their way. As an author, he could do that. He wanted to believe that people held the same power over their own lives.

"I tried to tell you," he sighed. He would have to do better than that.

"How ... where did you get all this information?" She ran her thumb across the edge of the manuscript, pages flipping rapidly under her touch. "Did you know Richard? Did *he* write this?"

"I'm not sure how to answer that," he replied.

"I want the truth." Her voice was stern, but quiet.

"Okay. I wrote it ... all of it. It's the story of *my* life."

"That's impossible."

Michael wondered if part of her wanted to believe him. "I came back for you."

"What?"

"Damn it, Emily," Tommy complained. "Let me see that."

Emily stared at Tommy for a moment, then tossed the manuscript in his direction. As Tommy moved to catch it, Michael picked up a brass lamp from the end table and swung it at his head. It wasn't a direct hit, but enough to send him reeling backward. Michael followed, raising the lamp for another strike. Tommy quickly caught his balance. In one fluid motion, he reached behind his back, pulled a gun from his belt, and leveled it at Michael's chest.

"Tommy!" Emily yelled.

Michael stopped in his tracks and brought the lamp down slowly. Tommy squeezed his eyes shut for a second as he tried to shake off the effects of the blow to his head. He motioned with the gun for Michael to put down the lamp. Michael complied.

"That's going to cost you, Riordan," Tommy growled.

"For God's sake, Tommy. What are you going to do? Shoot him?"

"If I did, it would be self-defense," he said, rubbing his temple with his free hand.

"Then what? Are you going to shoot me, too? What's gotten into you?"

He glared at her, the gun still pointed at Michael. Tommy may have been following orders from Emily before, but now he was clearly taking matters into his own hands. Perhaps Phillip was still calling the shots and gave Tommy the green light to step in if Emily appeared to be losing her nerve. Michael was witnessing a mutiny of sorts, one that wasn't in his best interest. His chances were better with Emily in control.

"Put that away," she demanded.

"Did you see what he just did?" he replied, eyes wide. "I told you he was dangerous."

A silence descended on the room as Michael stared at the gun in Tommy's hand.

Emily broke the silence. "Richard."

Instinctively, he turned toward her. "What?"

Their eyes locked, and he knew immediately what she'd done.

Tommy was having a hard time keeping up. He frowned as he looked from Michael to Emily and back again. "Somebody tell me what the hell is going—"

Before he could finish his sentence, Michael attacked again. He brought the lamp down hard on Tommy's forearm, knocking the gun to the floor. Both men scrambled for the weapon, reaching it at the same time. Tommy had a significant weight advantage and considerably more upper-body strength, which was evident as the two fought for control. Michael struggled to pry Tommy's fingers from around the gun. Emily's attempt to stop them resulted in her being thrown to the floor just before the gun went off.

The noise startled the two men, and Emily, who was getting back on her feet, slumped to the floor. Michael let go of the gun and moved toward her.

"No!" he shouted as he turned Emily over and saw the widening circle of blood on her chest. She looked up at him momentarily before closing her eyes. Tommy sat back with his mouth hanging open. He set the gun on the floor beside him.

"Please, Emily. You have to hold on," Michael said, then

glanced over at Tommy. "Look what you did!"

Emily opened her eyes again. Michael looked for something he could use to put pressure on the wound and slow the bleeding.

"You can't leave me, Em," he pleaded. "I came back for you."

She looked into his eyes, "Richard ..." The faint smile that flickered on her lips looked morbidly out of place as a trickle of blood ran from the corner of her mouth.

"What? Emily ... what did you say?"

She closed her eyes and coughed. Michael wiped his face with his sleeve and looked over at Tommy, who still hadn't moved.

"Don't just sit there, you idiot," Michael shouted. "Call 911."

He looked back at Emily. "You can't leave me like this. Not now!" As soon as he said it, he remembered hearing Emily say the same words over Richard's lifeless body in the hospital. He closed his eyes. "You're going to be okay, Em," he said, struggling to keep it together. "You have to be."

The blood continued to flow. Michael applied pressure with the palm of his hand, but blood was everywhere. Too much time was passing. She would bleed out if help didn't arrive soon. He took a deep breath and gently brushed a few strands of hair from her face.

"Get that," Michael yelled to Tommy when he heard a knock on the door.

Tommy scrambled to his feet and opened it. Phillip pushed him aside, but stopped when he saw Michael and Emily on the floor.

"Oh my God," he gasped. "What happened?"

Michael turned. "What the hell are *you* doing here?"

"Tell me what happened," Phillip insisted, raising his voice.

Michael looked back at Emily. "Your hitman over there shot her," he said without looking up.

Phillip glared at Tommy. "It was his fault," Tommy said. "Did anyone call 911?"

"Yes," Michael yelled over his shoulder. Tommy nodded.

Phillip looked back at the two on the floor. "Get away from her."

Michael glanced at Phillip and back at Emily. "Hold on, Em. It won't be long now."

She opened her eyes and looked into his. Her lips moved, but no sound came out. Michael leaned his ear closer, but there was nothing. After a moment, he pulled back and looked into her eyes, now only half-open.

"I love you, Em," he whispered. "I will always love you. I'm so sorry ... for everything."

Phillip lunged. "That's enough," he said through clenched teeth. He grabbed Michael by the shirt and stood him up. "Now, look what you've done."

"I didn't do anything," Michael protested.

Outside, sirens blared. Within moments, two EMTs hurried into the room with a stretcher and Phillip loosened his grip. Michael pushed him away with both hands. Glaring at each other, they stepped aside to make room for the recovery efforts. An EMT strapped an oxygen mask around Emily's head before they lifted her onto the stretcher.

Michael followed as they made their way toward the door. Phillip moved in the same direction until Michael shot a glare that stopped him. When the stretcher rolled up to the ambulance, he watched the undercarriage collapse as it slid into the back. One of the EMTs climbed in next to Emily, and Michael attempted to follow. The other one held up both hands to stop him.

"I'm sorry. You can't ride with us," he said.

"But I need to—"

"Just let us do our job, sir," he insisted. "You can see her at the hospital."

Michael watched helplessly as the doors closed and the ambulance sped away, casting an eerie red glow on each house it passed. Icy fingers reached up his spine as he watched it disappear at the end of the block. The siren's cry faded slowly, and he closed his eyes.

He prayed she would hold on, but he had seen all the blood and the lifeless look in her eyes. Suddenly, images of their life together flashed in his mind. He was grateful for everything they had done together, but at the same time, saddened by the hopes and dreams that were now slipping out of reach.

He thought of her bucket list, and his stomach twisted as he remembered the look in her eyes whenever she spoke about traveling to Ireland. It was too much for his heart to bear. He had become adept at burying emotions that were too difficult to face, but this time, they overwhelmed him. A lifetime of tears poured out, falling to the pavement like a cleansing rain.

Eventually, he wiped away the tears to find the police stringing yellow tape along the perimeter of the front yard. As Michael scanned the small crowd gathering on the other side, his eyes locked onto a familiar face. *Arthur?* He walked quickly in his direction. A policeman followed.

"What are you doing here?" Michael asked as he approached.

"I came to say goodbye."

Michael stopped. "Where are you going?"

"I'm not going anywhere," he said, shaking his head

slowly. "You are."

"Sir, you need to come with me," the policeman announced, as he neared the spot where Michael stood.

"I just need a minute," Michael replied without turning around. "But Arthur, I can't leave Emily. She needs me."

"You're right, Richard. Emily needs *you*."

Michael frowned. "What?"

"We need to go back inside. *Now*." The voice behind him was firm.

"Arthur. Please. Help me."

"It's time," Arthur replied.

The policeman grabbed Michael's arm, attempting to pull him back toward the house. Michael looked at Arthur, confused, his eyes pleading for help.

"Dawn is coming," Arthur said softly.

The tugging on his arm continued. Michael tried to pull away.

"Richard!" the man behind him called. It froze him for a second. When he turned around, he saw his friend John from the homeless shelter.

∞∞∞∞

John tugged again on the arm of his friend who lay face down on the bed. "Richard! C'mon, man. Wake up."

"Huh?"

"Damn, you had me scared," John said, as he let the arm fall back onto the sheet. "I've been trying to wake you for the past five minutes."

Richard's eyes moved from side to side, trying to get his bearings. Everything was still hazy. He turned over onto his back and lifted his head off the pillow a few inches. Looking around, he noticed the purple walls. The shelter, he thought. *Purple again.*

He looked at John, eyes wide. "What's my name?"

"Say what?" John studied him through squinted eyes.

"Humor me."

John hesitated. "Richard ... your name's Richard."

"What day is it?" Richard propped himself up on his elbows, a sudden urgency in his voice.

"It's Tuesday."

"The date. What's the date?"

John hesitated and rubbed his forehead. "July nineteenth."

Silence.

"You got the year figured out yet, or do you need that, too?" John asked with a nervous smile.

"Do you know if Emily is okay?"

"Your wife?" He shook his head. "I don't know, but if I had to guess, I'd say she's probably pissed off at you right now."

Richard said nothing, his eyes drifting. Pissed off, he could deal with—bleeding, not so much.

"Maybe I should take you to the emergency room to have you checked out."

"Look, John, I appreciate the concern, but I'm fine."

"You don't sound fine."

"I'm better than fine. Believe me." Richard looked across the room at the empty bed. There was no sign that anyone had slept in it last night. "Where's Arthur?"

"That guy?" John asked, hooking a thumb toward the empty bed. "He left early this morning. Said he was just passing through."

"He slept here last night?"

John frowned. "Yeah, Richard. You brought him in. Are you sure you're okay?"

Richard said nothing. A few seconds passed.

"Let me ask you something," John said, looking puzzled again. "How well did you know that guy?"

"I just met him. Why?"

"He left you a message."

Richard pulled himself up to a sitting position. "Really? What did he say?"

"I wrote it down so I wouldn't forget." John pulled a folded piece of paper from his pocket. "He said to tell you, 'It's never too late to be what you might have been.'" He shrugged.

"Arthur wanted you to tell me that?"

"Yeah. Do you know what he's talking about?"

Richard paused before a faint smile crossed his lips. "I think I do now."

Chapter 38

Normally an early riser, Emily fought to keep her eyes closed, but the morning sunlight, an unwelcome intruder, crept silently across her bed, making it virtually impossible. She lifted her head far enough to see the clock on the nightstand; six forty-five. A bottle of tequila and an empty glass stood beside it.

Emily squeezed her eyes shut and tried to will herself back to sleep. It didn't work. She tried pulling the sheet over her head, but her mind was already spinning with thoughts of what happened last night and what the future might hold. *Did I really throw him out last night?*

A sound interrupted her thoughts.

"Who's there?" she called. Nothing. Could it be Richard? Was he here to apologize ... or to pick up his things?

She pulled the sheet down below one eye to take a look. A pair of sad eyes stared at her from across the bed. Bogey's head rested on the edge, drooling on the sheet.

"Gross!" She looked at the closed door. "How did you get in here?"

Bogey stared without making a sound.

Emily vaguely remembered him following her into the bedroom last night. She closed her eyes. Ironically, she had been the one to break her long-standing, number one dog rule. Before she let Richard bring a dog into the house, she had made it clear that under no circumstances would the dog be sleeping in their room.

She opened her eyes and gave him a scornful look, but

it had no effect. His eyes moved to Richard's pillow as if to say, "Where is he?"

You've GOT to be kidding. I'm NOT going to try to explain this to a dog. She ducked back under the covers.

Her head throbbed. She only remembered drinking a couple of shots before falling asleep. Was her present condition a result of the tequila, the thousand thoughts of last night that raced through her head, or maybe the fact that her life was now officially falling apart? *All of the above.* She had awakened to the harsh reality that she was alone.

Emily pulled back the covers and stared at the spot where Richard once slept. She looked around the room— *their* room—thinking of all they had built together. Her eyes stopped at the flowers on her dresser and a chill ran through her veins as a painful memory resurfaced.

She was seven years old, skipping back to the campsite with a handful of beautiful wildflowers to take home. Her smile disappeared when she arrived at their cabin and found it deserted. She called for Mom, then Dad, then Uncle Mike. No one answered. The cars were gone, her things were gone, and the doors were all locked. Surely, they would be back for her any minute. She waited.

Evenings by the lake were cool when the sun went down. Emily huddled near the door of their cabin, shivering in her tank-top and shorts. The tears would not stop. Night was falling and no one was coming back for her. She felt alone, abandoned by the people who were supposed to love her.

She shuddered to think that those feelings were back. I made him leave, but this is not my fault, she thought. He's the one who decided he wanted something else—someone else.

Staying in bed and feeling sorry for herself wasn't going to help. She pulled herself up, slipped into her robe, and headed for the stairs. As she passed her dresser, she pulled the flowers from the vase and threw them in the wastebasket.

The coffee seemed to take longer than usual as she waited, cup in hand. Once ready, she took the carafe from its plate, poured the steaming brew, and held her nose just above the rim of the cup to inhale the aroma. She lingered in the kitchen for a moment to hold back a tear before moving to the patio, her morning sanctuary.

The sun had risen above the peak of the garage, illuminating the area where she sat. Its soothing warmth had often helped to heal whatever ailed her. But today she found little solace there. Her current heartache was not one of those rudimentary problems that presents itself from time to time as one's life unfolds. No, this was much bigger. This was one of those life-changing dilemmas that couldn't be washed away with a little sunshine and caffeine.

The birds sang and went about their normal routine in the trees around her, unaware of her distress. She asked herself some hard questions. *Have we changed that much over the years? I used to feel like I was important and Richard loved me. What happened? Is there really someone else?*

She couldn't remember a time in the recent past when Richard had professed his love and commitment to her, and it troubled her. Sure, he was still affectionate from time to time, but even then, she didn't seem to command his full attention. It was as if he had other places to be and other things to do. *I'm just not a priority any more.*

Judging by the number of magazine articles on the subject, their situation was not uncommon. She never thought it could happen to them. *Could this be my fault? What could I have done differently?* She wondered if perhaps it was the squeaky wheel thing, and she hadn't been squeaking loud enough.

Emily longed to feel special again—to see the look in a

man's eyes that made her feel wanted. She had hoped and prayed those eyes would belong to Richard, but she was losing faith.

A single tear that had been clinging to her chin fell into her cup. With trembling hands, Emily set it on the table. She didn't know what to do or to whom she could turn. She felt abandoned and betrayed.

After a few moments, she turned her face toward the sun. The soothing warmth reminded her that we are never alone. Her faith taught her that. She shifted uncomfortably as she remembered several times in her life when she felt somehow beyond its reach. This felt like another one of those times.

Emily's phone vibrated on the table. She considered letting it go until whoever it was gave up, but she recognized her boss's number on the screen. "Hello, Scott," she said, forcing a smile.

After she'd had her children, Emily had taken a job at Pendulum Publishing, a well-established company specializing in mainstream novels and self-help books. She enjoyed the freedom of working from her home office, reading manuscripts and doing some editing. She was determined to raise her children herself, rather than farm them out to daycare, and the extra income helped with the growing family's expenses. Her employers were happy to increase her workload after the children had grown.

"No, Scott. I didn't forget." She closed her eyes. "Something has come up at home. I'm afraid I'm not going to be able to make the meeting. I'll stop by later and explain."

She checked the time on the phone before she set it on the table. The weekly staff meeting should have started ten minutes ago. She took a deep breath and exhaled slowly before gathering her phone and coffee cup and heading into the house. On her way, she couldn't help wonder where the last two hours had gone.

"Damn him," she said under her breath as she headed upstairs to the shower. Emily stayed longer than usual, letting the warm water wash away her tears. She pushed in the faucet and leaned against the tile wall for a few moments before reaching past the curtain to grab her towel.

Emily dressed quickly and made the bed.

Bogey barked downstairs. She walked to the window and peered through the blinds. A strange car had pulled into the driveway.

Chapter 39

That's one hell of an imagination you've got there," John said, eyes glazing over.

"Yeah, I guess so," Richard replied, hoping Emily would see it differently. He wondered if that might be asking too much. Perhaps he would have to proceed with a bit more caution.

After breakfast, Richard stepped out the front door of the shelter and stopped for a moment on the top step. A smile crossed his face as he looked at his car—still in one piece— exactly where he'd left it the night before. He hurried down the stairs, placed his hand on the fender and let it follow the contour of the car as he walked around to the driver's side. He opened the door and looked up at the clear blue sky. *What a fantastic day!*

On the drive home, he thought about what he would say to Emily. Yesterday seemed like a lifetime ago. He still couldn't believe it had come to this. These things happened to other couples, not to them. He had to find a way to turn it around. This was a new day and, in some ways, a new Richard. The past was, well, the past. What he did next was what really mattered.

An unfamiliar car sat in the driveway of his home. He pulled in and glanced at it through the side window. An expensive car. A BMW. He'd seen it before, but he couldn't remember where or when.

Richard stared through the windshield at his house. It looked the same as it always had, right down to the missing coach lamp that Josh had broken playing basketball two ... no, three ... summers ago. *Was it really that long?* He made a mental note to replace it.

Everything was just as he remembered, but he couldn't shake the feeling that something was different. Perhaps it was he who had changed. Whatever it was, he didn't understand it yet, but he could feel it.

He walked to the front door and cast another glance at the Beemer. Though the middle of July, a chill descended on him, as if a frosty breeze had blown up the back of his shirt. He tried the door. It was locked. He rang the doorbell.

All at once, he remembered the car. *You've got to be kidding me.* It belonged to Carolyn. His pulse quickened as he tried to sort out what was real and what was ... he wasn't sure what to call it. A dream? No, it felt like more than that. He slipped his hands into his pockets and waited. Memories flashed past, but could they be trusted?

"Good morning, Richard," someone called.

He looked up. Gail Jensen stood on her front porch, waving so hard he was sure her hand would fly off her wrist.

He nodded. "Morning, Gail."

His hand touched something unusual in his pocket, and he pulled out a small piece of Tiger Eye. He rang the bell again. Still no one answered. He shrugged, forced a smile in Gail's direction, and ran to the back of the house. He found Carolyn sitting alone on the deck.

"Hello, Richard," she said when she saw him walking up the steps. "Emily went to get the door. She'll be right back."

"What the hell are *you* doing here?"

She frowned. "I ... I came here to talk to you."

He stopped at the top of the stairs, took a deep breath, and looked toward the house. Emily had not yet returned.

"You just show up at my house? What was so important that you couldn't have told me over the phone?"

"I've been trying to call, but there's no answer."

He didn't remember hearing his phone ring. He would check later. "I think you knew I wasn't home. I think you came here to meet Emily."

"What?"

"I know what you're up to."

She tilted her head to one side. "What I'm up to is finding a way out of this mess. I've got a proposition for you."

I'll bet you do. "I think you should leave."

Carolyn shook her head slowly. "Richard, I—"

Emily opened the door and stepped onto the deck. She stopped when she saw Richard. "Was that you at the front door?"

"Yes," he said softly as he studied her. It was good to see her again with all her blood on the inside.

"What the hell are *you* doing here?"

"I guess I deserve that," he whispered.

Carolyn smiled briefly before lowering her head.

"I came here to talk."

Carolyn stood. "I really should be going." She fumbled with her keys. "It was nice meeting you, Emily."

Emily nodded. Richard couldn't tell what, if anything, had transpired between the two women before he arrived, and it made him uneasy.

They watched her leave, then Emily turned to him. "Well?"

He didn't know where to start. In fact, he wasn't entirely sure he understood everything that had happened in the past twenty-four hours. Whatever it was, he was glad to be back, glad to see her again, even if the feeling wasn't mutual.

"You said you wanted to talk. I'm listening."

Richard's eyes narrowed. "What did Carolyn want?"

"She wanted to tell you something, which I imagine she did while I was inside."

He opened his mouth to say something, but thought better of it.

"I'm sure that's not what you came here to talk about," she said, folding her arms.

"You're right." He took a deep breath. "I have so much to say ... I don't know where to begin." Richard shifted uncomfortably as Emily waited.

"Just pick a place and start talking."

"Okay," he said before taking another deep breath. "Let me start by saying that I know I've been absent lately from our relationship."

"That's an understatement."

"I'm sorry, Em. I fell asleep at the wheel, but I'm awake now. You're looking at a new and improved model."

"People don't change overnight, Richard."

"That's what I used to think," he said. "In fact, I used to think a lot of things that just don't make sense any more. To you, it must feel like I've only been gone for one night, but to me, it's been much longer. It's like ... like I lived a lifetime last night."

"What are you talking about?"

"I'm not even sure. It's like, I visited some alternate reality where we were the same, but different. I know it sounds crazy, but I spent months, maybe years, in this place living out the consequences of the choices I made—or didn't make—in this life."

Emily was silent, but the look on her face told him that she wasn't sure what to make of all of this. He went on to tell her about Arthur, careful to withhold some of the more bizarre events for another time.

"Think about it, Em," he said. "You've known me for a long time. Haven't I always been very logical and practical? I'm sure a few other words come to mind, but the point is, I couldn't make this stuff up if I tried."

Emily held up her hand. "Before you go any further, I need to know something. And I want you to think before you say anything. I don't want any bullshit. If you're hiding anything, you need to come clean right here and right now."

Richard held his breath.

"Are you having an affair?" she asked.

He exhaled. "No. I am not having an affair."

She looked directly into his eyes. "No bullshit, Richard. I'm going to find out one way or another."

"No, Emily. I am not now, nor have I ever been, unfaithful."

"Sam was there."

"Sam was where?"

"At the restaurant." She studied him. "Adrianna's."

Richard nodded. "When was this ... about three weeks ago?"

"So you *were* there."

"Yes. I had dinner with Carolyn. She owns the restaurant."

"Carolyn?" Emily looked away, as if she needed a moment with this unexpected information. She closed her eyes and shook her head before looking back at him. "According to Samantha, there was clearly something more than business going on—champagne, laughter, a certain look in her eye ..."

"Yes, I admit we were laughing, and we did have a bottle of champagne. We were celebrating."

"Really? What were the two of you celebrating?"

"A nightmare, as it turns out." He looked down at his feet.

"You're not making any sense."

"It's what I came here to tell you," he said, looking at her again. "It's why I've been so distracted lately. I really screwed up, Em, and I didn't have the courage to tell you."

"Tell me what, Richard?" Her voice began to rise.

Richard sat and motioned for Emily to do the same. "The money we've been saving ... the twenty thousand dollars ... it's gone."

"What do you mean it's gone?"

"I mean, I lost it. Well, most of it, anyway."

She remained silent, waiting for an explanation.

"I invested it ... along with Carolyn." He leaned forward, perched on the edge of his chair. "The tip came from a reliable source—someone Carolyn knew, someone close to the company. I even did some research." Richard sighed. "It smelled like a sure thing, Em. I guess I need to get my nose examined along with my head, huh?" He forced a smile.

Emily did not reciprocate. "What happened?"

"At first, we started to make money—the reason for the celebration that Sam witnessed—but then I got greedy. It was easy money and I wanted more. I thought we could redo the kitchen *and* go to Ireland *and* do a whole lot of other things. We might even be able to relax and enjoy life a little more."

Emily took a deep breath. "Do you know what would make me enjoy life more?"

"Please. Tell me."

"If I could trust my husband."

Richard felt the weight of his indiscretions. He opened his mouth to respond.

"Let me finish," Emily said as she raised her hand. "Maybe if I didn't have to question his love and commitment—if I just knew. If spending time with his wife was more important than chasing a few extra bucks. If he could realize, once and for all, that love was more important than any of it. That, Richard, is what would make me enjoy life more."

He didn't know what to say. It wasn't the first time he'd heard it, but it was the first time he listened. He understood now and hoped to God that it wasn't too late. "I am *so* sorry, Emily. Can you forgive me?"

She stared at him silently for a moment. "Perhaps I can forgive you ... eventually. But it's going to take time. Maybe you didn't sleep with anyone—I haven't decided yet whether to believe you—but even if you didn't, what you did was wrong. You had no right to make that decision alone."

For a moment, he wondered if she would feel any differently if he had walked in and dropped a pile of cash on the table in front of her. Perhaps, but that wasn't the point. There were some things money couldn't buy, and it seemed like Emily had always known that. She valued things like love and trust over money. It occurred to him that some place deep down inside, he knew it, too. Everyone did. It just took some people longer than others to remember.

"Please, Em. I love you and I want to come home."

She looked down at her hands in her lap before looking back at him. "I'm not ready to do that just yet."

"Why not?"

"I need some time."

"Time for what?"

"Seriously, Richard?" Her eyes drilled into him. "Do you know how hard it was to push you away, to make you leave like that?"

He assumed it was a rhetorical question. He couldn't

possibly have known the answer.

"It was a huge step—one I never wanted to take—but now that I did, I'm not willing to undo it too hastily. You haven't exactly been showing me that I'm the most important thing in your life. I have to be sure. I'm not going to put myself in a position where I need to do something like that again."

He saw the pain in her eyes and backed off. "I guess you deserve that much."

Bogey, who had been lying in the grass listening to everything, wandered over and stood between them. He looked at Emily for a moment before walking over to Richard's chair. Richard stroked the back of Bogey's head. "What do *you* think, boy?" he whispered.

"He doesn't get a vote," Emily said.

Richard looked at Emily. "I'm going to find a way to make it up to you, Em. I promise."

"Right now, the only thing you need to find is your way out. Please ... just go."

Chapter 40

E mily sat at her kitchen table, pushing food around on her plate, so lost in thought that it took a moment to realize her phone was ringing. She decided dinner was over, walked to the counter, and picked up the phone.

"You've got to tell me what's been going on over there," Samantha said.

"What do you mean?"

"I just got a delivery. Flowers. From Richard."

Emily turned around and leaned back against the counter. "Richard? Why would he do that?"

Samantha hesitated. "We had a little chat at Frank's party. Well, *he* didn't actually say anything. I read him the riot act, Em. I told him I knew what he was up to and—"

"Did you?"

"Did I what?"

"Know what he was up to?"

"I told you about that night at the restaurant. Isn't it obvious?"

"I'm not so sure."

"The note with the flowers said he was sorry and that he told you everything. So, come on. Spill it."

Emily paused, deciding how much to tell her. "He was hiding something, but I don't think it was an affair."

Samantha waited. "Well?"

"He invested all the money we've been saving and lost it."

"And you knew nothing about this ... investment?"

"Nope. He never said a word."

"He must have been crapping his pants."

"Small consolation."

"So how did he know that woman? I told you, she was pretty hot."

"He admitted being there with her that night. She's a client of his. She was in on the investment. Apparently, they were celebrating how well it was doing before the whole thing went south."

"Do you think he was sleeping with her?"

"I'm not sure."

"What are you going to do?"

"I don't know, Sam. This whole thing has made me think about a lot of things."

"What are you thinking about? Divorce?"

The word hung there for a moment. "Is that what you're hoping?" Emily asked.

"No, absolutely not. I wouldn't wish that on anybody." She took a deep breath and Emily waited. "Even though you're my little sister, I've always looked up to you, maybe even envied you for what you've done with your life. After my divorce, it became obvious that you had what I wanted. I guess it's why I've been so hard on Richard. Now, I don't know what to think."

"Misery loves company, right?"

"It's not like that, Em. I guess I thought that if it could happen to someone like you, then maybe I wasn't such a loser, after all."

In her entire life, she had never heard her sister cry. "Sam?"

"I'm sorry, Em."

"It's okay." She sighed. "I'm not thinking about divorce, at least not at the moment. I'm thinking more about who I am and realizing that I don't even know any more. Richard and I have been together so long and, now that the kids are gone, I need to figure it out."

Neither said anything for a moment.

"Perhaps that's what Richard has been doing." Samantha offered.

Emily sighed. "You think?"

"I love you, Sis," Samantha said. "I'll support you whichever way this goes."

"Thanks, Sam. I love you, too," Emily whispered. She set the phone down and closed her eyes.

Emily pulled the cork from a bottle of Pinot, poured a generous glass, and headed for the sofa in the living room. She stopped to look at the picture of Richard and her that sat on the piano and turned it face down before she continued to the sofa. Sam's call gave her something to think about. Halfway through her second glass of wine, the hard edges of her anger began to soften and she suddenly had the urge to play the piano.

She put her glass down next to the overturned picture and sat on the bench. Playing had always helped her relax. She found it easy to get lost in the music and let her cares melt, drifting away on the sweet sounds that filled the room. She thumbed through her music, looking for a song to play.

She opened an old book of Carole King songs, a gift from Richard. The songs had been favorites back in college, but now she had difficulty finding one whose words didn't feel like a knife in her heart. Songs like *It's Too Late, So Far Away*, and *Will You Love Me Tomorrow* just made her feel worse. She began to cry.

While the lyrics seemed to bring only pain, the songs themselves invoked memories of happier times—meeting Richard, falling in love, and starting a family, the foundation upon which her life had been built. Now, that foundation showed signs of deterioration, and she wondered how long it would be able to support the weight of the dreams that once rested securely upon it. She didn't really believe it was beyond repair, but she was smart enough to know that if it wasn't tended to, it would crumble. If that happened, nothing would ever be the same again.

The weight of her sadness was painful, but her fear of the unknown was crushing, and she found herself unable to sit any longer. She emptied her glass, walked slowly to the sofa and collapsed. With a blanket pulled over her head, she closed her eyes. They didn't open again until morning.

Chapter 41

Richard had not heard from Emily in two days. He wanted to give her some space, but he also wanted to keep the lines of communication open. She'd been spending more time with Samantha, and he was pretty sure that wasn't helping his case. He drove to the house to see if she was home.

He found her washing dishes at the kitchen sink. Richard watched for a moment through the screen before knocking.

"Come in," she called.

Knocking on his own door felt strange, but he had agreed to respect Emily's privacy while they figured out how to proceed. He believed it would be a temporary arrangement. A few awkward moments followed as they made small talk while she continued with the dishes.

Richard cleared his throat. "I feel like you've been avoiding me."

"That's not true," she said without looking up. "I've been busy at work."

Richard walked to where she stood and leaned against the counter. "I'd really like to move back in. Not everyone is lucky enough to have what we had ... *have.* I don't want to lose that, Em. And I certainly don't want to throw it away because of a misunderstanding. Do you?"

Emily picked up a towel and dried her hands. "I wish you felt that way two years ago." She walked to the kitchen table and sat down.

"So do I," he admitted and sat in the chair next to hers.

"The sad part is, I did. I just didn't know it. I lost sight of what really mattered. It was a careless mistake. One I won't make again."

"You told me you would always be there for me ... and you weren't. That feels like betrayal."

Richard couldn't un-ring that bell. The damage had been done. It wasn't even about the money any more. It was a matter of proving she could trust him again—about making her feel safe. "I'm sorry, Em."

"Why did it take you so long?"

Richard looked away. "What if everything Arthur said was true?" he asked after an awkward silence. "What if I was given a glimpse of what the future might be like if I continue down the same road?"

"Arthur?"

"The old man I told you about from the shelter."

"Do you know how crazy that sounds, Richard?"

"Of course, I do," he said. His eyes widened as he continued. "But I was there. I felt it. It was real. It makes perfect sense now. I've been missing the point. It's a wonderful life if you appreciate what you have. I haven't been doing that."

"I can't argue with you there." She breathed a heavy sigh. "It's what I've been trying to tell you for almost two years. I've racked my brain to find a subtle, yet compelling, way to get through to you. Then you talk to some homeless person one night and suddenly you 'get it'? How do you think that makes me feel?"

"I don't know ... grateful?"

"Did you even hear what I just said?"

"I heard you. Does it really matter *how* I get there, as long as I get there?"

Emily stood and walked to the kitchen window. After looking outside for a moment, she turned, leaned back against the counter, and folded her arms across her chest.

He saw an opportunity for a healing moment and he took it. He walked over and wrapped his arms around her. She lowered her head, arms still folded in front of her.

"I want us to be *us* again."

Emily nodded.

He kissed the top of her head before letting go. "So what do you think?"

"About what?"

"About me moving back."

"I'm sorry, Richard." She looked away for a moment. "I'm not saying it won't happen ... just not now."

"C'mon, Em—"

"No. I've been thinking. All this happened for a reason. Maybe it's not just about you. Maybe I need a break, too. To be honest, I've been feeling a little lost, like I don't know who I am any more."

"We can figure it out together."

"I don't think so. It's something I have to do on my own."

He saw a vulnerability in her eyes that he had not seen in some time, and it disarmed him. He waited for an explanation, but she seemed to feel no need to elaborate. She looked at the floor, and he took a deep breath, accepting her answer without further debate.

It could have all gone down like dominoes with one more push, but he wasn't going to let that happen. He didn't get the answer he wanted, but what he got was encouraging. Richard took a few steps toward the door, then turned around. "When can I see you again?"

"I know it's hard to believe, but my social calendar is pretty open. Oh, except for Saturday night," she said without looking up. "I have a date."

"A date?" Richard's heart sank.

She looked at him. "Do you have a problem with that?"

"Well, I ..."

"Relax." Despite the tension, Emily smiled. "I'm going out with Samantha. It's just some political fundraiser."

Richard exhaled. "Since when are you interested in politics?"

"I'm not, but it's for a friend of Tommy's, so Sam and I agreed to go. It's not like I have anything better to do on a Saturday night."

Richard swallowed hard. "A friend of Tommy's?"

"Yeah, some guy who's running for District Attorney."

"You can't go," he blurted out.

"Excuse me?"

"Uh ... what I mean is ... I've got something special planned ... for us, for Saturday." It was a lie, but he had to convince her to cancel her plans.

She looked at him curiously. "What is it?"

"I can't tell you. It's a surprise."

"Really?" she said tilting her head. "Are you asking me out on a date? I'm not sure I remember what that sounds like."

He ignored her sarcasm and smiled. "It's more than a date. But you won't know unless you go."

"Can we do it some other night? I promised Sam—"

"No. It has to be Saturday."

She wrinkled her brow. "If you're trying to make up for our anniversary—"

"I apologize for my careless oversight, but that was the past."

Silence.

"So?"

"I'll think about it," she said.

A tough nut to crack.

Chapter 42

S he's not with anyone right now," the receptionist said as she stared at her computer screen. "Your name is ...?"

"Richard Dunham." It felt good to be able to say that again.

Richard had raised the stakes when he told Emily that he had something special planned for Saturday night. What else could he have done? He had to keep her from attending that damn fundraiser and meeting Phillip Morgan. Sure, it sounded crazy, but he wasn't about to take any chances. He'd been gambling enough lately.

So, why was he here? He wasn't sure, but he needed to talk to someone. He would have given anything to be able to chat with Arthur again, but since that probably wasn't going to happen, he decided Helena would be the next best thing. After meeting Arthur, he was a little more open to the idea that some people had certain ... *abilities* ... that allowed them to communicate with a higher power.

While he believed such things were possible, he didn't fully understand what it meant. Did she talk to God? Perhaps. Were Angels sending her messages? He couldn't be sure. Whatever the case, it was clear that, unlike his occasional attempts at such conversations, whomever Helena was talking to talked back. He also recalled her matter-of-fact reaction to Michael's news that he was Richard disguised in another man's body. He trusted her intuition.

"She's not answering her phone," the receptionist said as she replaced the handset in its cradle. "I'll go see if I can find her."

Richard thanked her as he shoved his hands in his pockets and looked around. He'd never set foot in the room before, but it seemed strangely familiar. He examined the merchandise in the display cases, and the memory became vivid. Everything was the same. *How could I have known this?*

He picked up a can of tea marked China White just as someone called his name. Richard turned around to find Helena smiling at him.

"I'll bet this one is a real trip," he said, holding up the can.

"Now, Richard," she said with a little wink, "everything I sell is perfectly legal."

"You have some pretty interesting stuff here."

"I like to think so." She walked to one of the shelves and searched through the gemstones. She picked one up and turned around.

"Here. This is for you."

He held up his hand. "Don't tell me. Tiger Eye for insight and clear thinking."

Helena stopped, clearly stunned by his remark. "How did you know?"

Richard grinned. "What? You think you're the only one around here with supernatural powers?" He reached into his pocket and pulled out the piece she had given Michael. "Look. I already have one."

Helena eyed him suspiciously.

"Does the name Michael Riordan mean anything to you?"

"No." She frowned. "I don't think so. Why do you ask?"

"Never mind. Can we talk?"

"Sure."

Richard made a sweeping gesture with his right arm in

the direction of the arched doorway. "After you."

They sat down in Helena's office and Richard told her everything he could remember about his experience that night and the events leading up to it. He made sure to mention the part where Helena gave him the Tiger Eye.

"So, that explains your supernatural powers."

Richard grinned.

"Well, it's quite a story, Richard. You should write a book."

"I did."

Helena's eyes widened.

"Unfortunately, I left it in the other world."

They both laughed.

"So what do you make of all this?" he asked.

She thought for a moment. "It's all very intriguing. There are actually quite a few *parallel universe* or *other worlds* theories. You can Google it. I'm not making this up." She smiled.

Richard waited for her to continue.

"I think what you are referring to is one of several mainstream interpretations of quantum mechanics," she explained. "It says that all possibilities or potential outcomes to a situation exist. We can only focus on one of them, and that one becomes our reality. Each decision we make determines which one of the many worlds we live in."

He lifted an eyebrow. "So is that what Arthur meant when he said our thoughts create our reality?"

Helena smiled. "There's more to it than that, but yes."

"And the other potential outcomes make up these parallel universes?"

"Yes. For example, suppose a die is thrown that contains six sides. All six possible ways the die can fall correspond to six different *universes* where life goes on, so to speak, based on each one of the potential outcomes. You only get to experience one of them."

"Until that night," he added.

"Apparently."

"So, if this sort of thing doesn't happen very often," his eyes narrowed, "why me?"

"Well, Richard, I believe we are all guided by a higher power that is not of this world. However, we are not separate from this power. It is a part of us—our higher self—and knows all, seeing things we can't. It guides us and makes certain adjustments if we get too far off course."

"Isn't that like someone else telling us what to do? What happened to free will?"

"It's still you making the decisions, only at a higher level."

Richard frowned as he thought about it for a moment. "If there are countless other versions of me running around in all these parallel universes, does that mean—"

"Someone or something keeps track of them all."

Again, Richard took a moment to process. "That must be one hell of a spreadsheet, huh?"

Helena laughed. "You're such a nerd sometimes."

"It's my job."

They both laughed again before Helena's expression became serious. "What do you plan to do now?"

"I want to move back in with Emily and work this out together. I asked her yesterday, but she said she wasn't ready." He swallowed through the lump in his throat. "What is she waiting for?"

"These things take time, Richard." Helena paused, looking him in the eye. "We're talking about deep emotional scars that need time to heal. You need to be completely honest with her. She has to feel safe with you again."

"I came clean, told her everything. I'm not sure she believed all of it. I guess I'm going to have to find a way to prove it, huh?"

"Find a way to make her feel like she's the most important thing in your life."

"She is."

"Good. Remember, what you say is important, but it's what you do that matters."

Richard ran a hand back through his hair and Helena must have seen the worried look in his eyes.

She leaned forward. "Do you have a problem with that?"

"No ... there's something else." He cleared his throat. "She told me last night that she's planning to go to a political fundraiser on Saturday."

"And?"

"It's for Phillip Morgan. That's how they met."

"I see. Do you think ..."

"I told her she couldn't go." He shrugged. "It just came out."

Helena attempted to conceal a smile. "How did *that* go over?"

Richard paused. "Well, you can imagine, but I didn't know what else to do. I told her I made plans for us for Saturday night—something special."

"Let me guess. You have no idea what those plans might be."

He raised his eyebrows, grinned, and shrugged.

"Did she accept?"

"Not yet."

"You better be ready in case she does."

Richard nodded.

"Think big. Don't hold anything back. If she agrees to go with you, it means there's hope. Believing in something and then acting as if it were already true is the process that will ultimately bring it forth into existence. It's a self-fulfilling prophecy, Richard, and you are the prophet."

Richard smiled. "You really have a way with words, don't you?"

"It's my job." She flashed a smile. "But seriously, you need to stop thinking like the old Richard and start thinking like the new one."

He inhaled, then slowly exhaled. Helena waited. "So, I guess it's true," he finally said.

"What's true?"

"The past is past. It's what we do next that matters."

"Well put," she said.

"Arthur told me that."

They both stood and Helena held out her arms for a hug. Richard obliged.

"It wasn't a dream, Richard," Helena whispered in his ear, "it was a gift."

Richard smiled.

Chapter 43

E mily looked across the table in the small outdoor café, hoping she was making the right decision.

"So, you took me to lunch to let me down easy. Is that it?"

"No ... well, maybe," Emily admitted.

"I was really looking forward to Saturday night."

"You were looking forward to not walking in there alone." Emily knew her sister had an ulterior motive for inviting her to the swanky affair, especially after she offered to pay her way. "I know you, Sam. After the first drink, you were going to drop me like a bad habit and start working the room."

"That hurts, Emily." Samantha lowered her eyes and waited. Emily remained silent. She raised her head and flashed a devious grin. "I'll have you know, I planned to stick around for two drinks this time."

"Well then, I just might have to reconsider," Emily said, and they both laughed.

Samantha finished the last bite of her sandwich and washed it down with some iced tea. Her expression became serious. "Believe it or not, I understand, Em. You have to do what you think is right. It's different than Matt and me. You still have a chance."

"I know," she sighed, "but now it appears I'm the one who has to make the final decision. I don't like that kind of pressure."

Samantha's eyes darted back and forth as she leaned in closer to Emily. "I know. You want to make the right decision." She lowered her voice. "That's why I had Tommy look into Richard's activity over the past few months."

"What?"

Samantha leaned back. "I wasn't going to risk *my* job doing something like that, but Tommy—"

"Sam!" Emily glared. "I thought I told you—"

Samantha held up her hands. "Too late. It's done." There was a moment of silence as they stared at each other. "Do you want to know what he found or don't you?"

Emily knew she should say no, but ... "I don't know, Sam."

"Relax," she said. "It's good news."

Emily remained silent, but her eyes told Sam to continue.

Samantha explained that Tommy had found nothing suspicious in Richard's phone or credit card records. "Carolyn's number showed up a few times, but I think we can assume it was about the investment thing. Other than that, I think he's been behaving." She smiled.

"It feels a little sleazy, you know, checking up on him that way, but I guess I'm relieved to hear what you found."

"You're welcome."

Emily forced a smile. She finished her tea and absently chewed on a piece of ice as she stared past Samantha at nothing in particular.

"You want my advice?" Sam asked.

Emily's gaze met hers.

Sam didn't wait for her to answer. "Take it slow. Don't rush into anything. If he's sincere and this is what he truly wants, he'll wait for you."

"I suppose you're right. There's no hurry," she said, her eyes drifting. "He still needs to prove himself before I let him back."

The devious grin returned to Samantha's face. "You

might even want to make him sweat a little. You know, show him—"

"That's enough, Sam." Emily raised her eyebrows. "I get the point." She reached for her purse.

"So what time do you want me to pick you up Saturday night?" Sam asked.

Emily looked at her sideways.

Sam held up her hands. "Okay. You can't blame a girl for trying."

∞∞∞∞

Richard leaned against the rail of the Overlook and watched the activity below—business as usual. Everyone acted so *normal*. He thought about how his life had become anything but normal.

A young couple stood on the other side of the platform, and Richard couldn't help but steal a glance every now and then. They spoke in hushed tones and gazed into each other's eyes. It reminded him of the times he and Emily had stood in the very same spot.

He didn't love her any less now; in fact, he loved her more. A deeper love, one that came from a place of understanding that they meant more to each other than a simple human relationship. They were soul mates. That's what Arthur had said. They had a cosmic connection that wasn't limited to this lifetime. Sure, it sounded a little *out there*, but in the last couple of weeks, *out there* had become much closer.

Now he stood on the Overlook alone, devising a plan to win back Emily's heart. *Back? How could I have lost it?* It didn't matter now. He knew what he had to do. He just wasn't quite sure how to pull it off. Emily was the most important thing in his life, and he had to make sure she knew that. Given their current situation, it seemed like a tall order. However, he would not be discouraged. Where there's a will, there's a way ... and there is definitely a will.

He scanned the park below and noticed a man sitting alone at one of the Chess tables. From this distance, he looked a little like Arthur. Richard squinted for a better look. When he remembered that Michael had found Arthur playing Chess by himself at the very same table, he took off down the path.

Richard's shoulders sagged when he reached the tables and found them empty. They'd only been out of his sight for a minute or two on his way down from the Overlook—not enough time for someone to pack up and leave. He scanned the area, looking for any signs of activity. Nothing. Here one minute, gone the next. The man was a ghost ... or perhaps an angel. Had he even been there at all?

Richard sat at the nearest table, rested his elbows on his knees, and stared at the ground, still reaching for each new breath. His normal rhythm returned and, as he straightened up, his peripheral vision picked up something out of place. A blue Chess piece stood alone in the middle of the table. It looked familiar, and he searched his memory for a time and place. Technically, *he* hadn't seen it before; Michael had.

Richard didn't know much about Chess, but he remembered what Arthur had said when he'd first showed the piece to Michael. Arthur had made a move where he intentionally sacrificed that piece. A *gambit,* he called it—part of a larger strategy.

"That's it!" he said aloud. *How could I have missed it?* He stared at the blue knight standing alone on the table and a faint smile crossed his lips. Without hesitation, he pulled his cell phone from his pocket, scrolled through his list of contacts, and tapped one of them. Moments later, Richard smiled as he ended the call and slipped the phone into his pocket. He grabbed the piece off the table and left the park in a hurry.

Chapter 44

A black limousine pulled up in front of Emily's house at exactly seven o'clock on Saturday night. The driver exited the vehicle and opened the rear door. Richard stepped into the street and buttoned his jacket.

His breath caught in his throat when Emily opened her front door wearing an off-the-shoulder, champagne-colored dress that shimmered in the evening sun. She hadn't worn it since Josh's wedding, and he remembered how he'd been unable to take his eyes off her at the reception. They'd made love that night as soon as they'd returned home.

"I'm sorry," he said.

Her expression went blank. "Sorry? For what?"

"I'd forgotten how absolutely beautiful you are."

Emily smiled briefly before lowering her gaze. "Thank you, Richard."

"Shall we." He offered his arm.

Champagne and roses awaited them in the limo. Richard instructed the driver to take the scenic route.

When the limo pulled to a stop in front of *Autour du Monde*, Emily glanced out the window and back to Richard. "This *is* a surprise."

He flashed a confident smile. "Expect the unexpected."

She held his gaze. The driver walked around the car and opened their door. Richard placed his hand on the small of her back, and they walked toward the restaurant. The doorman smiled.

"Bonsoir." He tilted his head and held open the door.

Emily returned the smile, and Richard nodded as he followed her in.

Small wooden tables sat on a large checkered tile floor. The plaster walls and wainscoting showed their age gracefully in the low light. Richard turned, half-expecting to catch a glimpse of the Eiffel Tower through the front window. They walked past the bar to the main dining room, where the maître d' greeted them.

The dining room was more elegantly appointed without sacrificing any of the old world charm. Tables for two with fresh flowers on white linen sat beneath reproductions of famous French paintings. Muted colors and soft lighting added to the intimate atmosphere. The maître d› held Emily's chair, and she sat, her eyes wide and sparkling.

She unfolded her napkin and placed it on her lap before glancing around the busy room. "I heard it takes months to get a reservation here. How did you—?"

"I had a little help," he admitted.

Emily was right. You couldn't just call *Autour du Monde* and get a reservation for Saturday night, but Richard knew someone who could. Actually, he knew someone who knew someone.

At first, Tommy McKenna had not been happy to hear from Richard. Surprised, but not happy. Richard explained his side of the story while Tommy listened. After Richard made his case for their reconciliation, Tommy reluctantly agreed to help him out. He told Richard that he had a good friend with enough juice to get him a reservation for Saturday night.

Emily leaned forward. "Who are you, and what have you done with Richard?" A smile crossed her lips.

He returned her smile, thinking it a fair question. "Richard, the new and improved model." he reminded her.

"The upgrade was long overdue."

Richard had pulled out all the stops. The restaurant was just the beginning. They took their time with dinner—the best meal either had eaten in a very long time; maybe ever. Likewise, conversation was the most comfortable it had been for some time. They ordered Cherries Jubilee for dessert and another drink after the table had been cleared. His plan seemed to be working.

From the corner of his eye, Richard saw a familiar face, and his dessert nearly made a second appearance. Phillip Morgan, wearing a suit that probably cost more than Richard's car, crossed the room toward them. He stopped at their table and looked at Emily.

"You must be Emily," he said.

She glanced at Richard then back. "Yes. I am. Have we met?"

"My name is Phillip Morgan."

Richard shifted uncomfortably in his seat.

Phillip turned. "I'm sorry." He held out his hand. "Phillip Morgan, Assistant District Attorney."

Richard hesitated. He assumed that Phillip was the friend Tommy used to secure their reservation, but this scene brought back some unpleasant memories. He cleared his throat. "Richard Dunham."

"I'm sorry to intrude, but I just wanted to make sure Pascal was taking good care of you."

Richard nodded. "Everything's perfect."

"Enjoy the rest of your evening."

"We will," Richard said, and watched him walk away.

When he turned to Emily, she stared at him through squinted eyes. "What was that about?"

He raised his eyebrows as a faint smile played on his lips. "Like I said, expect the unexpected."

When they left the restaurant, Richard instructed the driver to kill some time before their next stop. He held the champagne bottle up to the light. Enough for a couple of glasses remained. They settled into the soft leather seats, and he offered a toast to a new beginning. Emily smiled, but said nothing. Their glasses met and he quickly emptied his.

Richard reached into his breast pocket. "I have a present for you," he said with a nervous smile and held an envelope between them.

Emily set down her glass. Her eyes narrowed. "What for?"

"No reason. Just something I thought you might like."

"First dinner ... and now a gift." She tilted her head. "If I didn't know better, I'd say that you were trying to—"

"Go ahead, open it."

Emily took the envelope, slid the contents out, and examined it.

Two first-class airline tickets to Dublin.

She drew in a quick breath and looked at Richard, eyes wide.

"We leave in a week. You can cross it off your bucket list."

Her expression fell. "I can't just jet off to Ireland ... I have responsibilities."

"What happened to spontaneity?"

"I'm sure I couldn't get time off from work on such short notice."

"I thought you might say that." He smiled. "I talked to Scott and he agreed to give you the time off."

She held the tickets to her chest, closed her eyes and took a deep breath. Her bottom lip trembled, and she lowered her head.

He waited patiently for a response. When she said

nothing, he put his hand on her shoulder. She didn't resist, so he bent over in an attempt to make eye contact. "Em?"

She opened her eyes without looking up. "I don't know what to say."

"How about: This is awesome, Richard. I'm going to start packing as soon as I get home?"

"I wish I could say that ... but I can't."

The smile slid off his face. "Yes you can." He placed his index finger sideways under her chin and gently raised her head. She avoided his eyes.

"Do you really think this is a good time to do something like this?" she asked, looking past him over his shoulder.

His head told him: *Maybe she's right. Maybe I'm rushing things*. That's when his heart stepped in. "Absolutely. It's the perfect time. It's what we need right now. A new beginning, new memories."

Emily twirled a lock of hair around her finger.

"I know there are places you want to see and people you want to meet. You can do it all. I won't hold you back from any of it. It's what you said you've always wanted. Let me give that to you."

She looked at him, and he didn't like what he saw in her eyes. "Of course, it sounds wonderful." She looked down at the tickets and then back at him. "But I'm just not sure we're ready for this."

"Please, Em, what's it going to take?"

"I know we can't afford to do this. How did you even pay for these tickets?"

He winked. "A magician never reveals his secrets."

"But Richard—"

"No buts. Just say *yes*."

She hesitated. "I'm scared."

"What are you afraid of, Em?"

"What am I afraid of?" She had that look in her eyes again. "I'm afraid I'm being naive if I blindly trust this sudden change of heart."

He paused, looking her in the eye. "I know it's a lot to ask, but please trust me on this."

"Why did it take something so drastic to make you understand?" Her head moved slowly from side to side. "I have to protect myself, Richard. I can't let this happen again."

"Is that what love is about now ... protecting yourself?"

Instead of answering, she placed the envelope in his hand.

"Will you at least think about it, Em?"

"Yes, Richard. I will think about it."

He opened the envelope, examined the two tickets, and slipped one of them into the pocket of her purse. "I'll be on that plane, Emily. I guess the rest is up to you."

He leaned over and kissed her forehead as the car came to a stop in front of The Paradise Club. Emily looked out the window, then to her lap. "Richard, I don't feel much like dancing tonight."

"C'mon, Em. The night is still young."

"Let's not spoil a lovely evening." Her voice was firm.

His stomach told him that it might be a little late for that.

The driver remained in the car when they reached the house. Richard let himself out to open Emily's door. She avoided his eyes as she stepped out of the car, and he followed her up the front steps.

When she turned around, he played Bogart again. "If that plane leaves the ground and you're not with him, you'll regret it. Maybe not today, maybe not tomorrow, but soon. And for the rest of your life."

Emily closed her eyes and smiled. "You'd better go," she whispered when she opened them.

The smell of her perfume caused him to linger for a moment before he turned to leave.

"Richard," she called after him.

He stopped.

"Dinner was lovely. Thank you."

He forced a smile as she paused for a moment before closing the door.

Richard held his head high as he walked to the waiting limo. Once inside the car, he slumped into the seat, shoulders sagging. *Let's hope you didn't blow it, Richard.* He second-guessed his decision to surprise her with the tickets. Was it too much too soon? Had he underestimated her recovery time? Would she recover?

He knocked on the privacy screen that separated the front and back seat. An electric motor whirred and the glass lowered.

"You got anything else to drink?" he asked the driver.

"There might be some Scotch in the—"

"I don't drink Scotch," he said to the eyes that watched him in the rear view mirror.

"You're probably better off," the driver said, eyes on the road again.

"How's that?"

"Mark Twain said, 'Too much of anything is bad, but too much good whiskey is barely enough.'" He turned from the road to the mirror. "Alcohol's not the answer."

"I suppose you know the answer?"

"I do."

"Care to enlighten me?"

He paused and their eyes met again in the mirror. "Life is a self-fulfilling prophecy."

Richard nodded. "Yeah, I've heard that one, but what does it mean?"

"I think you already know." The whirring noise returned and the privacy screen rose.

Richard leaned forward and knocked on the glass. No response. He settled back into the seat and looked out into the night. The ending of *Casablanca* played again in his mind. In the scene at the airport, Ilsa wanted Rick to board the plane with her, but he wouldn't go. The roles were reversed now. His story would end differently—they would be on that last plane out of Casablanca *together*.

Chapter 45

Emily stepped inside the Starbucks on Mission Street and looked around. An attractive Latino woman watched from a table near the window. She stood as Emily approached.

"Emily?"

"You must be Helena."

"Yes," she smiled. "Thank you for coming." Helena gestured toward the counter and they placed their orders.

Emily spoke first. "I was a little surprised to get your phone call ... more than a little, actually." Emily hesitated. "Did Richard put you up to this?"

"No. Richard doesn't know I'm here."

An awkward silence descended between them as they sipped their coffee. When their cups were back on the table, Emily spoke. "Before we go any further, there's something I need to ask you."

"Of course."

"Richard spent a lot of time with you a year ago. He said you were working together, but I suspected something more." She hesitated. "Did anything else ever happen between the two of you?"

"No, Emily." She offered a reassuring smile. "I don't think that would have been possible. All he ever talked about was you. It may not have seemed like it at the time, but Richard loves you very much." The sincerity in her voice made it nearly impossible not to believe her.

"I don't understand. If he loves me so much, how

could he leave me?"

"Everything happens for a reason, but it's not always evident at the time what those reasons are. Oftentimes, it's to create a new space for something bigger and better for one or both of you. What has this created in your life so far?"

Emily looked out the window. "I guess it's made me take a hard look at who I am and what I want. I'm confused. I still love him, but I'm afraid to give in, to trust him again. I want to move past all this somehow, but I'm not sure what's holding me back."

"Love will never hold you back," Helena responded. "Your unwillingness to forgive is what will hold you back. Forgiveness is not for the other person, Emily. It's for you."

Emily took a sip of coffee and slowly set the cup down. "So is that why you're here? To convince me to forgive him?"

"Honestly, Emily, I didn't know what I would say to you, but I knew that we had to talk. I have learned over the years not to question my guidance—just follow it."

Emily studied Helena. Once again, she saw nothing but sincerity. "Did he tell you about the big trip he planned to Ireland?"

Helena's face lit up. "He did. I think it's wonderful. When do you leave?"

"The flight leaves at six o'clock tonight."

"Oh. Then I should let you get home and finish packing."

"I'm not going."

Helena's expression fell. "But, Emily ..."

Emily leaned over the table. "He must have told you about that first night ... about the *dream*."

Helena cleared her throat. "I believe it was more than a dream."

"So, in your professional opinion, this kind of thing is possible?"

"Absolutely."

Emily stared at her cup, turning it back and forth in her hands. "I thought he was crazy at first," she said without looking up, "but he's been different since then." She looked at Helena. "I want to believe him. I want to trust him like I did years ago, but I'm having a hard time. It seems too soon."

"What are you waiting for?" Helena asked.

"I don't know. I guess I'm waiting for some kind of sign that I'm the most important thing in his life again. I haven't felt that way for a long time."

"My advice. Don't wait too long."

Emily said nothing.

"It's your turn, Emily. What are you going to do?"

Emily stood and pushed in her chair. "It was nice meeting you."

"A wise man once told me that the past is past; it's what we do next that matters."

Emily picked up her purse. "Who told you that?"

"Richard Dunham."

As Emily pushed through the door and stepped outside, she thought she saw Richard's car parked across the street. She looked again—definitely his car. A man walked up to the driver's side, looked briefly in her direction, and opened the door. She raised her hand to her forehead to block the sun and get a better look. The man was not Richard.

"Excuse me," she called across the street as the stranger entered the vehicle. He paid no attention to her.

"Wait!" She ran across the street toward him as he started the car. Just before he pulled out, she put both hands on the driver's door as if she intended to hold the car in place. "What are you doing with this car?"

The driver stepped on the brake and looked up at her.

"Excuse me?"

"This is my husband's car. What are you doing in it?"

"I bought this car last week."

"Where?"

'From Richard Dunham."

"Huh?" She straightened up, removing her hands from the door. "That's impossible. Richard would never sell this car."

"And you are ...?"

"I'm his wife."

The man turned and looked through the windshield, hands still holding the wheel. He took a deep breath. "I'm sorry, but he sold it to me," he said politely. "Told me he needed the money to travel ... overseas, I think he said."

Emily froze, unable to speak.

A few seconds passed before the man looked up at her. "Is it okay if I go now?" he asked.

Emily nodded slowly as she stepped away from the car. She watched him pull out, then hurried back across the street.

Chapter 46

"Delta Flight one-seven-three to Dublin will begin boarding in five minutes. Please have your boarding pass ready."

Richard examined every face in the busy terminal. Emily's wasn't among them. Not yet. *She's going to be here. She has to be.* Everything in his life had led up to this—the moment she walked into the terminal. The rest of their lives together depended on it.

Passengers began to board the plane, but still no Emily. Richard held his boarding pass in his hand and bit his lower lip as he scanned the faces coming and going. "Please, Em," he whispered as they called the next group of passengers.

When the last call was announced, he looked around one more time before heading for the jetway. He believed he'd done everything he could to convince Emily of his love and renewed commitment. It was up to her now. He also believed that, however this played out, chance or coincidence would have nothing to do with it. If he ended up in Ireland alone, there would be a good reason for it. That, however, was not his intention.

The walk down the jetway grew more difficult with each step, and he turned around every few feet for another look. *Stop it. Have a little faith, man. Believe in yourself and what you're doing.* He thought of Emily and the times he'd criticized her stubbornness. She called it determination. In that moment, he borrowed some of her determination, deciding on the lonely walk to the plane that fear would no longer be an option. Love would be his strength.

Richard inched down the aisle, stopping while passengers stowed their carry-on luggage in the overhead compartments. He checked his ticket against the numbers printed at the end of the rows until he found a match, then sat down next to the window. He glanced sideways at the empty seat next to him and then watched the last few passengers make their way from the front of the plane. Once again, Emily was not among them. His heart sank.

Through the window, he watched as the ground crew made the final preparations for take-off. After a few minutes, the passenger activity on the plane decreased as the crew began their final pre-flight preparations.

"Click ... click ..." The sound reverberated in his ears as the flight attendants made their way to the front of the plane, closing the overhead compartments.

"Excuse me," Richard said to one of them when she reached the end of his row. "Have they closed the doors yet?"

"No, but they will be any minute now," she replied. "Is everything all right?"

'Yes." It was a lie. "How soon before we take off?"

"We should be getting underway in about five minutes." She smiled and continued up the aisle.

Richard attempted to adjust the air vents above his head before looking out the window. The empty baggage cars headed back toward the terminal. He felt the plane move, and he slumped a little lower in his seat. Another plane lifted off the tarmac in the distance, climbing into the low gray clouds.

The flight attendants went about their routine, pointing out the emergency exits and demonstrating the overhead oxygen masks. He watched their scripted performance as the plane pulled away from the terminal and taxied toward the runway.

I could use one of those masks right about now.

It appeared that he would be flying alone.

∞∞∞∞

Richard sat in the terminal at JFK International Airport with a single red rose on the seat beside him. He had a two-hour layover in New York City before changing planes for the trans-Atlantic leg of his flight. The sheer number of people passing through the terminal made him feel even more alone.

Emily should have come around by now and been on that plane. He had no clue what his next move would be, only that there would be a next move. He wouldn't give up. He pressed speed dial for Emily's cell and held the phone to his ear, not sure what he would say. A few seconds later, it didn't matter. Voicemail. He didn't leave a message. A more pressing question needed to be answered. Should he continue on to Ireland without her? What would be the point?

After twenty minutes of deliberation and two more attempts to reach Emily by phone, he decided to inquire about canceling the rest of the trip and booking a flight back to Springfield. He would cut his losses, lick his wounds, and live to fight another day. He walked up to the ticket counter.

"Can I help you?"

"Hi. My name is Richard Dunham, and I wondered how I might—"

"Oh, Mr. Dunham," she interrupted. "I have a package for you."

Richard watched her bend down and reach under the

counter. She stood up holding a large envelope that she slid across the counter.

Richard looked at the envelope and then back to the woman. "What's this?"

She shrugged. "I don't know. Someone dropped it off for you a few minutes ago. I was just about to have you paged to pick it up."

"Someone? What did they look like?"

"An older gentleman. Short. Gray hair."

"Did he leave his name?"

"No. He just said he was a friend and that you had left this behind." She pointed to the envelope. "He said it was important."

Richard picked up the envelope and thanked her, still staring at his name on the front.

"I'm so sorry, Mr. Dunham. I interrupted you." She smiled apologetically. "What was it you wanted to ask me?"

Richard looked up. "Uh ... never mind." He shook his head. "It was nothing."

When he returned to his seat, he flipped the package over and squeezed the clasp. A large stack of papers held together at the top by a metal binder clip slid out onto his lap. He recognized his manuscript immediately—the manuscript he had written as Michael—but hesitated to believe his own eyes. He lifted his head and scanned the gate area for any familiar faces. There were none to be found. Rubbing his chin, he tried to imagine how this was even possible.

Slowly, he peeled back the cover sheet and looked at the words spread out across the page in neat little rows. Tens of thousands of them, and he remembered writing every one. The only thing missing was the title. How does one sum up a lifetime of love and loss and emotional chaos in a few little words? It didn't seem possible at the time. It still didn't.

Richard sat thumbing through the pages, stopping from time to time to read a particular passage before moving on. He thought about Michael's sister Angela and wondered if their paths would ever cross in this lifetime. And Michael, with whom he shared a most unusual relationship, was most likely still alive. He thought about looking them up, but what would he say to them?

About three-quarters of the way through the manuscript, he heard a familiar voice behind him.

"Can I tell you a story, Rick?"

He froze, unsure whether the sound came from somewhere in the terminal or somewhere inside his head. Faith made him set the manuscript down and stand. He turned, believing with all his heart that she would be there.

Their eyes locked and time stood still. Richard cleared his throat, mustering up his best Bogart voice. "Does it have a wow finish?"

Emily slowly closed the space between them. "I don't know the finish yet," she said, her eyes as green as he had ever seen them.

"Go on. Tell it. Maybe one will come to you as you go along."

They stood locked in each other's gaze. He searched those eyes until he found what he was looking for. The eyes don't lie.

Their lips met. Everything around them seemed to fade away. Their kiss was fueled by every embrace they had ever shared.

When they came up for air, Richard took her hand and they sat. "I've missed you so much, Em."

"Richard, I'm sorry for the way I've been—"

He put his finger to her lips to stop her. "The only thing

that matters now is that we're together."

"There's something I need to say that I haven't said in a while." She paused. "I love you, Richard."

Richard made no attempt to hide the tear that slid down his cheek. He silently vowed to make sure nothing would ever change her mind again. "What happened, Emily?" he asked, his eyes searching hers. "When did we stop being *us*?"

Her expression softened. "Somewhere along the way, we stopped talking, stopped communicating," she said. "I didn't know what you were thinking, and I feared the worst."

As soon as she said it, he realized that he'd been shutting her out. He shifted uncomfortably in his chair. "That's not going to happen again. I've been—"

"I know. You've been telling me for the past two weeks, but I was the one who wasn't listening."

Richard held the rose between them.

Emily smiled. "What's this for?" She took it from him and held it below her nose.

"A new beginning," he said, watching as she closed her eyes and inhaled. He paused for a moment as she opened them again and met his gaze. "The past is the past—"

She cut him off. "It's what we do next that matters."

Richard smiled and picked up the manuscript. He set it on his lap and took a deep breath. "Can I tell you a story, Emily?"

Acknowledgements

My heartfelt thanks go out to all those friends and family who supported me on this journey. While writing is oftentimes a solitary practice, publishing a novel can not take place in a vacuum.

I am grateful to Dan for his storyboarding help and access to the lake house in Canada where a good deal of this book was written. Diane, whom I've spent more years with than without, provided inspiration and a key female perspective. Kevin and Katie with their keen eyes were instrumental in reviewing my work along the way. The remaining early readers and other staunch supporters are too numerous to mention here, but you know who you are.

Finally, I would like to thank Tahlia for a wonderful job editing my words and showing me how to be a better writer.

A Note From The Author

Thank you for investing your valuable time in reading my novel. I hope you enjoyed the story.

Word of mouth is the most powerful promotion any book can receive. If you enjoyed this book, please tell your friends, and consider writing a review on Amazon.com and Goodreads.

A Discussion Guide for book clubs is available for download from my website at **www.davidhomick.com.** You may also subscribe to my mailing list to receive information about new releases and special events.

CPSIA information can be obtained at www.ICGtesting.com
Printed in the USA
BVOW04s0926281014

372607BV00002B/6/P